In a fit of panic, she lunged at the door, slammed it shut and twisted the lock into place

Kelly laughed at herself, seeing humor in her sudden paranoia. The legend of Moore House was actually getting to her. What was next? Would she hear bumps in the night? Rattling chains at midnight moving down the hallway?

Her home was miles from town. She savored the isolation, using Moore House to hide from prying eyes. Not many people were brave enough to step inside the black wrought-iron gates surrounding the property. Very few would willingly approach the massive Victorian mansion. Hardly anyone dared to grasp the brass lion's head knocker in their hand long enough to see it.

They were afraid of ghosts.

The dead didn't bother her. She was more afraid of the living.

Dear Harlequin Intrigue Reader,

At Harlequin Intrigue we have much to look forward to as we ring in a brand-new year. Case in point—all of our romantic suspense selections this month are fraught with edge-of-your-seat danger, electrifying romance and thrilling excitement. So hang on!

Reader favorite Debra Webb spins the next installment in her popular series COLBY AGENCY. *Cries in the Night* spotlights a mother so desperate to track down her missing child that she joins forces with the unforgettable man from her past.

Unsanctioned Memories by Julie Miller—the next offering in THE TAYLOR CLAN—packs a powerful punch as a vengeance-seeking FBI agent opens his heart to the achingly vulnerable lone witness who can lead him to a cold-blooded killer.... Looking for a provocative mystery with a royal twist? Then expect to be seduced by Jacqueline Diamond in *Sheikh Surrender.*

We welcome two talented debut authors to Harlequin Intrigue this month. Tracy Montoya weaves a chilling mystery in *Maximum Security,* and the gripping *Concealed Weapon* by Susan Peterson is part of our BACHELORS AT LARGE promotion.

Finally this month, Kasi Blake returns to Harlequin Intrigue with *Borrowed Identity.* This gothic mystery will keep you guessing when a groggy bride stumbles upon a grisly murder on her wedding night. But are her eyes deceiving her when her "slain" groom appears alive and well in a flash of lightning?

It promises to be quite a year at Harlequin Intrigue....

Enjoy!

Denise O'Sullivan
Senior Editor
Harlequin Intrigue

BORROWED IDENTITY

KASI BLAKE

HARLEQUIN®

TORONTO • NEW YORK • LONDON
AMSTERDAM • PARIS • SYDNEY • HAMBURG
STOCKHOLM • ATHENS • TOKYO • MILAN • MADRID
PRAGUE • WARSAW • BUDAPEST • AUCKLAND

ISBN 0-373-22752-3

BORROWED IDENTITY

Visit us at www.eHarlequin.com

Printed in U.S.A.

ABOUT THE AUTHOR

At twelve years of age Kasi Blake decided to be a writer and modestly rewrote the ending of a popular classic. She has an insatiable desire to read everything she can get her hands on. When she isn't writing or reading, she spends time with her favorite nephew, paints with oils, travels and shops until she drops. She resides in Missouri with her two cats.

Books by Kasi Blake

HARLEQUIN INTRIGUE
676—WOULD-BE WIFE
752—BORROWED IDENTITY

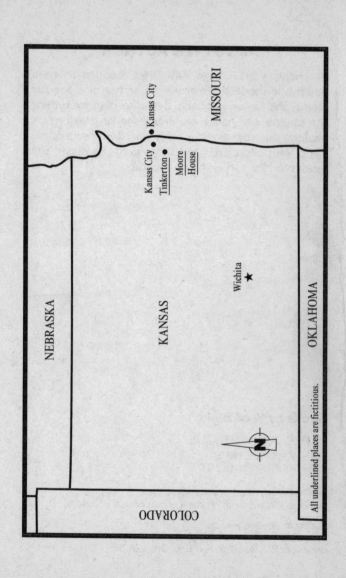

NEBRASKA

COLORADO

KANSAS

Kansas City • Kansas City
Tinkerton •
Moore House

MISSOURI

Wichita ★

OKLAHOMA

N

All underlined places are fictitious.

CAST OF CHARACTERS

Kelly Hall—Either she's losing her mind or someone is trying to make her think she is.

Michael Taggert—He has a job to do, and he can't let anyone get in his way. Not even the beautiful blonde down the hall.

John "Paddy" Paddington—The private investigator has gambled away his future, but ten million in diamonds might be the ticket to his freedom.

Margo Lane—Kelly's neighbor has disappeared, leaving her dog to fend for himself.

Mona Hall—Kelly's mother is in a mental hospital for life.

Zu Landis—The assassin has been sent to do a job, but did he kill the wrong man by mistake?

Elvin Grant—His "boss" wants Kelly to sell her house. How far is he willing to go to convince her?

Wade Carpenter—This mildly retarded man has a way of finding things. Did he see something the night the killer struck?

To my mom for supporting my writing habit when everyone else thought it was a waste of time. And for all the "mom" things you do. Love you.

Chapter One

"Kelly."

The whispered name pulled Kelly Hall out of her blissful sleep. At first she thought it was her husband calling to her. *Husband.* What an odd word. Married for mere hours as she was, it was going to take some getting used to. She smiled serenely, her eyes closed.

Her hand went to the other side of the bed, reaching for him, and found it empty. She forced her heavy eyelids open a slit, enough to see the illuminated numbers on the clock. Just minutes past four in the morning. Panic shot through her, setting every nerve ending on a razor's edge. Where in the world could Michael be?

Her memory sported holes the size of baseballs, but not enough to keep her from remembering she was a married woman. Nothing short of brain damage could make her forget that.

She switched on the lamp and stared at the vacant side of the bed. There wasn't even a telltale dip in the pillow to signify Michael had rested his head next to hers last night.

Her lips twisted into a grimace. Three generations of her family had lived in Moore House and not one had had a happy ending. She had been raised on stories of curses and doomed love. Everyone in the small town of Tinkerton,

Kansas, knew about the legends of Moore House. Only the truly morbid and superstitious considered them fact.

Kelly didn't believe the rumors surrounding her home. Michael hadn't been carried off by a goblin in the dead of night. He was somewhere in the house, possibly the bathroom. Or maybe he was in the kitchen getting a snack.

She struggled to her feet in the enormous master bedroom, wobbling slightly. A wave of dizziness washed over her. Her stomach churned and her head throbbed painfully. Fearing she was about to be sick, Kelly headed for the master bath.

Halfway to her intended destination, she spotted her reflection in the vanity mirror out of the corner of her eye. A streamlined white satin-and-lace gown hugged her body like a mummy wrap. Why had she slept in her wedding dress?

She frowned as she struggled to recall going to bed, but her memory was a blank. She took a long look at the facts. Michael hadn't made love to her. It didn't make sense. He'd been so insistent they marry at once instead of next month as per the original plan. Why would he walk out on her, leaving her an untouched bride?

Who would want you?

She shoved the haunting words aside, knowing they must have come from a dream. Michael wouldn't say such a hurtful thing to her.

Her rush to get to the bathroom forgotten, Kelly crossed the cold hardwood floor to the closet. She wanted to get out of her grandmother's wedding gown, hang it up before it was ruined. Later, she would have it professionally packed once again.

She opened the door and reached for a hanger.

Michael was hiding in the closet like a ghoul ready to pounce.

Gasping in fright, she nearly jumped out of her own skin.

"Michael! You almost gave me a heart attack!" Nervous laughter bubbled up in her throat.

Kelly moved closer and the other side of his face came into view.

Blood formed an intricate design on his cheek, around his eye. The red lines wove a pattern over the hard planes, starting deep in his hairline and ending at the base of his jaw. Droplets rained down on his blue chambray shirt.

She screamed and reached for him, grasping the front of his shirt in her desperation to hold him.

The body had been propped against the door but now it rocked as if disturbed by her outburst. He fell forward. Kelly jumped sideways to avoid the crashing body and tripped over the bottom of her dress.

Her head bounced against the hardwood. Pain shot from the back of her skull to the sensitive point just below her eyes. She wanted to scream, but only managed a small whimper.

A thousand thoughts raced through her mind, but she couldn't isolate one long enough to focus on it.

Her husband was dead. She didn't need to check his pulse to know for certain. His unblinking eyes confirmed what she felt in her gut.

He'd been murdered.

Kelly pressed her back against the wall, using it as leverage to raise herself up. Her eyes refused to blink or to stray from Michael's body. Taking a deep breath, she bolted out of the bedroom, running as if the devil were on her heels.

The long hallway yawned before her, riddled with doors. Every bad nightmare she'd ever suffered sprang to mind, visions of killers hiding in the shadows and waiting for their next victims. What if the killer was in her house?

She stopped.

Her feet froze as if glued to the blood-red carpet that lined the several intersecting hallways. In her mind she saw the path she would take. She planned her route quickly, begging her legs to move. Fortunately, she knew the house, every inch of it, by heart. It didn't matter that the corridor was windowless. She didn't need the moon's light to find her way out.

All she had to do was run down the hallway and turn left along another long, dark passageway. Eventually she would make it to the dual winding staircases that led up from the foyer, meeting on the second floor in front of an illuminated stained glass window.

Once she made it down the stairs, she would be safe.

Breathing hard, she silently screamed at her legs to move. They trembled beneath her, but she forced them to obey. Somehow she was going to make it to the front door.

She turned at the next hallway intersection and stopped again. A shadowy figure moved out of one of the rooms. It pulled the door shut. A flash of lightning escaped through the crack between wall and door, illuminating his features.

Michael?

She screamed.

Michael's ghost turned in her direction and started straight for her. His hands stretched out before him as if he wanted to choke her.

Blackness shrouded her. She fell and her eyes rolled back, seeking the darkness. Her body turned to vapor. She collapsed into a pair of strong arms.

KELLY WOKE SLOWLY, drifting through several layers from dream to reality until she was fully conscious. A horrible vision of Michael popped into her head. He was dead, then he was alive. She'd seen him in the hallway coming out of his bedroom. Her heart thundered like a dozen horses galloping down the homestretch.

Drawing a deep breath, she took a personal inventory of

herself. She was under the covers in her own bed, wearing a T-shirt instead of a wedding gown. But her relief was short-lived. Michael wasn't anywhere in sight. Fear clotted her throat as nightmarish images surfaced. Her eyes strayed to the closet door.

It was closed.

She struggled out of bed, holding on to the mattress until her feet were firmly on the ground. As if drawn by a magnetic force, she went to the closet door. Each step was a silent march into madness. Her fingers trembled on the cold knob. It turned slowly in her grasp. She held her breath and tugged, automatically preparing to scream.

The door opened to reveal her wardrobe. Nothing sinister, just a full rack of clothing and a line of shoes at the bottom. She took a moment to search for blood, but she didn't look very hard—partly because she didn't think she would find any, partly because she feared she might.

Kelly left her bedroom in a rush to find Michael. A small doubt would linger until she saw him for herself. Only then could she be sure he was safe.

She stopped at the top of the double staircase and glanced up at the stained glass, unable to avoid it. An angel towered over her, shielding two young children beneath her cloak. It was meant to signify protection. However, something about the depiction of the angel made Kelly uneasy. Its eyes were dark and stormy, filled with something akin to hatred.

Kelly tore her gaze away from the haunting picture. She glanced over the hand-carved banister to the massive foyer below. The floor was marble, a shiny, almost transparent stone that reflected light from the crystal chandelier. The double staircase curved up both sides of the semicircular room. There were cutaway arches descending with the stairs, arches that held statues of Greek gods and noblemen. The statues, like everything else in Moore House, were old and chipped. Small lights behind each statue illuminated them at night.

The foyer had four doors, one per wall, beginning with the sturdy entrance, a thick door with two deadbolt locks and an old-fashioned brass knob. The parlor was directly to the right and the kitchen to the left. Both rooms were connected to the hallways that led to various rooms such as the formal dining room, the study and the billiard room. All were sadly withering from lack of use.

Below the point at which the two staircases met, underneath the stained glass, a pair of doors blocked the entrance to the library. The library, Kelly's favorite room, was designed by a genius in her opinion. The walls curved slightly, yet held reams of books along endless shelves to form a complete oval. The library was the largest room in the house, built on a grand scale that would have pleased the wealthiest of kings. It was the only ground level room that didn't have a second floor above it. The ceilings reached high to form a dome. The stained glass angel, a mirror image of it, stood high above the doors with a lightbulb attached to the top, a light that glowed day and night.

The second floor mainly housed bedrooms and bathrooms. There were a few small exceptions, like the sewing room.

The third floor had three short staircases. One led to the attic and the other two went to the long, rectangular ballroom. Both rooms were locked as far as Kelly knew.

She hesitated, hearing a noise.

Michael entered the foyer and stood near the bottom of the stairs. Hands shoved deep into the pockets of his jeans, he turned hard brown eyes in her direction. They were cold, holding what appeared to be a trace of contempt. For a long breathless moment he seemed a total stranger to her.

She sucked in a painful breath, wanting to flee to the safety of her bedroom.

Instead Kelly wrapped her arms around her body. A chill swept over her, and she felt vulnerable standing there in nothing but a long T-shirt. They were married now and she shouldn't feel awkward. But she did. Michael had only seen her fully clothed before. Their dates had ended with chaste kisses. He'd been a perfect gentleman, not trying to push her further than she was willing to go.

Now his insolent eyes raked over her seminude body. The desire in his gaze was easy to define, but there was something else she couldn't identify. The unfamiliar expression on his face frightened her.

She took an awkward step backward, desperately wanting to go to her room and dress properly before attempting a conversation with him. Forever the klutz, she tripped over her own feet and bumped into the wall.

Michael raced up the stairs, taking them two at a time. His expression had turned to concern. Gone was the cold stranger, replaced by the old warmth of Michael Taggert.

"Careful," he said, catching her by the arms and steadying her.

"You're here." It was the only thing she could think of to say.

"You were expecting somebody else?" The harmless smile didn't quite reach his eyes. "Santa Claus, perhaps?"

He bent forward, placing cool lips on her forehead, branding her with fire. His fingers momentarily tightened like steel clamps on her shoulders.

"I wasn't sure you were here." She shivered, picturing Michael's bloody face. "I was afraid something had happened to you."

"Why?" He pulled her pliant body into his arms, holding her against his solid chest. He stroked her back. Obviously he wanted to comfort her, to reassure her.

So why did his touch have the opposite effect?

"It was…I saw you… Never mind," she said.

"Bad dream?"

"Horrible." She cringed at the memory of it, not understanding how her own mind could invent something so awful. "You were dead. You'd been murdered and placed inside the closet."

"Do you know who killed me?" His eyes sharpened on her upturned face. "Did you see them?"

She laughed nervously, thinking he was making a joke, but he seemed serious. He wanted the awful details of her nightmare. His interest in the morbid dream filled her with dread. Some things were better left in the dark.

"No," she replied. "After I found you in the closet, I raced down the hallway. Then I saw you coming out of your bedroom."

"You thought I was in the closet?" Michael frowned at her as if he thought she was losing her mind.

"You were," she insisted. "But you were in the hallway, too." She rolled her eyes. "Now that I've said it, I can hear how ridiculous it sounds. It seemed so real at the time."

"Dreams usually do."

Changing the subject, she asked, "Why didn't you wake me this morning?"

"Was I supposed to?" He shrugged. "I figured you needed the rest."

"I don't know what to say to you."

Kelly walked away, needing time to plan her next words. She didn't want to embarrass herself. Thinking about time reminded her that she hadn't fixed her father's favorite clock in days.

She descended the stairs, crossed the foyer and stepped into the parlor. The room had been decorated by her grandmother in dark colors and antiques before Kelly had taken her first breath. Kelly was reluctant to change anything. There was no need for her to redecorate, seeing that she seldom used the room, anyway. In fact there were only a few rooms in the house that she did occupy on a regular basis. Her bedroom and bath, of course. Also, the kitchen, and once in a great while she used the library.

The parlor's high cathedral ceiling boasted a mural of a cloudy sky. Three windows with arches over them stood tall, nearly but not quite reaching the ceiling. They were concealed with heavy, dark green draperies. Not much sunlight filtered into the parlor. Her grandmother had preferred it that way.

Most of the furniture, all original pieces from her grandmother's day, hid beneath dusty sheets now. When Kelly felt like sitting down, she went into the library or out to the solarium. Since she didn't employ a staff there wasn't anyone to help her keep the place clean.

Kelly went to the old grandfather clock, opened it and moved the minute hand to the correct time. The timepiece ran a bit slow, but it still worked. She had been brought up to value family heirlooms and some day she might have the clock fixed.

Kelly performed the task of setting the time in an effort to avoid looking directly at Michael. She couldn't allow him to see the tears of confusion swimming in her eyes. Being near him made her nervous. It didn't make sense to her. Michael had put her at ease with a simple smile, but that same smile chilled her now.

"I thought things would be different between us today. Why didn't you make love to me last night?"

"I didn't know you wanted me to." He closed in on her, cutting off her escape route. His fingers caressed the slope of her neck.

A thousand tiny tingles shot through her body.

She turned to face him, purposely knocking his hand away. The parlor seemed smaller than usual, almost as if the huge room was closing in on her. Tension kept her body rigid. She needed answers, even if they hurt.

"I may not be as worldly as you, but I do know that men make love to their brides on their wedding night." She stared at the top button of his jersey rather than meeting his gaze, embarrassed by her own words and a bit resentful that she should have to say anything. "Didn't you want to?"

"Okay," he sighed, rubbing his forehead as if he, too, had a headache. "Let's start over. From the top."

"I want to know if I made a mistake last night."

"What do you mean?"

Kelly counted to ten under her breath. She had known Michael for only three months. He had appeared out of nowhere. One day she'd been returning from a visit with her neighbor Margo Lane, and Michael had been standing on her front porch, peeking through the window. She neither liked nor trusted visitors, but Michael was different. He was charming, too charming, and he seemed to honestly enjoy her company. He was working on a book about infamous houses and the stories behind them. Of course he'd wanted to know about Moore House, but she was reluctant to tell him anything. The last thing she needed were more visitors and a book like his would bring them in droves. They would trample over her flower garden, invade her privacy and basically disrupt her whole life. Michael had agreed to drop the idea, but his interest in her seemed to grow with each passing day, no matter what she said to dissuade him. He'd pursued her with flowers and gifts, using one smooth line after another until she'd agreed to marry him.

"Last night, out of the blue, you begged me to elope with you—"

"Begged?" He interrupted her, a look of pure arrogance transforming his handsome features. "I don't beg, sweetheart."

If she didn't know better, she would think she was talking to a complete stranger. His gorgeous face hadn't changed. He had the same square jaw, the same chiseled nose and sculpted cheekbones. The change was in the eyes. They were the same deep brown, like warm brandy, but they seemed different, wary, as if they were holding dark secrets. Why hadn't she noticed it before?

"You said you couldn't live without me. You dared me to throw caution to the wind and elope with you." Her forehead wrinkled with the memory. "You had everything ready. You brought my grandmother's wedding gown down from the attic."

"Your grandmother's wedding gown?"

"You had a ring and a dozen white roses. You even had a minister from Kansas City."

He shook his head. "A minister?"

"Stop repeating everything I say!" Hands on her hips, she exclaimed, "You weren't like this before. You were nice to me. More than nice. You told me you couldn't wait to marry me, and wanted to do it right away." She blinked away the tears. "Why are you treating me like this? You said you loved me."

Michael held his hands up and she thought he was going to surrender, admit to the joke, but his words took her on a twisted detour. "Look at your hand. Where's the ring? Where's the dress? Where's your proof?"

She glanced down at her left hand, finding the fingers completely bare. Another realization hit her. When she had looked inside the closet that morning, her gown hadn't been there. In fact, she hadn't seen it since the nightmare.

She stepped across the parlor and plopped down on the sofa, questioning her own sanity.

"This is not happening," she mumbled. "I didn't imagine getting married. It was real. I remember every detail."

"Relax," Michael said, hovering over her. "Nothing to get upset about. It was just a dream."

"It wasn't a dream, dammit!"

"Don't you think you're overreacting to all this?"

"Let me get this straight," she said with a sigh. "We didn't get married last night? We didn't elope?"

"No," he said with a firm shake of his head. He crossed his muscular arms over his chest. "But there's got to be a logical explanation for your confusion. Did you drink any alcohol last night? Are you taking any medication?"

"I took a couple sleeping pills," she admitted. "I haven't been sleeping well lately."

"Why not?"

"You know why!" She glared at him. "The house has been making more noises than usual. It keeps me awake, and I was tired. I took the pills before you asked me to marry you."

"Listen to yourself. Why would I ask you to marry me so late at night? And why would you say yes when you'd just downed a couple sleeping pills?"

"I don't know," Kelly said. He was right. She would have to be messed up to say yes to a proposal that late at night, and when she was so tired. But she remembered him pushing her to do so. He wouldn't take no for an answer. "It seemed so real."

"You suffered an unfortunate side effect from a drug. It happens."

Could it be that simple? She grabbed on to the explanation, desperate to believe. Relief spread through her like rays of warm sunshine. She wasn't losing her mind.

"Maybe your pills reacted with something else in your system," he said. "It would also explain why you're feeling poorly this morning."

She felt silly. She would have to be more careful with medication in the future.

"I'm going to go upstairs and take a shower," she announced. "I need to get dressed."

"Okay." Michael said, with a pleased smile on his handsome face. That smile lit up every corner of her heart. "I'm glad we cleared that up."

"We're still getting married, right?" She watched his expression carefully, looking for revulsion. "Next month? Like we planned?"

"Just like we planned."

She was being a total idiot, doubting him when he hadn't given her reason to. What sort of wife would she make if she couldn't trust the man she was marrying?

"I'm sorry about the misunderstanding," she said. "I feel like a big heel for jumping all over you."

"Don't give it another thought." He smiled once again—a warmer smile this time. It almost reached his eyes. "Call me if you need anything."

He walked off. She didn't relish facing her bedroom alone. Knowing it had all been a dream didn't evaporate the horrid feeling of spiraling out of control. It would take a long time for the images of Michael's dead body to vanish completely.

She went upstairs.

Kelly entered her room and headed for the bureau. She needed to dress warmly. Moore House welcomed the chill of winter, holding on to the cold like a small child clinging to her favorite doll. Even in the summertime the house was cooler than most other places. It would cost a fortune to keep it warm, so she only heated the rooms she used on a regular basis.

She retrieved a pair of jeans and a light sweater. Kelly padded across the wood floor in her bare feet to the bathroom. Passing the closet, she purposely focused her eyes straight ahead. She would not look at the closed door again. It had been a dream. Michael wasn't dead. Everything was great.

So why did she feel as if she were standing in quicksand and sinking fast?

KELLY DIDN''T GIVE a thought to the bathroom door until she'd been in the shower a good ten minutes. A noise startled her as she shampooed her hair. It sounded close by, close enough to be in the same room. She always left the door wide open when she showered, because the bedroom door was closed.

But it wasn't locked.

Michael wouldn't dare enter without invitation.

She peeked through squinted eyes, trying to see through the foggy shower glass. Shampoo dripped down her forehead, and her eyes burned painfully.

Kelly opened the shower door a few inches and stuck her hand out. A mental image of someone there, someone attempting to grab her arm, almost made her pull it back. Clutching a towel, she brought it inside far enough to wipe her face. Her eyes continued to sting. Closing them firmly, she rinsed the shampoo from her hair.

Another noise made her jump. She shut off the water and retrieved the discarded towel. Wrapping it securely around her wet body, she exited the shower. There was no one else in the steamy bathroom.

In a fit of panic she lunged at the door, slamming it shut. Kelly twisted the lock into place.

She laughed at herself, seeing humor in her sudden paranoia. The legend of Moore House was actually getting to her. What was next? Would she hear bumps in the night? Rattling chains at midnight moving down the hallway?

She had inherited Moore House from her father upon his early death. She had moved into it immediately, feeling instantly at home. She and Moore House shared common ground. The people in Tinkerton gossiped about them both, spreading nasty rumors and half-truths. They were both considered freaks. Somehow she felt as if Moore House accepted her, even wanted her.

Her home was miles from town. She savored the isolation, using Moore House to hide from prying eyes. Not many people were brave enough to step inside the black wrought-iron gates that led to the property. Very few would willingly approach the massive three-story, forty-seven room Victorian mansion. Hardly anyone dared to grasp the brass knocker shaped like a lion's head long enough to use it.

They were afraid of ghosts.

The dead didn't bother Kelly. She was more afraid of the living.

She turned toward the foggy mirror and reached for the blow dryer.

She froze instantly, terror shooting through her limbs.

Someone had penned a note for her, using a finger to write one word on her mirror. The three letters dripped water. They were already beginning to fade, but she could read the word clearly.

Die.

Kelly's back hit the tiled wall and she screamed at the top of her lungs like a banshee. Once she started screaming, she couldn't stop. One shriek after another vibrated through the large bathroom, bouncing off the walls.

She bolted from the room, fright leading to flight.

She rounded the corner on slippery feet and ran out the bedroom door.

Hands came out of nowhere. They grasped her wet shoulders in a steel grip.

Another scream ripped from her sore throat.

Chapter Two

Michael Taggert's fingers closed over Kelly Hall's creamy white shoulders. He swung her around and pressed her spine against the wall, his heart pounding at a marathon rate. Fearing the worst, he visually inspected her from top to bottom, reassuring himself she was all right.

A short towel was the only thing between him and her naked, glistening body. The green cotton ended at her upper thighs, exposing them to his avid gaze. Her blond hair hung in wet waves around her heart-shaped face. She was pale, for all of the color had drained from her cheeks.

Her blue eyes were wide, but they didn't focus on him. Instead, she stared past him at the wall as if she wasn't aware of him.

She continued to scream as if she couldn't stop. She fought desperately to break his hold.

Michael pulled her into his arms and held her close. He whispered reassuring words into her hair while stroking her back until the shaking subsided.

After a few minutes, she pushed him away. Reason surfaced in her eyes. She blinked at him as if stunned, probably seeing him for the first time.

"I…" Her neck swiveled and she stared at the open door of her bedroom. Her teeth chattered violently. "I was taking a shower and…"

"What? What happened?"

"I thought I was alone, but I heard something. There's a word written on the mirror. Someone was in the bathroom while I was showering!"

Suspicion colored her expression and Michael knew she was wondering if it had been him in the bathroom.

"I was downstairs when I heard you scream." His gaze slowly moved down her towel-clad body. He released her shoulders, taking a step back for his own peace of mind. He needed to keep focused on the job at hand, had to remember to play the part of the devoted fiancé without getting carried away. "What frightened you? What's written on the mirror?"

Kelly wrapped her arms around her body in a form of self-protection.

His gaze went to the scars on her forearms. This woman was no stranger to horrible circumstances. She'd been hurt badly.

"'Die,'" she sobbed. "The word *die* is on the mirror, written in the steam. Someone was in the bathroom with me." Her hands shook as she wrung them together. "Do something."

"Stay here while I check it out."

"No." She shook her head adamantly and latched on to his arm. "I am not going to stay out here alone. I'm coming with you."

"Stay behind me then," he said, entering her bedroom.

At the moment he would have given every cent in his bank account to have a weapon. If there was someone dangerous nearby, how was he going to protect Kelly?

He felt her hands at his back, holding on to his waist with trembling fingers. Kelly was standing so close to him as they entered the bedroom together, he doubted a breath could slide between them.

She was too close. Everything about her was an unwanted

distraction. The weight of her hands on his spine. The amazing floral scent of her skin and hair. The whisper of breath as she inhaled and exhaled at a steadily increasing rate.

They stepped into the bathroom and Kelly gasped. There were two words on the mirror now: *Die Michael.*

He turned on her. "Is this your idea of a joke?" Anger clouded his vision. He had a job to do. He didn't have time to play games with the local head case. No matter how beautiful she was.

"But…I didn't do that…I swear." Kelly hugged herself again. Her entire body shook like a leaf in a strong wind. "There was only one word before. You have to believe me."

Michael sighed. If she was acting, she deserved an Oscar. His gut told him she believed what she was saying. But Michael knew no one could have gotten into the room. They had both been standing in the hallway.

"You think I did it!" Her slender hands clenched into tight fists. She shook them at him. "I am not crazy!"

"Maybe the pills you took—"

"Get out!" She pointed at the door. "Get out of my room."

When he didn't immediately leave, she threw a bottle of shampoo at him.

He ducked, allowing the plastic bottle to hit the door behind him. He didn't want to leave her alone in her present condition. He had no idea what she was capable of.

He could tell her the truth, but the truth could put her in even more danger. His hands were tied right now. There was work to be done. Afterward, he could tell her everything.

"Get some rest. The sleeping pills will be out of your system soon and you'll feel better."

"Don't patronize me," she snapped. "You think I'm losing my mind."

"No, I don't." He raked a hand through his dark hair, searching for the magical words that would put her mind at ease. "I think the drugs are causing this reaction. I also think you'll be back to normal within the next few hours."

She stared at him through sky-blue eyes that glistened with mistrust. Michael had learned early not to care what others thought about him, but the angelic blonde cut him to the quick with her suspicious gaze. For some reason he wanted her trust and respect. Unfortunately, he hadn't earned either one.

"I want you to go," she stated firmly.

"Are you all right?"

"Yes!" she hissed between clenched teeth. "I'll be fine once you're gone."

Michael reluctantly left her to her own devices. Closing the door softly behind him, he stood there for several minutes, waiting for another frightened cry that never came. The dimly lit hallway remained silent. When he heard her walking across the bedroom floor, he left. She was safe in her room.

HAD SHE WRITTEN the words on the mirror?

No one else could have done it. She strained to picture the mirror in her mind again, trying to see it as it was before she'd left the bathroom to find Michael. There had been one word when she'd stepped from the shower. She was sure of it.

Maybe Michael was right in thinking she was losing her mind. He didn't have to utter the words. It had been evident in the way he looked at her.

She'd seen the pity in his eyes. Avoiding that look was the reason she chose to live in isolation at Moore House. When she was growing up in Tinkerton, going to the local schools, she'd learned to hate the smell of pity. People in town knew the tragic story behind her scars. Most of them were kind, trying not to glance down, but it didn't matter. She didn't need their pity or Michael's.

Returning to the bathroom, she splashed her face with cold water. She was lost, confused, with no idea what to believe. She prayed Michael was right about the sleeping pills. If her problem was that simple, it was easily remedied. She wouldn't take them anymore.

She got dressed in a frantic rush, wanting to escape the four walls of her room. She purposely wore a long-sleeved sweater to hide her scars.

Kelly hurried down the hallway, but froze at the top of the stairs. She had an unexpected visitor.

Wade Carpenter, her best friend, was tiptoeing across the large foyer, heavy toolbox in hand. Wade was mildly retarded, but he was a genius when it came to carpentry work. He was larger than the biggest football player in the National League, an intimidating figure in faded coveralls.

"Wade," Kelly called out.

Startled, he jumped at least a foot in the air. His toolbox hit the floor with a loud clang and the tools scattered across the marble with an awful noise, as if an entire orchestra had dropped their instruments at the same time.

"W-what?" His wide blue eyes snapped up to find her on the landing. "Oh, Kell. Hi. Were you sleeping?"

"It's nearly noon," she pointed out. "Why would I be asleep?"

He shrugged his large shoulders and kicked at an invisible rock. "I dunno. I knocked. I knocked real hard."

"I didn't hear you." Kelly descended the stairs to stand beside her friend. Wade didn't feel sorry for her or for himself. She felt most people could learn a lesson from him. He was nice to everybody.

"I have a key. I'm sorry." Wade banged his head against the wall, punishing himself. "I knocked. I really did."

"Don't be silly." Kelly stroked his back. She could

barely reach his enormous shoulders. "I gave you the key so you could come in anytime you wanted to work on the house. Don't apologize for using it."

Wade was going to restore Moore House to its original beauty, although he worked for a construction company part-time, so he wasn't always available. He didn't believe in ghosts any more than she did. He loved hearing the old stories about the house's origins.

Wade sank to his knees, grabbing a hammer and a wrench in his large fists. "I dropped my tools. I take good care of them."

"I know you do, Wade." She placed a hand on his shoulder. "Here, let me help you."

"That's okay. I can do it. I can take care of my tools." His curious eyes turned in her direction. "Are you sad?"

She felt as if he was talking Greek to her. "Why would I be sad?"

"I dunno." He placed the last tool in the metal box and stood, towering over her. "'Cause Michael left. You're lonely. Huh?"

He thought Michael was gone. Why would he think that? She opened her mouth to correct him.

Before she could say anything, Michael appeared in a doorway off the foyer. Wade stiffened beside her. His eyes were glued to her houseguest, with a hostile emotion evident. It didn't surprise her. Wade hadn't liked Michael from the beginning. Although he hadn't said anything bad about him. Wade didn't speak ill of anyone.

Wade stuttered, "I—I d-didn't know y-you were here."

Michael shrugged without comment.

Wade took a step backward, fear in his gaze as if he was looking at the devil himself. Did he see the change in Michael, too? From Jekyll to Hyde, or vice versa, her fiancé had exchanged personalities sometime during the night.

Did he think he could fool her, pretend to be something

he wasn't? Which one was the real Michael? The animated, generous listener she'd spent so many hours with or the cold, magnetic man she saw standing in front of her now?

If she didn't know better, she would think they were two entirely different people.

Wade turned abruptly and headed for the door. "I gotta go."

"But you just got here," she said.

"I gotta go now," he insisted, dancing around as if he had to use the bathroom. He charged toward the exit. "Bye-bye."

Kelly chased after him. She managed to reach him before he made it out the door. Her hand landed on his arm, tugging him to a stop. "You didn't do anything wrong, Wade."

"You mad at me?"

"Of course not."

"Don't listen to him." Wade looked pointedly at Michael. "I'm not bad."

"I know," Kelly reassured him. "Don't worry. I could never be mad at you."

A smile tilted Wade's mouth. He stepped out into the cold autumn day, and Kelly stood at the door, watching him go. Halfway to his truck, he bent over. He plucked something from the ground and turned to her, holding it high with a bright smile.

"I found a penny for my collection." He began to chant. "Finders keepers. Losers weepers."

She forced a smile. Wade's hobby was finding things that other people lost. He kept them in a box in his room at home, watching over them as if they were actually worth something.

He waved at her, obviously excited about his find.

Michael spoke from directly behind her, far too close. His warm breath caressed the back of her neck. She wanted to swat him away like a pesky mosquito. His newfound attitude made her nerves tighten to the point of snapping.

"What was that all about?"

"You tell me." She turned on him like a cornered animal would. "I haven't seen Wade so upset before. What did you do to him?"

"I didn't do anything. I didn't say a word to him. You were here the whole time."

"I wasn't talking about today." She put distance between them, choosing to stand near the staircase. "You must have said something or done something when I wasn't around."

His lips compressed into a tight line.

She added, "I don't even know you, do I? You're a stranger to me. Were you pretending to love me these past few months? Was it all an act?"

He stared at her, his eyes cold chips of dark ice, and she knew he wasn't going to answer her. He hid behind a stoic expression, not saying a word. He hadn't been like this before today. Was it possible for a person to overhaul his personality overnight?

This Michael was like an exposed negative of the original photograph. He walked differently, stalking his prey like a hungry panther. Gone was the amusing swagger. He moved with a purpose now, walking with a quiet grace that was at odds with his big, muscular body. But it didn't stop at the way he walked. There was the way he held himself, his gestures, the way he spoke. Everything about the man was different.

It made her want to scream in frustration.

For the first time since she'd moved into the old house, it seemed too small. His menacing presence devoured the oxygen. What could she do to protect herself against him if he attacked her?

Michael closed the gap between them with quick and easy strides.

"Are you afraid of me?" He asked the question with a look of wonder in his eyes. It gave her hope. He was stunned by her reaction, by her need to get away from him.

"Should I be afraid of you?"

A harmless smile tilted the corners of his mouth, but it didn't touch his eyes. "Do I make you nervous?"

"Answering a question with a question is an outdated and impolite way to avoid answering."

"You started it," he said. "How do you feel now?" His fingers stroked the side of her face. "Better?"

Her skin burned where he touched it, igniting her nerve endings. She realized, too late, that she was in danger of a different kind. Now she wondered what it would be like to kiss him again. Would it be different? Everything else had changed about him. Would his kisses be different, as well?

She feared she knew the answer already.

She gently pushed his hand away. "I feel fine."

"Then why is your breathing erratic?"

Kelly swallowed hard. What was wrong with her? Michael hadn't cared about her scars. Outside of Wade, he had been the one person she could open up to. So why did she feel uneasy with him all of a sudden?

"It was a rhetorical question," he said. "I don't expect an answer."

"Good." She inched her way along the wall, moving sideways past the staircase. "Can you tell me something?"

"What?" His eyebrow arched.

"Do you love me, Michael?" she asked.

There was an obvious hesitation, as if he was trying to figure out how to answer her question.

"Yes or no!" A voice at the back of her mind screamed at her not to ask. "It's a simple question."

"Sure I do." He said the words without feeling or depth. He replied as one would to a child in need of humoring.

I never wanted you. It was a joke. You're a joke.

The words shot through her like a bullet, bringing a searing pain with them. Kelly's hands flew to her temples. Palms pressed hard against the sides of her head, she held it tightly, fearing it would explode. A soft whimper floated to her ears.

It was her. She was moaning while slowly sliding down the wall.

Hands enclosed her upper arms and tugged her up again. Her back scraped against the wall behind her as Michael used it to keep her from falling.

"What's happening? Talk to me!" he demanded.

The pain receded, and she gasped for breath. Every thought had been forced from her mind. She couldn't remember what she'd been thinking at the time the pain had hit, striking like a bolt of lightning out of a pure blue sky.

Michael held her close to his chest as if she was a precious treasure, and she could feel his heart beating beneath the palm of her hand. She was afraid to speak, afraid to break the spell of the moment. The tension she'd been feeling in his presence was gone now. She felt safe and cherished. She didn't want to move.

Kelly rested her head against him. Her equilibrium hadn't returned yet. A few more easy breaths and she would be fine.

"Kelly, are you all right? Can you talk to me?"

She looked up at him. His dark eyes were filled with concern. He couldn't possibly be faking the emotion. It was too raw, too powerful. Michael really did care about her.

"What's wrong with me?" She asked the question in wonder, her mind a mass of confusion.

"You need to lie down," he said. "I'll help you upstairs."

She wanted to argue with him. The idea of being in her room filled her with dread, but her vocal cords didn't cooperate.

Michael swung her into his arms and carried her. She

wanted to fight him, fight her deepening dependence on him, but she rested her head against his hard shoulder. He was a good man, and she was a paranoid dope for suspecting him of being anything less than wonderful.

The feel of his strong arms holding her close was too good to be real. She could happily close her eyes and melt into him. They would become one entity…

She silently berated herself. Was she a hopeless romantic or what?

Michael left her on her bed after asking if she wanted anything from the kitchen. She felt bereft, abandoned without those strong arms around her. Part of her wanted to ask him to stay, but she wasn't going to be a clingy female. If he wanted to stay, he would.

She told him she just needed a bit of rest. The drug would clear out of her system and she would be able to focus once more. She longed to feel normal again. The woolly, disassociated sensation that dragged at her body soon would be a thing of the past. A little sleep and she would be fine.

When he'd left the room she groaned, realizing she needed to use the bathroom. Kelly struggled out of bed. She'd managed to take two steps when her bare foot landed on a hard, tiny, pebble-like object. It hurt.

She moved her foot and stared down, trying to find the offending item. She had bent over when a small white bead caught her eye. She picked it up and studied it. It appeared to be a small pearl. But where had it come from?

The answer floated up from the depths of her subconscious, an unwanted epiphany. She tried to deny it access, but her mind opened, spilling a recent memory. Her wedding gown had been covered with tiny pearls.

But the wedding dress had been part of a dream.

She knelt down on the floor. Sweeping her hands over it

with long, desperate movements. She managed to find three more tiny pearls.

Kelly scowled at the white beads in her hand. If her wedding was a dream, then where had the pearls come from? If it hadn't been a dream, why was Michael lying to her?

Chapter Three

The next morning, after pulling on faded jeans and a pink angora sweater, Kelly reluctantly went downstairs. Before leaving the sanctuary of her bedroom she placed the tiny pearls in a trinket box on top of her dresser. Asking Michael about them wouldn't do her any good if he was lying to her. She had to find a way to trick him into admitting the truth.

Kelly stood in the foyer and wondered about Michael. Where was he? A small part of her hoped he had left the house and her behind. But she knew if he was gone, she would miss him horribly. Her feelings for him were muddled, melding together in terrible confusion. Did she love him or didn't she?

It would be nice if she made up her mind before the wedding, she thought derisively.

She was tired, having spent the night tossing and turning, afraid to sleep for fear of nightmares. Several times she had heard strange noises in the walls. Most nights the sounds didn't bother her. They were to be expected in a place as old as Moore House. But last night, layered on top of her fears, every strange sound vibrated through her entire being, chilling her to the marrow.

Several times during the night she had almost gone running to Michael's bedroom, like a little child hoping to crawl into bed with her parents after a particularly bad nightmare.

Somehow she'd held her ground. She was an adult, not a child. She could handle a few bumps in the night on her own.

Michael stepped into the foyer, startling her. He stopped next to her, so close his proximity made her nervous. But he appeared to be going somewhere. He was wearing his denim jacket and his feet were encased in work boots. A set of keys was dangling from his hand. Good fortune was smiling on Kelly now. Maybe he would stay away. She was supposed to marry the man in a month. How could she? Being in the same room with him made her feel like a nervous cat in a dog pound.

"Leaving?" she asked, a thread of hope in her voice.

"I'm going into town for supplies. Is there anything you need?"

Privacy, she wanted to reply. Her uneasiness grew. She wanted him to leave, but at the same time she knew she would race after him if he did. She had too much invested in him to call off the wedding now.

"I don't need anything," she said with a sigh.

"Are you sure?" His piercing brown eyes stared straight at her, through her, as if he was trying to read her mind. "The forecast is for snow. I heard it on the radio early this morning. I don't know how reliable the weathermen are in these parts, but I think we should be cautious. If we get as many inches as they're predicting, we'll be trapped inside for a while."

She shivered. His last words echoed in her mind. She didn't want to be trapped in Moore House with him. There were more than forty rooms, yet the place felt far too small for the two of them.

"I..." She turned away, unable to look into those bottomless eyes and think at the same time. "I guess we need staples. Get food that won't need refrigeration in case the electricity goes out. Canned goods. Dried milk. The usual.''

His hand settled on her shoulder as if he sensed her need to put distance between them. She froze beneath the gentle pressure. Her breathing quickened. Why couldn't he leave her alone?

''I'll get a flashlight and some batteries, too, just in case.''

''Why?'' Her eyes narrowed, and she spun around to face him. ''We have three flashlights and you just bought batteries last week.''

''Well,'' he said with a shrug, ''you can never have enough batteries.''

She watched him walk across the foyer to the front door, and she thought about the changes in him. He was hiding something from her. She could feel deceit in his every word. She opened her mouth to mention the pearls she'd found. The accusation soured her tongue, filling her with bitterness.

He stopped at the door and smiled wryly at her. ''Will you be okay here by yourself while I'm away?''

''Fine,'' she said. ''Don't hurry back on my account.''

Then he was gone. The door shut softly behind him. She regretted not having the courage to confront him with her suspicions. Either she was losing her mind or he was lying to her, setting her up for a fall.

Kelly grabbed the phone and brought it to her ear. She wanted to call her only close neighbor, Margo Lane, and warn her about the coming storm. The elderly woman had a hard time getting around. She didn't have her own car, but relied on family and friends for transportation. She would need supplies, too.

Kelly remembered selling the guest house to Margo as one of the smartest things she'd done. At first she'd wanted an elderly couple to buy the place. She hadn't needed the money of course; she'd made that clear to the Realtor. She was willing to take a financial loss as long as she liked the people, feeling lonely after the loss of her father. Margo had fallen in love with the little house on sight and begged Kelly to sell it to her. Margo had family, but they didn't spend much time with her. Kelly remembered Margo's last remark to her that day, the reason she'd told the Realtor to let Margo have the house. "You and I, we'll look after each other."

And they did.

The phone line was dead.

Kelly slowly set the receiver down. Her eyes went to the front door. Margo lived in a small bungalow down the road from Moore House. Kelly considered walking there. The place had been part of the Moore estate at one time, a guest house for visiting relatives and friends.

John Moore had bought five hundred acres and then instructed the builders to erect the mansion. It was followed by the guest house, barracks for the workers, a detached garage and a barn. Each building stood separate from the other, spread out over the great expanses of land. Over the years, piece by piece, bits of the Moore estate had been sold off, the seven-room guest cottage among them.

The guest house was connected to the main public road right along with Moore House. John Moore, the original owner, had wanted his guests to have their privacy, wanted them to feel as if they were in their very own house, a house separate from his. But the guest house was also connected by a rocky path that wound past the detached garage and eventually traveled up a hill to meet the guest house's wrap-around porch.

Kelly grabbed her coat and headed out the door. There was a thin layer of frost on the ground. If she fell on the rocky path, there would be no one nearby to hear her screams for help. Margo was hard of hearing, and there wasn't another soul in the vicinity. Kelly couldn't rely on Michael to save her; he would probably be gone for quite some time.

Despite the slippery conditions, she arrived in one piece. Climbing onto Margo's porch, she rapped hard with her knuckles on the front door. She listened for activity inside the house, but didn't hear anything.

Kelly wondered how long it had been since Margo's relatives had checked on her. The woman lived alone, with a large golden retriever for company.

Kelly moved to the window and peered through, cupping her hands around her face to block the glare. Inside, the living room was empty, the television turned off. It was strange that Margo wasn't watching her favorite afternoon stories. There was no sign of her anywhere.

Suddenly a large form hit the window near Kelly's face, startling her. She shrieked and leaped away. Her foot caught the end of a wooden porch chair and she toppled backward. Pain lanced through her body.

Loud barking caught her attention. From her position flat on the porch, she peered upward. Margo's dog was at the window. Boomer yelped at her, raking his paws against the glass in his excitement at seeing her.

Kelly struggled to her feet, using the chair as leverage. Finding her balance took longer. She retrieved the spare key from the potted plant near the front door, then slid the key home and turned the knob.

Boomer barked happily and tried to jump on her.

"No." She pushed his front legs away. "Sit, Boomer."

The dog followed her command and Kelly moved from room to room, calling out to the elderly woman, who should have been somewhere in the house.

She wouldn't have left Boomer alone to fend for himself. A family member would have been called in to take care of him if Margo was planning to be gone long. Could her friend have gone for a walk alone and hurt herself?

Kelly hadn't seen the place in such bad shape before. Margo usually kept her home immaculate, but today it was a wreck. There were empty cans on the kitchen counter and table. Papers were strewn across the floor. It looked as if a tornado had ripped through the cottage.

Alarm spread through Kelly like wildfire. Something bad must have happened to Margo. Where could she be?

Kelly put the dog on a leash and took him outside with her. He was more hyper than he'd ever been, jerking on his leash, trying to force Kelly to run. As if he hadn't been outside in days, he ignored her firmly spoken commands and continued to struggle against the leash.

Kelly circled the house, calling Margo's name. She paused frequently, hoping for a response. There was no reply, just total silence. Margo seemed to have vanished without a trace.

There was nothing else Kelly could do on her own. She led the dog back along the path to Moore House. Fortunately, she kept a spare bag of dog food at her place in case Margo ever ran out. When she was almost there, she thought she saw someone duck inside the garage—a shadowy form without recognizable features. Her breath caught in her throat and fear gripped her once more. What should she do?

Her hand trembled, weakening her grip on Boomer's leash. The dog took advantage of her momentary distraction and bolted.

"Boomer!"

But the animal had raced around the garage, vanishing from sight. She wanted to call after him, but her mouth was as dry as the Sahara. Her respiration was labored, and she still had a long way to go to reach the safety of her front door.

First she had to check the garage, however. It was possible Margo had been on her way to see Kelly and had stopped in the garage. But why? What would her friend want in a deserted garage?

Kelly opened the garage doors and called, "Hello? Is somebody in here? Margo?"

The chains that had held the doors shut swung free, a padlock dangling from one end. Kelly never bothered to bolt the place. She didn't keep anything inside the decrepit structure worth stealing. She kept her truck in the newly built garage on the other side of the house. The lock had been purchased by her father when he'd kept his car inside, before a tornado had made the place unsafe.

The building was dark and seemed to be empty. She took a step inside, groping for the light switch. But when she found it and flicked it on, the place remained dark.

"Hello?" Her voice seemed to bounce off the walls, echoing eerily. Kelly limped inside, though she was unwilling to stray too far from the door. Her ankle was beginning to throb after her fall on Margo's front porch.

There wasn't anyone in the garage. Light streamed through gaps in the roof, highlighting certain areas. She planned on tearing the decrepit building down eventually; it was becoming a real danger. It had originally been a big red barn, but eventually was transformed into a white garage.

She turned to go, satisfied she was alone. But just as she did so the doors swung shut, startling her.

A nervous laugh escaped her throat. Sleeping in the legendary Moore House was finally getting to her. The stories had warped her mind from youth, desensitizing her. She had nothing to fear; there were no goblins hiding in the dark.

A soft click sounded like a thunderous explosion in the stillness.

She knew the origin of the sound before testing her theory. The doors were chained and locked. Someone had purposely trapped her inside the four-car garage! Besides the doors, her only escape route was a small window near the ceiling, too high for her to reach. Even if she could find a ladder or bench and climb up there, the window was painted shut.

Kelly banged her fists against the door, screaming for help even though she knew there wasn't anyone around to hear her frantic cries. If she was lucky, Michael would return from town soon. She would actually be glad to see him.

Of course, there was a good chance he wouldn't be able to hear her. The garage was set too far from the house for her peace of mind.

Rubbing her upper arms in an attempt to warm herself, she closed her eyes and prayed for a miracle.

FOR A SMALL TOWN, Tinkerton had more than its share of bars. Michael straddled a stool in one of them and ordered a cold beer. John "Paddy" Paddington was tardy. It was late afternoon and patrons were just beginning to fill the dimly lit room. Michael scanned the faces. He was relieved when he didn't recognize any of them. Mostly men, they appeared more interested in their alcoholic beverages than in him.

Michael was about to give up on his old friend when Paddy appeared in the doorway. Michael waved him over, ordering two more beers.

Paddy sat down with a tired grunt. He rubbed his back at the base of the spine and nodded at Michael without saying a word. The Irishman swallowed half his beer in quick chugs.

Michael waited, feeling impatient.

"Aw," Paddy said with delight, settling back. "That hit the spot. I did everything you asked of me. It all went as planned."

"Good." Michael asked, "Is there anything you need to tell me? I don't want to stay away from the house for too long."

"I spoke to our mutual friend. Zu Landis hasn't been

found yet. Sneaky devil. Wouldn't surprise me a bit if he was behind all of this.''

Michael blinked slowly, keeping his expression neutral. "Anything else?" He popped a pretzel into his mouth. Paddy was a good friend, but Michael trusted very few people these days.

"Yes.'' The Irishman grabbed a handful of pretzels himself. "You are to do anything you deem necessary. You have carte blanche. But our friend wants you to know that if you screw up, he's never heard of you.''

Michael nodded with a grim smile.

Paddy continued, "I'll keep an eye on the house from my vantage point down the road. If you need anything, just holler.'' He groaned, "I hope this doesn't take long. I'm not sure my back is going to hold up. Sleeping in a car will cripple you faster than anything.''

"I've told you for years, you need to hire a partner. That way, you could switch off with him.''

"I don't want a partner. I'm hoping to retire soon.''

"Aren't we all?'' Sarcasm dripped from Michael's tongue.

"What about the girl?'' Paddy asked. "Is she giving you any trouble? She looked like a little ball of fire to me. Am I right?''

"Kelly Hall,'' Michael stated. "That's her name.''

"Whatever.'' The man's ample middle shook like a bowl of jelly when he laughed, reminding Michael of a demented Santa Claus without the suit. "You always had a way with the ladies.''

"This one is different. I can't figure her out.''

"How so?''

"She seems so sweet,'' Michael said. "But I don't trust her as far as I can throw her.''

"Good man. Never trust a pretty face.'' Paddy shoved a

pretzel into his mouth. He stopped crunching long enough to ask, "Are you living in her house now?"

"Of course. I'm her doting fiancé." He waved a hand at Paddy as if to negate his dirty thoughts. "We don't share a bed, though. I have a room at the end of an entirely different hallway. I could probably shout my head off and she wouldn't hear me."

"That's convenient. Well, what about this Kelly Hall?" Paddy asked. "Do you think she had something to do with our current situation?"

"My gut tells me no, but I'll keep my eye on her. As far as I'm concerned, everyone is suspect." Michael drank half his beer in a few thirsty gulps. It felt good to relax and be himself. "I almost blew it today. I need to watch what I say. That lady is one sharp tack."

"You can do it," Paddy said. "I have faith in you. You can manage a cute little blonde with your hands tied behind your back."

That didn't sound like too bad of an idea. If he kept his hands tied behind his back, he wouldn't be able to touch her. Touching her would lead to more trouble than he could handle.

"That woman looks at me and throws me off balance," Michael admitted. "She's an enigma. According to the reports you compiled for me, her only friends are an old lady living in the guest house and a mentally retarded man who does handyman work around her place."

"Speaking of Margo Lane, have you met her yet?" Paddy winked. "She's a fine looking lady. Not that I've been looking. I'm happily married."

"Of course, you are." Michael sighed, focusing on the question. "No, I haven't met the neighbor yet. I saw the handyman. What was his name again? Wade something?"

"Carpenter." Paddy laughed and slapped the bar. "Carpenter. That's funny. Like a gardener named Plant or a baker named Baker. Funny, huh?''

Michael's jaw tightened. He rarely found life amusing. He didn't have time to ponder puns or think of jokes.

"Any news on where our buddy Landis could be holing up?'' Michael asked, his eyebrows raised.

"Oh yeah.'' Paddy smiled. "I was just about to get to that. Landis was spotted near Tulsa, Oklahoma. Keep your guard up. He's too close for comfort.''

"I'd better go.'' Michael glanced at his watch. "I have to get some supplies before returning to the house. Did you hear the weather? We may get snowed in.''

He finished his beer and stood up, searching the pockets of his jeans for money to pay for the drinks. His fingers came across a small circular object. He withdrew Kelly's wedding ring and stared down at it as if it were a snake. The last thing he needed was for her to stumble across a piece of evidence like that. He slapped the ring down on the bar in front of Paddy.

"Do me a favor. Take this thing and get rid of it for me.''

"What do you want me to do with it?''

"I don't care.'' Michael shrugged. "Toss it in the garbage. Pawn it. Whatever.''

The bartender approached with another cold beer. He set it in front of Michael along with a folded piece of paper.

"I didn't order this,'' Michael said.

"It was paid for,'' claimed the bartender. "A guy gave me a twenty to deliver the beer and the note.''

"Is that so?'' Paddy asked. "What man?''

The bartender briefly scanned the bar. "I think he left right after he paid me. Enjoy the beer.''

Michael unfolded the note and read it. It was simple and to the point, stirring fear deep in the pit of his stomach. "First the girl. Then you.''

"What is it?" Paddy grabbed the note, reading it for himself. He swore beneath his beer-laden breath.

"Kelly," Michael said, "I have to hurry. She could be in danger."

"Do you need me?"

"Not yet." He shook his head. "Stick to the plan. I'll call you."

Michael raced out the door, note in hand. He climbed into the Mustang and gunned the engine, determined to save Kelly. He told himself it was part of his job. He saved lives when possible. No one under his care died without a hard fight from him. He would die for the people he protected. He assured himself that Kelly was no more important than any of the others he'd guarded. It was nothing personal.

So why were his hands shaking like a tree in a hurricane?

THE GARAGE FLOOR was solid concrete. Smudges of dirt and oil stained the gray surface like an abstract painting. There were several holes in the ceiling, which was propped up on weathered wooden beams. Kelly rattled the door handles, but they wouldn't budge. Taking a deep breath, she ran at one door and delivered a karate kick.

A horrible sound that made Kelly think of a dinosaur screaming in rage forced her eyes heavenward. She watched helplessly as a large beam sagged, the metal sheeting groaning in protest.

She backed away slowly.

Wrapping her arms around her body to ward off the chill, she straightened her spine. Her teeth were starting to chatter. Hypothermia was the biggest worry on her list, next to being crushed to death by the collapsing garage.

Dying was a possibility she didn't want to consider. Her mind turned to other matters. Concentrating on facts, she thought about who had done this—and why.

Maybe it was a practical joke. It could have been Wade

playing a game with her. He would let her out soon. Or maybe local kids daring each other to get closer to Moore House. They might have locked her in the garage to keep her from reporting them as trespassers.

She couldn't think of anyone who would actually want her dead.

MICHAEL RACED THROUGH the house, yelling for Kelly at the top of his lungs. He searched the mausoleumlike mansion room by room, a thousand horrible thoughts flitting through his head. Something terrible could have happened to her. He imagined the worst.

When he made it upstairs and started searching bedrooms, he spotted a dog when he glanced out one of the windows. It was running around the garage, barking as if there was a rabbit inside.

Michael wished he had his .38 at his side. He took the fastest route to the garage, running down the back stairs. Within seconds he was outside.

A metal chain hung from one of the garage doors. A rusty lock had fallen to the ground nearby. He yelled Kelly's name, wondering where she could be. Was she inside?

"Michael?" Her quavering voice reached his ears. "Michael!"

Something was wrong.

Without hesitating he charged inside. Getting to Kelly, making sure she was safe, was the only thought in his head.

"No!" Kelly yelled a warning, but it was too late.

Above him, he heard the screech of metal giving way. He looked up. A heavy wooden beam fell, coming straight at him. There was no time to jump out of the way. No time to think.

No time for one last prayer.

Chapter Four

"Look out!"

Kelly shouted the warning as Michael blundered into the garage, loosening the wooden beam as he entered. She watched in horror as it fell. Time slowed and a surreal quality clouded her vision. The large beam would crush him.

She rushed forward, reaching out with her hands. There wasn't time to think about the consequences of her actions. She didn't consider the possibility that they might both die.

Before she could reach him, Michael flew toward her.

He tackled her, knocking her backward. His arms went around her as he tried to cushion their landing. One of his hands held the back of her head, saving her from an inevitable concussion.

They hit the concrete hard. Whether by accident or design, Michael landed beside her instead of on her. She felt her spine rattle as if every bone was shattering. Pain shot through her limbs. The impact shook her beyond belief.

Explosive noise deafened her. For a moment she feared the entire garage was going to collapse on top of them. Michael covered her body with his own, shielding her from the debris.

When her ability to hear returned, the first sound her ears picked up was Michael's harsh breathing. He turned his head slightly and his warm lips brushed her earlobe. The brief touch was comforting.

His entire body was warm, half covering hers, pressing her firmly against the cement floor. He lifted his head, and their eyes met. They were so different, polar opposites, but their bodies fit together like they'd been made to complement one another. Rough and smooth. Hard and soft.

A soft smile curved his mouth. Michael moved in for a kiss, and she closed her eyes in anticipation.

It wouldn't be the first kiss they'd shared. He had kissed her several times after taking her to dinner in dimly lit restaurants. Those had been chaste kisses, a brief touch and then it was over. Michael was a gentleman, and she'd appreciated his restraint. But she longed now to kiss him passionately, desperately wanted to take his breath away.

Something had changed inside of him recently. She didn't understand it, but she sensed it instantly. A mere look from Michael's smoky eyes burned her to a crisp. She wanted him to kiss her, wanted it more than she could remember wanting anything in her entire lifetime.

The sound of barking cut through their intimacy like a sharp knife. Boomer came bounding toward them, greeting them with loud yelps. He wagged his tail, as if happy to see them still alive.

Kelly laughed at Michael's wry expression as he rolled to one side.

"Boomer was alone in Margo's house and there's no sign of her. I'm worried."

"Why?"

"You know it isn't like her to leave without a word, much less to leave Boomer to fend for himself. She doesn't have a car. Where could she have gone?" Kelly shook her head, unable to understand why Michael wasn't concerned, too. "Her house was a mess, like it'd been ransacked. I guess she could have had family over and maybe they took off suddenly.''

"Or maybe they went to town for supplies and they'll be back soon,'' he said. "Perhaps they'd already heard about the snow. That's always possible.''

"Yes.'' She smiled in relief. "You're right. I'll call her later, if the phone starts working again.''

"What's wrong with the phone?''

"It's dead.'' She shrugged. "If I can't get her on the phone, I'll have to walk over there again later. I want to make sure she knows we have Boomer. I know I won't stop worrying about her until we find out what happened to her.''

"Understood.'' Michael didn't try to talk her out of her concern for the elderly woman as he stood and pulled Kelly to her feet. She wobbled slightly, trying to find her balance. His arm went around her waist to steady her, but she gently pushed him away. She didn't need to lean on him. She was a survivor. Molten steel hardened in her spine. She straightened, standing taller, chin held high.

They surveyed the damage together. The beam had fallen to the cement floor at an angle along with small pieces of debris, but the roof seemed to be holding strong.

"We should get out of here, just in case,'' Michael said. "Are you okay?''

"Fine.'' She forced a smile. "Thanks to you.''

"No.'' He jerked his head at the dog now sitting beside his feet. "Thanks to Boomer. He pushed me from behind. If it wasn't for him, I'd be a pancake.''

Kelly gazed up at him, not trusting her voice.

"How did you lock yourself in here, angel?''

His question floated through her mind. *Angel.* How could one solitary word pack such a punch? It seemed to hit her in the gut, knocking the air from her lungs. A memory connected with the word teased the back of her mind. She al-

most grasped it, but at the last second it faded into noth-
ingness.

"Hey!" Michael broke through her trance. "What's
wrong? Can you hear me?"

Kelly's eyes snapped up to meet his. He was staring at
her, his expression filled with concern again. He probably
thought she was losing her mind. He'd asked her a simple
question and she had zoned out on him.

"I'm fine, really. I was just thinking." She pointed at the
doors. "Someone locked me in. I stepped inside the garage
and the doors swung shut. I heard the chain being linked
together." She looked directly at him. "How did you get
past the lock?"

"The doors weren't locked." He raked a hand through
his dark hair, gazing around at the mess.

"They *were* locked," she insisted. "I tried them. I even
kicked at them. They wouldn't budge."

"Well, they weren't locked when I arrived. I only came
tearing in here like an idiot because you screamed my name
and I thought you might be hurt."

Kelly took a deep breath, then shivered. "I'm cold," she
said. "Let's go back to the house."

Michael helped her over the fallen beam and out the door.
As she started toward the house, Boomer fell into step beside her, with Michael tailing them. Kelly didn't dare look
back, feeling his perceptive gaze burning holes in her. He
had almost died trying to rescue her. She should be grateful.
She should be glad to have him around.

But her resentment grew.

He was lying to her, holding secrets in those dark eyes.
She saw it in his every glance. She had the horrible feeling
he knew exactly who had locked her in the garage, and he
wasn't going to tell her. He knew she wasn't crazy.

She wasn't losing her mind.

Or was she?

MICHAEL WALKED BEHIND Kelly as they followed the path to Moore House, ready to catch her if she stumbled. Neither of them spoke. There was a certain comfort to be found in silence. At least there was for Michael. It gave him opportunity to think.

At the house, he opened the front door and took a step back, allowing Kelly to enter first. He watched her limp up the steps, and realized she must have hurt her leg earlier. His hands itched to help her. Guilt flowed through his veins. She could have been killed. He should have been with her, but he'd gone to town to talk to Paddy. Following his agenda was important, but he wouldn't risk Kelly's life for it. Leaving her on her own was a mistake he wouldn't make again.

He followed her to the parlor. His concern for her escalated when she sank into the covered sofa and buried her face in her hands. He could tell by the way her shoulders shook that she was fighting tears.

Michael didn't know what to do for her. Comforting traumatized women was not one of his specialties. He felt helpless, and he didn't like it. Taking a seat next to her, he wrapped an arm around her and pulled her to his side. He hoped it would be enough. He wanted her to feel safe.

A soft sigh was her only response.

Michael looked around the room. The parlor was definitely not one of his favorite spaces in Moore House. It was bleak. A spider would have second thoughts about living in such a room. The sheet-draped furniture loomed around them like ghosts from the past. Michael wouldn't have been surprised to see them move.

He wanted to ask Kelly about the burns on her arms. He wanted to know who had hurt her.

She straightened her back and said, "I thought I was going to die. I know you don't believe me, but those doors were locked."

"It's possible… Maybe someone locked you in as a joke," he suggested. "Then they got scared and unlocked the doors without letting you in on their prank."

"Yeah. Maybe. Some joke. It was freezing in there and the stupid garage was falling apart." She took a deep, cleansing breath and regained her composure. "You saved my life."

"You would have been fine. Eventually you would have tried the doors again and found them open."

"How did you know to look in there for me?" she asked.

"Boomer was circling the garage when I got back from town. That's how I found you. You never mentioned what you were doing in the garage in the first place," he added.

"I thought I saw someone duck inside there. I went to check it out. I don't understand it," she said. "I was so sure I saw someone, but the garage was empty. I don't know how they got out without me seeing them."

"Maybe they walked around the corner of the building, and you just thought you saw them go inside," Michael stated.

"Yes. I guess that's possible," she said. "I heard the lock click shut soon after. I knew I was trapped before I tried the door. It was the worst feeling in the world." She turned to him, staring deep into his eyes as if searching for truth. "Who would do something like that? And why?"

He shrugged his shoulders. He wanted to tell her everything. He wanted to spill his guts, confess the real reason he was at Moore House, but he couldn't as he had to put this woman's well-being before anything else. He felt responsible for her. He had an overwhelming urge to protect her at all costs. The problem was he wasn't absolutely sure he knew who was behind all the trouble.

She shivered and he pulled her closer, trying to warm her with his body heat. His hand stroked her arm, heating her flesh with friction. She was chilled to the bone. If he hadn't found her so quickly, it was possible she could have died from hypothermia.

"Would you mind starting a fire?" she asked.

He looked at the fireplace with concern. Not long ago a friend of his had tried to light a fire in his hearth only to discover it had been booby trapped. Fortunately his friend had survived with only minor burns. Michael assured himself he wasn't that careless. He would be able to spot the wire before he triggered it.

Kelly's eyes burned holes in his back as he crossed the room to the fireplace. He quickly scanned the mantel for matches and found none. Bending his knees, he hunched down, checking the logs for a trap. Copper fireplace tools were on his right and there was a basket filled with logs to the left. Nothing looked tampered with. There were no matches here, either. What if they were in another room such as the kitchen? Did Kelly expect him to know where they were kept?

Was this a trick to slip him up? Did she suspect?

She rose slowly to her feet. He saw her approach from the corner of his eye.

Kelly pulled a box of matches from an opening at the side of the fireplace. She handed them to him without a word. She didn't need to say anything. Her suspicious expression spoke volumes.

"I'm sorry," he said. "Here I am taking my time and you're freezing."

"I'm fine."

"Would you like me to warm you?" He winked at her, causing her to blush.

"Not right now. Thank you."

"Okay. If you say so." He grinned up at her, playing his part to the hilt. "But you can have a rain check, redeemable any time you want."

Several long moments later the fire blazed to life. Michael

could feel rather than see Kelly hovering over him. Once he succeeded in his task he had no choice but to look at her. He stood, turning to face her. She wasn't looking at him.

Her blue gaze was focused on the fire. The light danced in her eyes, giving her the appearance of an angel in a trance. She was more than beautiful, he reluctantly admitted to himself. During his thirty-three years he had known his fair share of women, some of them beauties in their own right, but none could have held a candle to this lady.

Her eyes were bluer than the Montana sky. Her hair, the color of twenty-four carat gold, spilled over her slender shoulders in luxuriant waves. His hands itched to touch the silky strands. Her heart-shaped face and delicate features were a sculptor's dream. Her lips were sensuous and pink. Michael had a hard time keeping his gaze from dropping to that lovely mouth when standing face-to-face with her.

She hugged herself and stepped closer to the fire, then slowly turned to him as if feeling his eyes on her.

"You know something?" she said. "At first when the door locked I thought maybe I was hallucinating. Then I realized I really was locked inside. I don't know which is worse—thinking I'm crazy or knowing someone is trying to hurt me."

"Why would you think you were crazy?" His eyes narrowed on her face, he tried hard to understand what she was saying. "Because of the dreams you had the other night? That was the medication. I thought we already went over that."

"The dreams have nothing to do with it. It's my mother. I've always been afraid I'd wind up like her."

Michael froze, hearing the pain in her voice.

"You didn't press me to tell you about my mother before and I appreciate it, but I think you need to know." She continued. "I think I was six or seven the first time my mother went to the hospital. I barely remember it. Apparently she'd tried to kill herself—I'm not sure how. I think it was probably an overdose. I remember her medicine cabinet being filled to the point of overflowing with pills. My father called an ambulance, and the police came. She was gone for a week or so. When she came back, she was different.''

Kelly fell silent.

Michael chose his words carefully, afraid he might push her too hard. She could totally withdraw or freak out on him.

''How was she different?''

''She was a walking zombie.'' Kelly's fair eyebrows furrowed together with the memory. She stared into the distance. ''I don't think she even recognized me. She lived in a fog. No emotion whatsoever. I thought I'd done something wrong.''

''Didn't your father explain things to you?''

''I was a child,'' she reminded him. Her gaze swung to Michael. ''I couldn't possibly understand what was happening to her. When I was old enough, my father filled me in and I wished he hadn't. It turned my life upside down. I was so afraid of becoming like my mother.''

Was it possible to pass insanity from mother to daughter? For Kelly's sake, he hoped not. She'd had a rough life by the sound of it. She deserved better.

''My mother woke one morning and decided she wasn't sick anymore. She stopped taking her medication without telling anyone.'' Kelly's eyes fixed on his chest, but he knew she wasn't seeing him. ''We had no idea there was a problem until Mom decided I was out to get her.'' She swallowed hard. Michael watched with admiration as she pushed her pain down and went on. ''She was boiling water for something. Macaroni and cheese, I think. Without a word she grabbed the pot and threw the scalding water at me.''

Michael's sharp intake of breath went unnoticed. Kelly

continued talking, and he regained his composure. The last thing she needed was him railing at the world as if he had the right. She was the one who'd been burned. She was the one in pain.

"Luckily, I saw it coming." She forced a smile. "My mother was aiming for my face. I turned my head and put my arms up in an attempt to protect myself."

Kelly demonstrated, lifting her arms as she told the story. He stared at her burns now, seeing them in a whole new light. How could anyone do that to her own child?

Michael kept his feelings deep inside. What had happened to Kelly was in the past. He couldn't do anything about it. Getting upset, showing how angry he was that someone had hurt her, wouldn't help.

He wasn't psychic, but he knew what she was about to say. Her mother hadn't come home again. Good. He hoped the crazy woman would stay locked away forever. If he had any say in the matter she wouldn't get another chance to hurt Kelly. No one would.

"My mom is in the hospital and probably always will be. She was found insane by the court-appointed doctor. She has schizophrenia. A lot of people suffer from it but aren't locked up. They said my mom was different. She was dangerous. Lucky her."

Michael touched Kelly's chin, tilting it until her eyes met his and lost that blank stare. "There isn't anything wrong with you."

She let out a nervous laugh. "Thank you, Dr. Taggert."

"I may not be a psychiatrist, but I'm a good judge of character. You aren't insane."

"Not yet."

"Not ever." He released her chin, but his gaze held hers as a friendly hostage. "You are a strong, capable woman. Don't let a few bad dreams brought on by bad medication throw you. You aren't losing it."

"Well," she said, "today certainly wasn't a part of my imagination. Someone locked me inside the garage. I know it." She frowned. "Where are the supplies you went into town for? Are they in your car?"

Blast! The supplies. He'd forgotten his invented reason for going to town. Every time he thought he had Kelly a safe distance from the truth, she cornered him.

"I came back before getting the supplies." He smiled easily at her, another lie sliding off his tongue. "I forgot my wallet. Can't buy anything without money these days."

He was in the clear now.

Her eyes sharpened on him. "You usually charge it to my account."

Of course he did.

"Shopping was my idea." He shrugged. "There were some personal things I wanted to get, so I was planning on paying for them myself. I would go back for the supplies now, but in light of what happened I don't want to leave you alone."

"I don't need a keeper." She shrugged. "I can ask a friend to deliver whatever we need. You can make a list and pay him when he gets here."

Michael nodded. Now he was going to have to invent a list of personal items he just couldn't live without. He needed to keep on his toes around Kelly Hall. Her mind was a steel trap. One wrong move on his part and she would be all over him like a pit bull.

"I'll make a list later," he said. "I want to walk the grounds, make certain the intruder is gone."

"I can come with you if you want."

"I think I can handle it alone."

Michael left Kelly sitting in the parlor. He wished he could retrieve his gun but couldn't take the chance that Kelly might see it. Being naked couldn't have made him feel more vulnerable.

He stepped outside, with Boomer on his heels. Michael's gaze automatically traveled down the long road to where Paddy would be parked. He gave a short wave in case his partner was watching through the binoculars, then headed around the house with quick strides, anxious to get back to Kelly. He believed her about the garage being locked, even though it hadn't been when he got there. Michael hoped the intruder had vanished from their lives forever.

Unfortunately, his gut told him the opposite was true. The person who had locked Kelly in the garage was somewhere nearby, watching them. He could practically feel those evil eyes tracking his every move.

Boomer wagged his tail and stayed with Michael the whole time, not putting more than a few feet between them. He had found a new friend.

THE SOUND OF THE FRONT door closing gave Kelly permission to release the breath she'd been holding. The oxygen returned to the room in a dizzying rush. How did Michael's presence cause the walls to close in on her? It had never felt this way between them before. Within twenty-four hours Michael had altered drastically. His voice was the same, but his choice of words had changed and his mannerisms were different. In fact, his entire aura was different.

Or was it her imagination?

An insistent knocking on the front door drew her attention. She hurried to answer it, wondering if Michael had forgotten his keys. But the door was unlocked so it couldn't be him. Kelly pasted on a smile, thinking it was probably Margo coming for her dog.

Her smile froze.

It was a stranger—a tall, gangly man with a pointy nose and jutting chin. He wore a dark suit that must have been two sizes too small for him and held a briefcase close to his chest.

"Yes," she murmured, "may I help you?"

"I called a few weeks ago," he stated abruptly. "My boss wants to buy your house."

"I told you already, I'm not interested in selling. This house has been in my family for more than fifty years."

"My boss is willing to pay twice what the house is worth."

Her eyes widened. Why would anyone want to pay double?

"Who is your boss?"

"I'm not at liberty to say." He patted his briefcase. "I have all the papers in here. Say the word and we can sign them." He pulled a slip of paper from his vest pocket. "I also have a hefty check."

When he handed it to her she glanced down at the signature. It was signed "Natalie Gross." Kelly pushed it back at him.

"Okay," she said, attempting to remain calm, "I'm only going to say this once more. I am not selling Moore House. Not for twice the amount. Not for ten times the amount. Please leave."

She tried to close the door, but the man's hand slammed against it. There was a dark glint in his eyes behind the wire-rimmed glasses he wore. She sensed that this man was not only quite capable of hurting her, he would enjoy it.

Cold fear chilled her nerve endings. If he attacked her, would she be able to fight him off? If she screamed, would Michael hear her?

"My boss has her heart set on buying this house. I think you should consider her offer." He smiled calculatingly. "She will get the place one way or another."

"Is that a threat?" Kelly lifted her chin high, gritting her teeth to keep her jaw from trembling. "I want you off my land."

"You aren't listening." The stranger's voice rose.

"My fiancé is going to be back any second. He'll kick your butt all the way to the state line."

"I met your fiancé in town a few weeks ago. I don't think he'll give me any trouble."

"Think again, pal," Michael said. And immediately afterward, Boomer growled.

Kelly spotted Michael over the other man's shoulder and relief spread through her body, warming her. She hated the thought of being vulnerable and didn't want to be in anyone's debt, but there was a tiny guilty pleasure that came with being rescued. Michael was her very own hero, strong and courageous. He could handle the skinny man with one hand tied behind his back.

"You should stay out of this," the stranger said.

Michael stepped closer and the man's eyes almost bugged out of his head. He claimed to have seen Michael in town, but he looked like he'd just come across an unfamiliar and dangerous creature. He moved to the side, putting distance between them.

Michael held out his hand. "Show me your identification."

"Pardon?"

"You heard me." Michael snapped his fingers. "A driver's license. State identification card. Anything with a name and picture on it will do." His dark eyebrows rose. "Do you need help finding your wallet? I don't mind getting it myself." He moved nearer, closing in on him.

The stranger relinquished his wallet without another protest.

Michael flipped it open and read the name aloud.

"Elvin Grant." Michael handed the wallet back. "Okay, Elvin Grant, if I see you around here again I'll have the local authorities run your name through their computers. A man like you must have an interesting past."

"You'll regret this."

"No," Michael said with confidence. "You'll regret it if
ou harass the lady again."

The stranger scurried off, leaving Kelly and Michael
tanding on the porch in an uncomfortable silence. Kelly
lidn't know what to say. A quiet thank-you didn't seem
nough. She was certain Michael had saved her from harm.

Boomer barked happily and wagged his tail.

"Has that guy hassled you before?" Michael asked.

"Over the phone," she admitted.

"Well, he won't be bothering you again." Michael stared
ut at the dirt road, watching the dust float in the air as
Elvin Grant traveled back to the main road. "Why would
nyone want this house enough to threaten you over it?"

"Because of the legend of Fuller's diamonds, I imagine."

"Diamonds?" Michael's dark eyebrows rose slowly.

Kelly was certain she'd told him the story before. The
nan seemed to have a bad case of amnesia. He was con-
tantly forgetting things. She sighed, prepared to tell him
he sordid story again. The short version.

"Robert Fuller was thought to be a jewel thief. He lived
n this house, owned it in the 1930s." She shrugged. "He
vas accused of stealing a shipment of uncut diamonds on
heir way from South Africa to a big-time diamond dealer
n New York."

"Accused? So he wasn't arrested for it?"

"No." Kelly forced a smile. "Fuller died here. The di-
monds weren't recovered. Rumor has it the gems are hid-
len somewhere inside this house."

"I'm sure the police have searched the place thor-
ughly." Michael headed inside, apparently bored with the
onversation already. Boomer stuck to his heels like a loyal
oldier. Kelly followed them both.

"Well, yes," she replied, "Of course the police looked
or them. That's why it's just a rumor that they're here.
Jnfortunately, there are a lot of people who believe it. I

can't count the number of times I've had to run off a fortune hunter who thought he was going to dig up my yard or break into my house."

"I'll bet." Michael chuckled. "Must be a pain."

"It is. Anyway, Fuller had a mound of debts. He had nothing left to pass on to his only child. The state auctioned off this house. My grandfather bought it. It's been in our family ever since."

"Did you grow up here?" A curious light brightened Michael's dark eyes.

"I lived here until my mother went to the hospital for the last time. My father rented an apartment in town after that. He insisted I hold my head high no matter how much the other kids taunted me." She snorted, a small derisive sound. "Easy for him to say. He wasn't the one constantly stared at and mocked. Anyway, after my father died, I moved back into Moore House."

"You're hiding?"

"So?" She glared at him. "What if I am?"

"You're just punishing yourself. You shouldn't allow small-minded people to run your life."

"Now you sound like my father."

"Thank you," Michael said. "I take that as a compliment. He seems like an intelligent human being."

"He was." She stated quietly. Then she shrugged. " think I need a drink. Would you care to join me?"

"Sure."

She walked over to the wet bar and placed a couple glasses on the tabletop. "My father always liked a warm brandy before bed. I could use one after the day I've had."

"Kelly." Michael's smooth and sexy voice seemed to wash over her. "Would you like me to sleep in your bed tonight?"

Chapter Five

The look on her face wasn't exactly flattering. Shock reflected in the blue depths of her eyes. Michael had known the moment the query slid from his mouth that it was the wrong thing to say. It sounded like a blasted come-on. She thought he wanted to sleep with her.

Which he did, of course. What red-blooded American male wouldn't? But he couldn't make love to her, and he didn't want her to get the wrong impression.

"When I asked if you wanted me to sleep in your bed," he clarified, "I meant instead of you. Not *with* you."

Her eyes widened in confusion. "I don't get it. What are you saying?"

"You claim someone locked you in the garage."

"Someone did!"

He held up a hand, stopping what he suspected would be an angry tirade. "Okay. I'm not questioning that. I'm saying I'll trade beds with you if you want. That way, if someone is after you, they'll make the mistake of attacking me instead."

She gasped, and the remaining color drained from her cheeks. "I don't think that's a good idea." She turned her face away. Her slender frame trembled. "I don't want you to get hurt because of me. I'm not that selfish."

"I doubt it will come to that." Michael decided to change

the subject. The poor woman was on the edge of a mental collapse. She needed to get her mind off what had happened to her in the garage. "Tell me more about the jewel thief. It sounds like quite a story. How much is fact and how much is rumor?"

"Why don't I show you?" she offered. "Then you'll understand." An exuberant smile curved the corners of her mouth as if she was a child with a delicious secret she couldn't wait to share.

Boomer shot up the staircase and vanished from view just then.

"I guess he wants to explore his new surroundings," Kelly said.

She crooked her finger at Michael, gesturing for him to join her.

He trailed behind her, following her through the double doors beneath the point at which the two staircases met. They entered the library and hovered just inside the doorway for a few minutes, as if Kelly wanted to keep him in suspense. He couldn't believe his eyes as he took in his surroundings. They were standing in an enormous oval-shaped room with an endless wall of bookshelves wrapped around it. There were more books than he could count, stacked ten shelves high. The walls seemed to be in a straight line, but the room was round, each bookcase curving so slightly that it wasn't noticeable. Paddy's entire house could have fit in the room. Michael was sure of it.

He stepped to the side and watched Kelly slide an attached ladder along one section of the bookcase. She climbed the rungs and reached over, grabbing for one old tome. The book was huge, and she had to struggle to get a good grip on it.

Michael drew closer in case she fell. His eyes were on a level with her knees, and he couldn't help that the trousers that covered her lower limbs couldn't conceal their perfection. He remembered her legs, the way they had looked dripping wet from the shower. He envisioned how the towel had ended on her upper thighs, teasing him with a glimpse of what hid beneath the terry cloth.

Kelly teetered precariously.

She dropped the book a half second before she fell backward, a startled shriek bursting from her lips.

Michael caught her easily and cradled her in his arms. Holding her this time had a startling effect on him. Desire shot from his brain to his toes, leaving no part of him untouched. Electricity crackled in his veins. It had been a long time since he'd wanted a woman so much. Why her? Why now?

Eyes wide and unblinking, she stared up at him. She appeared to be as stunned as he felt.

Kelly pressed against his chest with her palms, and he let her slowly slide down his body until she was standing on her own two feet again. He still didn't release her completely. His hands remained on her arms, reluctant to give up the treasure they'd found.

"The book," she managed to say at last. "My grandfather compiled the history of Moore House and put it in that book."

Taking the hint, he went to the fallen book and picked it up, noting that it must weigh more than fifty pounds. Michael set it on a nearby desk and blew dust off the bronzed cover. There was a gold emblem on it, a circular pattern with a black design that seemed to be a family crest.

Kelly came to stand beside him, the top of her head barely reaching his shoulder. He could smell the shampoo she'd used that morning. The faint scent of wildflowers tormented his nostrils. Being this close to her was absolute torture, no doubt about it.

Kelly opened the book, and Michael tore his attention from her, trying to concentrate on the task at hand. Inside

there were pages of newspaper clippings, photographs and
journal entries. He didn't have time to go over everything.
He wouldn't find clues to solve his mystery in this book.
He was only looking at it to get Kelly's mind off of her
tiresome visitor.

"Give me the highlights," he said. "Break it down for
me. Start with the person who built the house."

"John Moore," she replied. "The house was erected directly after the Civil War ended. John and his brother Andrew were at odds. John was running a company up north
when the war began. His father and his brother expected
him to return to South Carolina and fight beside them."

"Of course he didn't," Michael guessed, trying to speed
things along.

"No. While his father's plantation—his brother's inheritance—was burned to the ground, John was becoming one
of the wealthiest men in the country. His father died of a
heart attack before the war ended. Andrew lost his wife and
unborn child in the fire that took the plantation house."

"Then what?"

"John moved here with his wife, Anabella," Kelly said.
"He wanted to get away from everything that reminded him
of the war. He bought five hundred acres. He planted wheat
and invited his brother to see it. John planned on offering
half the land to his brother, but he never got the chance."

Michael had a bad feeling he knew what had happened
next. The house seemed to shudder around him with the
resurrected memory of John Moore. If there were ghosts in
the world, Michael had no doubt this house would be the
perfect place for them.

He waved Kelly on, wanting her to continue.

"Before John could make the offer, Andrew killed him.
It happened in the middle of the wheat field. Andrew picked
up a rock and bashed his brother's head in. The soil drank

his blood. Rumor has it the land became cursed after that. It hasn't grown a decent crop since.''

"Right.'' Michael laughed. "How much of this is true? Is there any solid evidence?''

"There are papers. The only thing that can't be proved here is if the land is cursed. Everything else is true.''

"Okay. Who owned the estate next?'' Michael couldn't help it. Curiosity grew like a seed in his belly. Now that he had a taste of the legends of Moore House, he wanted to know everything. Every detail, no matter how minuscule.

"Well, Anabella inherited the house from her husband, of course, but she sold it a year later. A man by the name of William Smith bought the estate. He wanted to farm the land. Unfortunately, something happened every year to ruin his crop, and he lost money fast. The bank eventually foreclosed on him.''

"That doesn't sound particularly strange,'' Michael commented. "Stuff like that happens all the time.''

"True.'' She smiled smugly. "William Smith seemed like an ordinary farmer to the outside world. However, some people believed he rode with Jesse James. In fact, there are rumors that Jesse James hid out at Moore House for a few weeks while a stubborn posse was trying to track him down.''

"Jesse James?'' Michael smiled, remembering his boyhood fantasies concerning the historic outlaw. "Cool.''

"Yeah. They say Jesse hid in secret passages, but to my knowledge no one has ever found a hidden entryway. It's probably bogus information. Just another rumor that grew into legend.''

"Have you seen the blueprints?''

"No,'' she said. "They must have been lost a long time ago.''

"That's too bad.''

As she continued to speak about the old mansion, Michael

found himself becoming more and more involved in the legends. Kelly was a natural storyteller and she obviously felt passionate about Moore House. Her face and tone were animated, drawing him in.

He found himself smiling, watching her face light up as she spoke. The urge to reach out and stroke her cheek grew stronger with every word she uttered. But touching her would mean interrupting the stories. His professional curiosity was piqued. He had to know about the people that Moore House had supposedly destroyed.

COLD FINGERS OF EXCITEMENT mixed with fear of the unknown tingled Kelly's spine. She felt she should be whispering the tales to Michael under a blanket while holding a flashlight. Or not talking about them at all. These stories, the darker side of them, still had the ability to frighten her. Although she didn't believe in ghosts, she did believe in evil. She'd seen evil, had felt it as her mother turned on her with that scalding pot of water.

A tiny thrill came from talking about the legends. If Michael was going to marry her, live with her at Moore House, then he had every right to know the truth. She hoped he would come to appreciate the house as much as she did.

"William Smith sold off parts of the estate to try to keep his head above water," she continued. "Ten acres here, another twenty there." She shrugged. "That's why the estate is so much smaller now."

"Who bought the house after Smith?"

So he was bored with William Smith already. She felt as if she was losing her audience, but she knew how to kindle his interest. "It's all right here." Kelly turned a few pages of the book. "A rancher by the name of George Monroe bought it. He had three grown sons. One of them was married. The wife had an affair with one of the brothers. When her husband found out, he and his brother fought over her.

In the process, they fell over the banister where the stained angel is and both died.''

Michael cut in. ''What happened to the girl?''

''George Monroe was overcome with grief. He had the girl hanged out back, from a branch of the tallest oak tree. Those were odd times. The father managed to convince the townspeople she was a witch and had put a spell on his sons.''

''That's brutal.''

''Yes,'' Kelly agreed. ''It is.''

Next came her favorite owner of Moore House. ''Monroe sold the place after his sons were killed. It stood empty for a short time. Then an heiress named Elizabeth Barrington bought it in the 1920s. She was young and beautiful, full of life. She threw the most lavish parties here. People came from all over the state to attend her gatherings.''

''I get the feeling something bad happened to her,'' Michael said.

''Oh, yes. Elizabeth caught her boyfriend in bed upstairs with one of her closest friends during a party.''

''Ow.'' Michael perched on the edge of the desk. His knee accidentally bumped Kelly's thigh. A shock of recognition shot through her. She was more aware of him than ever before. With the awareness came uncertainty and a growing excitement.

She plunged on, continuing with the story. ''Elizabeth killed her boyfriend using a silver candlestick.'' Kelly took a deep breath before adding, ''But people that were at the party claim the boyfriend and best friend weren't even in the house at the time Elizabeth said she saw them together. Her boyfriend showed up late. Elizabeth took him straight upstairs with her. He probably thought he was in for some loving, but she killed him.''

''Were there any witnesses to the crime?'' Michael asked.

''More than one. They caught her with the bloody candlestick in her hands. She dropped it, screamed and ran from the room, leaving her stunned guests to marvel at what she had done. They looked for her, searched the entire property.'' Kelly shrugged. ''No one ever found her. She disappeared. Eventually the house was auctioned off by the state to cover her debts.

''The next owner of Moore House was Walter Fuller. He was the alleged jewel thief. He was also the last owner before my grandfather.''

Michael shut the book, staring down at the Hall family crest as if waiting for it to speak. His dark, sultry eyes swung up to meet hers, filled with a hint of skepticism. ''Amazing. So tell me, why would you want to live here now? After everything that's happened?''

Kelly wrapped her arms around her middle and forced her eyes to focus on his. She would not let herself look down at the scars on her forearms.

''This is my home,'' she stated. ''I'm not afraid of a curse. I live here because I want to.''

''You're hiding. Just like Jesse James.''

Hurt filled her chest. ''Why are you being so mean?''

''I'm not.'' He took her hand. ''I'm sorry if it sounded that way to you.'' He stood before her and brought her hand to his lips, kissing the tips of her fingers. ''You are an incredibly beautiful woman. I just hate to see you lock yourself away in this fortress. You have so much to offer the world.''

''I'm not locked away. I visit with Margo and Wade. I go into town sometimes.''

''Have you ever thought about getting a job?''

''I'm independently wealthy,'' she said. ''I don't have to work.''

''But it would give you some sort of fulfillment. You need that.''

"Stop telling me what I need!" She lowered her voice. "I thought you liked me for me. Just the way I am."

"I do."

Michael slid off the edge of the desk and stood next to her. He lifted his hands to her hair, slipping his fingers into the tangled curls. She wanted to bolt like a frightened horse. Her feelings didn't make sense to her anymore. She was engaged to Michael. She was going to be his wife. So why was it hard to be in the same room with him now?

Why did the thought of kissing him send her spinning into flight mode?

He lowered his head and touched her lips with his own, but the familiar velvety softness of his mouth hardened instantly, sweeping her into a maelstrom of sensation.

Kelly gasped, her expectations of a kiss changed forever. Michael's kisses usually played like a gentle melody from beginning to end, but this was a thundering crescendo.

Kelly welcomed the kiss and deepened it. The smooth feel of his tongue gliding against her own sent a thrilling current of electricity through her veins. She wasn't sure which of them had let out a groan, a throaty sound of primal desire. It didn't matter. Her mind was swirling with colors, and she reached for him, running her hands up his back. Her fingers curled, digging into the muscles beneath the thick wool of his jersey.

The world around her ceased to exist. There was nothing but Michael. Nothing else mattered. Passion stirred within her and she was swept away on a tidal wave of pleasure.

She wanted more. She wanted to touch his bare flesh, but didn't dare. The fear of rejection kept her from burrowing her fingers under the hem of his sweater. Instead, she savored what Michael was willing to give to her. She tugged at him, wanting him closer, and barely remembered the doubts she'd had about him.

But slowly, the little things that bothered her floated to

the surface. The changes in him. The secrets and lies lingering in his eyes. Did he really think she was so stupid that she couldn't see them?

And there was the matter of those tiny pearls she'd found....

With a mighty shove, Kelly pushed Michael away.

He fell back, bumping into the desk, and a startled look crossed his face. It vanished in a second, replaced by a carefully neutral expression. It was so easy for him to cover his true emotions. She both envied and resented him for it.

"What's wrong?" he asked calmly. But a tiny muscle in his jaw tightened visibly.

"I need to know something." She hugged herself. It was a bad habit. She did it every time she felt weak or vulnerable. "I found pearls on the floor in my bedroom."

"So?" His eyebrows arched, and he sighed. "What is that supposed to mean?"

"My grandmother's wedding gown has tiny pearls on it. You told me we didn't get married. Therefore, there shouldn't have been little pearls on my floor. I haven't once taken my grandmother's gown from the box in the attic." Dropping her hands on her hips, she dared him to lie to her again. "Care to explain?"

He shook his head slowly. "I have no idea what you're talking about."

"Fine," she said. "Come with me then. I'll show you."

Kelly didn't wait for his consent, but bolted out the doors, turning to the stairs on the right side. She felt rather than saw Michael follow her. His eyes burned into her back, making her feel as if she was on fire. She hurried her pace and practically ran up the staircase.

"Slow down," Michael said. "It's not important enough to break your neck over."

Moving even faster, Kelly raced into the master bedroom and went straight to the heart-shaped trinket box on the vanity. That was where she'd put the pearls. She flicked off the lid, practically shoving the box under his nose.

"Explain these, okay? Where did they come from if not from my grandmother's dress?"

Michael glanced inside and shrugged. "Explain what?"

"What?" She looked into the box. There was nothing there. She reached in and felt around with her fingers, hoping the tiny pearls had simply blended with their surroundings, but she didn't find any. The box was empty. How? "I know I put them in here!"

Was she losing her mind? Had it been this way with her mother in the beginning?

Kelly threw the offending box across the room. It hit the wall, shattering into several pieces. The fragments fell to the floor, white shards on dark wood. They represented her life. She was going insane....

Michael's hand caressed her shoulder.

She slapped it away. She didn't want or need his pity. She hated him seeing her like this.

"I found pearls on the floor and I put them in that box. They were pearls off my grandmother's wedding dress." She repeated what had happened in a clear, disconnected voice. She wasn't sure if she was trying to convince Michael or herself. "I wasn't sleeping. I wasn't dreaming."

Her upper body began to shake and tears filled her eyes. "I don't want to be crazy," she cried.

He opened his arms and she automatically stepped into the comforting circle. He had strong, reassuring arms, hard muscle and warm flesh. She pressed her face to the groove of his throat, squeezing her eyes shut. Tears escaped, sliding down her cheeks.

"It's okay," he murmured while smoothing her hair. "You are not losing your mind. I'm sure of it. Believe me on this one, okay?"

"It feels like I am," she sobbed.

"No, honey. I'm sure there's a logical explanation for it."

"Like what?" She pulled back, staring at his face through a watery film of tears. "How did the pearls disappear from my room? Either I imagined seeing them or I got rid of them and forgot doing so. Any way you look at it, I'm losing my mind."

Michael opened his mouth as if to argue the point, but then closed his lips firmly, compressing them into a straight line. He obviously wanted to tell her something. So why didn't he? Why was he holding back?

She withdrew from his embrace. She couldn't trust him. He proved that fact over and over again.

She went to her bed and lay down, turning her back to him. She didn't need him. She didn't need anybody.

She heard the door close softly behind him as he left her alone. Fresh tears filled her eyes. Her mother had hated it when Kelly cried. She remembered her mother screaming at her to grow up and stop acting like a baby. Kelly had grown up thinking crying was a sign of weakness, but now she saw it differently. She needed to cry. It was a cathartic.

She thought about her mother and choked back a sob.

MICHAEL PEERED INSIDE the fully stocked side-by-side, stainless steel refrigerator. As far as he was concerned there was one clear explanation for Kelly's hallucinations; she was being drugged. If that was the case, the drug would have to be in something she consumed on a daily basis.

Michael chose the midnight hour to dump the pitchers of iced tea and lemonade so Kelly wouldn't walk in on him and demand answers. He cleaned out the refrigerator, throwing away anything and everything that could have contained a drug. Someone, anyone, could be lacing her food or drink with a drug that causes hallucinations. He would make certain the delusions stopped now. She wasn't losing her mind.

He'd stake his reputation on that. Someone had to be drugging her. *Damn the situation!* He wanted to hold Kelly close, tell her the truth, help her deal with it.

But he couldn't risk it. Not yet.

A sound in the hallway brought his head out of the refrigerator. He closed the door softly and glanced around in the dark, adjusting his eyes to it like a panther. Once again he longed for the security of his gun. He went to the open doorway and looked down the hallway.

A giant shadow moved, growing closer like a demon sent from the depths of hell.

Michael tackled the man, shoving him into the wall.

The man grunted.

"Please, don't hurt me," cried a familiar voice.

It was Kelly's friend, Wade Carpenter.

"What are you doing here?" Michael released the giant, putting enough space between them so they could both breathe.

"I...I have a key," Wade stated in a frightened tone. "Kelly gave me a key."

Michael turned on the light and watched the intruder blink in the sudden glare. "Why were you skulking around in the dark?"

Wade shook his head without replying.

"I think you should leave now," Michael said. He had no reason to hold the man, and Wade obviously wasn't going to tell him anything. He held out his hand. "Hand over the key."

"Kelly gave it to me," the man whined.

"Yes, she did. But she didn't think you were going to use it in the middle of the night. Give it to me. Now."

Wade reluctantly handed the key to Michael. Head bent low, he walked away, tripping over his own big feet on the way out. As he did so, a pair of glasses fell out of one of his pockets. The lenses broke, scattering tiny pieces of glass across the floor. Wade continued on, not picking them up.

"Wait," Michael said. "You dropped something."

"I found them. Finders keepers. Losers, weepers."

"Where?"

"In the study," Wade replied. "They were on the desk. I found them. I didn't steal them."

Michael waved him on, wanting the giant to leave. He almost disposed of the glasses in the kitchen garbage pail, but as he did so a fragment of glass nicked his thumb.

"Ow. Damn." He sucked it into his mouth, cleaning the wound with his tongue. He slid the glasses into his pocket, figuring they could turn out to be an important clue. His eyes went to the ceiling as he wondered if Kelly was asleep yet. He imagined her in bed, pictured how she would look with her hair spread across the pillow. A new ache began in the lower part of his anatomy. It was going to be a long night.

SOMETHING WOKE KELLY a little after two that morning. She heard a noise, a faint, raspy sound. Freezing in fear, she lay immobile beneath the heavy covers. She didn't dare breath. Straining her ears, she listened for the slightest noise.

She wasn't alone in the room.

Quiet footsteps moved across the floor toward her bed, coming closer and closer. She imagined herself running to the light switch and flicking it on. The light would make all demons disappear. But her body refused to obey her brain. No matter how hard she tried, she couldn't get out of bed and run. She lay there, stiff as a board.

Were the footsteps real?

The feeling of having an intruder in her bedroom was oppressive. She couldn't breathe. The walls seemed to shrink around her.

Michael? If she called for Michael, he would come. He would save her from danger, real or imagined.

She opened her mouth to scream, but something soft wrapped around her throat, looped around her neck, squeezing her windpipe. She couldn't see the man's face, but she could feel his stinking breath on her. He smelled like cheap wine.

Kelly fought like a tiger gone mad, striking out at anything within reach. Her fingernails clawed at her attacker's face, but he moved his head backward. She went for his hands then, digging her nails into them.

He cried out in pain.

Kicking furiously, she struck her intended target several times with her foot and was rewarded with another grunt of pain.

Yanking free, she finally tumbled off the bed and screamed.

Boomer barked in the distance.

The intruder was gone in an instant. Footsteps raced across the hardwood floor. A light flared and then faded into darkness.

She pulled the material the stranger had tried to strangle her with away from her neck, letting it fall to the floor. She gasped. Drawing air into her lungs proved to be a painful endeavor.

A second light appeared. With it came Michael's voice. "What is it? Are you all right? Did you have a bad dream?"

She couldn't speak. Her throat was raw, aching from the brutal pressure. Michael lifted her from the tangled sheets on the floor. His arms wrapped around her, strong arms that could keep the demons at bay. She knew as long as she was in his embrace nothing could hurt her.

She was safe, if only for a moment.

Chapter Six

Michael held Kelly to his chest, feeling the rapid tempo of her heart through his jersey. Something had scared the poor woman nearly to death. The fierce trembling turned to gentle shudders. He continued to hold her while stroking her thick blond mane. It didn't matter if her demons were real or imagined. He would willingly slay them for her.

Michael wondered if this new need to protect came from lust or from a deeper emotion. The last woman to share his bed had been a spy intent on prying information from him through pillow talk. She had tried to kill him when he'd discovered her true identity. It hadn't taken him long. His trust was not easily won.

Even now, while holding this beautiful angel in his arms, he took a mental step backward, away from the situation, and watched it unfold like an epic novel. Kelly Hall appeared to be a sincere, genuine person of strong character. She was a complicated individual, a mixture of frightened child and determined adult. His gut told him she was on the level.

But he would sleep with one eye open in case he was being deceived.

He wouldn't be the first poor sap to be swayed by a pretty face. There might be treachery hiding behind those innocent blue eyes. Could he trust her with the truth? He wanted to, but his past had slowly poisoned him. The idea of trusting anyone, even Kelly, filled him with a sickening dread.

Kelly snuggled closer as if she couldn't get near enough. He tucked her head under his chin and tightened his arms around her. He wanted to shove his suspicions aside and believe this woman was the real thing. But he couldn't. Not yet. He'd seen the dark side of humanity too many times to allow a pretty face and soft hands to make him forget his true purpose.

He had a job to do.

"Tell me," he whispered into her hair. "What happened?"

"He tried to kill me." Her voice was barely audible.

"Who?"

"I don't know." Fresh terror tinged her words. "There was someone in here with me. I didn't imagine it. I'm not crazy."

"Okay. I believe you. Tell me everything. Start at the beginning."

"He tried to strangle me." She broke off for a moment, swallowing hard in the darkness. He waited for her to continue, holding her tight as if his strength could seep into her flesh and bones. "He came out of nowhere. I hit and I kicked and I scratched. He started choking me. I couldn't breathe."

If this woman was lying, then he was a fool, because he believed her.

"I need to check things out. I'm going to let you go now. Okay?"

"Yeah." She disengaged from his embrace. "Go ahead."

"Are you sure?"

"I'm okay now. Really." A brave smile curved her lips.

Michael switched on the bedside lamp and quickly scanned the room. Everything seemed to be in order. His gaze went to Kelly. Her face was still pale but from the stubborn tilt of her chin and the defiant sparkle in her eyes, he could tell Kelly's fighting spirit seemed to be reemerging.

Returning to her side, he gently pulled her white night-gown away from her neck and looked for evidence of an attack. Her throat appeared blotchy and sore. There was some sort of abrasion, but it didn't look like marks left by fingers. She could have done it herself if she was clever and wanted his trust.

His damn training was a nuisance at times. It would have been nice to take things at face value for once instead of looking for hidden truths.

Determined to give her the benefit of the doubt, Michael held a finger to his lips, and motioned for her to be quiet. He stepped over to the closet and jerked the door open. It was empty. His next stop was the bathroom. He checked everywhere, including behind the glass shower door. No one was in sight.

He didn't want to leave Kelly alone for a second longer than he had to, so he returned to her. She hadn't moved a muscle and was shaking uncontrollably again. The glimmer of her old self he'd seen moments earlier was no longer evident. He realized she'd only been putting on a brave front for his benefit.

Without a word he swept her into his arms and carried her down the hall to the bedroom he was using. She would be safe there.

Boomer joined them. The dog settled at the foot of the bed, curling into a ball.

Michael tucked her securely into bed. She was still trembling. He had to help her. Surely there was something he could do for her.

"Would you like some water? I could get you a glass."

He made a move for the door, but her hand shot out to stop him, grabbing his forearm. She possessed amazing strength for a girl of her stature. He wouldn't be able to break away without a struggle.

"I don't want anything," she said in a barely audible voice. "Can you stay with me?"

He could tell be the tone of her voice that she hated admitting to her fear. That asking him to stay hadn't been easy. He climbed on the bed beside her. She automatically turned to her side, facing the opposite wall. He stretched out and put an arm around her, pressing against her length in an effort to warm her, resting his face in the curve of her neck. Her hair tickled his nose, but he didn't move, not even to scratch.

She smelled incredible, like nothing he'd known before. It was a clean, fresh scent, like flowers after a spring rain. And she was soft. His hands itched to move, to stroke and explore. If he hadn't been working—and if she wasn't on the verge of a mental collapse—he wouldn't be able to stop until he lost himself in her beauty and warmth.

"I told you about my mother," she said, breaking into his thoughts. "Remember?"

"Yes." He waited patiently for Kelly to make her point. He would lie there quietly all night if he had to, not pressuring her in the slightest to hurry her words. He would give her whatever she needed.

"But I don't know anything about you," she said. "Tell me about your family, your childhood. What was it like?"

The request caught Michael off guard.

Tension invaded his body like a spreading disease. He hated talking about himself. He didn't believe in dwelling on things a person couldn't change. Getting him to talk, he'd been told, was a nearly impossible task, fraught with frustrations. He didn't open up easily to anyone and rarely spoke about his feelings. Probably one of the many reasons he hadn't married.

He told himself this situation was different. He could talk

to Kelly. She wasn't trying to find ammunition to use against him later. She could have been killed by the intruder. *If there was an intruder,* a dark voice whispered in his head. She needed to get her mind off the terror she'd felt when the stranger's hands closed around her lovely throat. The least Michael could do was talk to her. He didn't have to tell her anything radical.

"Okay," he sighed. "What exactly do you want to know?"

"Where were you born? Who are your parents? Are they still alive? You know, the usual stuff."

He would rather have a root canal operation than discuss his past life.

"New York," he said shortly. "And I don't have parents."

"I'm sorry I asked." Her voice grated with sudden anger and she stiffened.

Women! He wouldn't understand them if he lived to be a hundred. She wanted to stick her pretty little nose in his business, so he'd answered her questions. Now she was angry because she didn't like his tone of voice? "What do you want from me? I gave you the facts."

"Yes, you did." Kelly sat up straight and glared down at him. "'Just the facts, ma'am.' Give me a break. We're supposed to be engaged. You asked me to marry you, but you can't even talk to me. I don't know who you are."

"That didn't seem to bother you until now. Why didn't you ask these questions before you agreed to marriage?"

"I did," she said. "Don't you remember? You always changed the subject back to me. You wanted to know everything about me. You listened like you were writing a book, but you wouldn't return the favor. I need to know who you are. If I'm going to marry you, I have to know you." Her lower lip trembled. "I guess I didn't want to rock the boat before. I was relieved I wasn't going to end up alone. You have no idea what my life was like before you entered it. I couldn't believe someone actually wanted to marry me—scars and all.''

She had no idea how beautiful she was. How perfect.

"I'm sorry," Michael said. "You have every right to know about the man you're going to marry. Ask me anything you want. I'll try to be honest with you."

As honest as he could be without blowing his cover.

She lay back down beside him, facing him now. A small smile played across her lips. She was incredible. She'd been through so much and yet she still had the ability to smile, to laugh and be happy. He would sacrifice anything to keep the smile in place. Even his own life, if it came to that.

"What was your childhood like?"

"Well, it wasn't ideal. My father was a drunk. I guess you could say I was spunky when I was a kid. I followed him one day, thinking he was going to work, and I found him in a bar getting sloshed. For a long time I thought sitting on that stool, tossing back cold beers, was his job. Denial, I guess." Michael paused. "My parents split when I was about thirteen. My father was abusive. He beat my mother on a pretty regular basis. I wanted to kill him."

Kelly gasped. "I'm sorry. I had no idea."

"He didn't hit my brother or me very often. He used words instead. Every day I got to hear what a disappointment I was to him."

"That's horrible." Kelly said, "You don't have to go on. You don't have to tell me any more if it's too painful."

"No, I want to." He was amazed to hear the words spill from his lips. He actually wanted Kelly to know about his past. "My mother tried to leave my father once. She took me and my brother with her that time, but the old man caught up with us. He put her in the hospital for a week. After that she wasn't allowed to take my brother and me out at the same time. She always had to leave one of us behind.

"Finally she couldn't take it anymore." Michael shrugged with a derisive laugh. "One day we went to the store and she told me we weren't going back. I just happened to be the one with her that day. I got lucky. Otherwise I would have been raised by the old man instead of Jimmy."

"What happened to your brother?"

"I saw him a couple of times after we were fully grown," Michael replied. "We were so different. Had nothing in common. We went our separate ways."

"That's sad."

Michael stroked a finger from her nose to her mouth, following the groove. Her compassion called to him like a siren's song. The intimacy of the situation wasn't lost on him. They were in bed together, lying face-to-face. He wanted to kiss her, but he didn't dare. He wasn't a complete idiot. Kissing would lead to touching. Touching would lead to making love.

She deserved better from him. She thought they were getting married. In the end he would have to hurt her. But he wasn't going to complicate matters, wasn't going to make things worse by making love to her.

"I suppose," he said. "But I didn't know any other life. It seemed normal to me at the time. Kids will accept almost any situation as long as they don't know any better."

"Did you ever see your father again?"

"No," he replied. "He died of cancer some years ago. Good riddance."

"Oh." She grew braver. Her fingers went to his face, tracing lines and smoothing over the planes. She seemed lost in what she was doing, as if she was trying to memorize his features. He didn't speak for fear it would distract her.

After several long minutes she added, "Neither one of us

had an easy time of it. I think you have scars, too. They just aren't as obvious as mine."

He was taken aback by her observation. Could she be right? Was he hiding as she was, too?

"You want me to leave the light on while we sleep?"

"If you wouldn't mind." She smiled wryly at him. "Are you trying to tell me to shut up and go to sleep now? Stop asking questions?"

"Not at all. We can talk as long as you want."

"As long as we don't talk about you," she said. "Fine. I'll drop the inquisition. For now."

"Thank you."

He sat up, leaning his back against the headboard. He wasn't planning on sleeping. Just in case there was someone in the house, someone stalking Kelly, he was going to stay awake tonight. It wouldn't be the first time he'd gone without sleep for a forty-eight hour period. It probably wouldn't be the last.

She relaxed against him. "I don't know what it is about you, but I feel safe in your arms." She blushed. "Maybe I shouldn't have admitted that. Don't men like women who are mysterious?"

"Not all men." He remembered Wade's visit. "By the way, I caught your friend Wade sneaking around in the dark earlier."

"I'm sure he wasn't sneaking around." She sat up again, her spine ramrod straight. "Wade has a key. I hope you didn't scare him. I told him he could come over anytime he wanted to."

"Yeah," Michael said. "So he could work on the house. But he wasn't fixing anything tonight. He was in the hallway in the dark. There's no telling what he was doing before I caught him."

"Would you stop saying you caught him!" She sighed.

"I've known Wade for a long time. He's a good guy. He's harmless."

"I'm sure someone said the same thing about Ted Bundy at one time."

"Let's just agree to disagree. Okay?"

Her tone was defensive. She was obviously loyal to the people she cared about. It was another virtue on a growing list. In his line of work he didn't come across many people of strong character, and he was sure he hadn't met a woman like Kelly before.

Of course, how he felt about her was a moot point. Once she learned the truth about him, she'd want nothing to do with him.

"Wade collects things," she added. "That's probably why he was here."

"What sort of things does he collect?"

"Things he thinks people lost. He has a 'lost-and-found' box at home. I saw it once. He had an assortment of keys, loose change and various objects in it."

"Are you sure he only takes lost things?" Michael rolled his eyes. "If not, they have a word for it: *stealing*."

"Wade doesn't steal. He has the mind of a young child."

"He knows right from wrong," Michael insisted.

"Maybe he does. So what? He's a good man. He isn't hurting anyone."

"Hmm." Michael was unconvinced. "We'll drop it. For now."

Kelly rested on her side, facing away from him again. She didn't move for several minutes. He started to think she'd fallen asleep. He closed his own eyes, resting, but her soft voice reached into his self-imposed darkness.

"Will you answer another question?"

Another one? "Yes."

"Will you be honest? I don't want you to simply tell me what you think I want or need to hear."

"Okay." Michael tensed, holding his breath.

"Do you think I'm losing my mind?" She flipped over to face him. Her eyes were wet from tears. "Is it possible that I'm becoming like my mother?"

"I don't know." He wanted to say something that would comfort her, but he didn't have the words. He wasn't a doctor. He didn't know anything about her mother's disease. "I saw red marks on your neck earlier. You could have been attacked. On the other hand, I was nearby. I didn't see anyone leave your room. How could they have gotten in and out of your bedroom without being detected? They didn't go out the window."

She sank back on the pillow and slung an arm over her face. Her chest rose and fell with her shaking breaths. "Well," she whispered, "maybe Moore House is haunted, after all. That would put me in the clear."

An idea occurred to Michael, shocking him with its simplicity. Why hadn't he thought of it before?

"You mentioned secret passages in your story about Jesse James. Could there be a secret door going into your room?"

"No way." She shook her head emphatically. "Two out of four of the walls in the master bedroom are exterior ones. Then there's the wall next to my bed. It shares a wall with a guest bedroom. No secret door there—no room for one." She twirled strands of hair around her finger. "The only remaining wall has the bathroom and closet. Wade and I expanded the bathroom a few years ago. We cut into the closet, making it smaller, in order to accomplish that feat. We had to knock down a couple walls. We would have found a passageway if it existed."

Michael didn't say a word. She was right. If there was something to be found, she would have noticed it by now.

"Besides," she continued, "no one could possibly know about the passages if there were any. As I said earlier, the blueprints were lost long ago. In my grandfather's day, or maybe before.'' She shrugged. ''Anyway, all the people who have lived here are dead now, except for my mother. She's in a mental facility. So I don't think she broke into my house.''

Michael slowly digested the information. ''Maybe we should visit your mother,'' he said.

''Why?'' Kelly hugged her body and shivered.

''Your mother may have told someone about the passages...if there are any.''

''I don't want to see her. I can't.''

Her fear was understandable. She'd paid a high price for her mother's insanity. Of course she didn't want to have to face the woman again. Michael considered leaving her out of it. He could approach her mother on his own, ask her questions if the woman was coherent enough to make sense. He didn't have to have Kelly at his side.

But he wanted her there. It was the best thing for her. She would face her fears head-on instead of running from them. Perhaps she would be able to gain some kind of closure. Michael hated seeing Kelly in pain. This new protective instinct rose up in him again like a three-headed monster. The urge to take her into his arms, hide her from whatever demons lurked in the shadows, threatened to overwhelm him.

''I think it's important,'' he said. ''I'll be with you every second. She won't be able to hurt you. You don't even have to talk to her. You can stand in the background, let me question her.''

Kelly remained silent.

''Think about it,'' he offered. ''Finding out your mother told someone about hidden passages would be preferable to being crazy. Wouldn't it?''

''Do you know anything about schizophrenia?''

She had him there. He shook his head in answer to her question.

"Well, I do." She spoke quietly. Each word was pronounced with a cold finality. "I read about it after my mother burned me. If you have a parent who suffers from schizophrenia, you have a one in ten chance of getting it, too. Most of the time it can be controlled by drugs. But not always."

A sudden noise vibrated through the room. Michael jerked, sitting up straighter. His heart hammered against his rib cage. His hand automatically went for his .38, but his fingers closed around air. Then he remembered he'd put the gun in the bottom dresser drawer beneath a ton of ancient, dusty quilts.

"It's okay." Kelly grasped his upper arm. "It's an old house. It makes strange sounds sometimes. The furnace in the basement probably just kicked in. It's normal."

Michael settled back against the headboard. He was definitely leaving the light on tonight. All night.

"Oh my gosh!" Kelly's hand flew to her mouth. "I just remembered something."

"What?"

She leaped off the bed, coming around to his side as if she was too excited to be still. A new light sparkled in her eyes.

"I wasn't choked by hands," she replied. "The person who attacked me wrapped something around my throat. I fell off the bed, and you came running. Whoever it was took off, but didn't take the material with him."

Michael listened intently.

Her hand went to her throat as she relived the event. "I removed it myself. It must be in the bedroom. That's my proof!"

He stood, his eyes automatically moving to the dresser drawer where his gun was hidden. He longed to retrieve it, but didn't dare. He didn't want Kelly frightened any more than she already had been.

"Stay here," he ordered. "I'll take a look."

"I'm going with you. I know where I dropped it. You don't."

Michael grabbed her by the shoulders. "You're staying here. Lock the door behind me. I'll be right back." He nodded toward the dog. "You'll be okay. Boomer is with you."

Maybe the dog could protect her if someone was still in the house, but who was going to look after Michael? He would be alone.

Kelly swallowed but didn't speak. Her eyes were glazed with doubt.

He tapped her on the nose and added, "Trust me."

Michael left Kelly in the bedroom, pausing outside the door until he heard the soft click of the lock being engaged. He reached the master bedroom in several quick strides. He wanted to hurry and get back to her before she panicked. She wouldn't stay in his bedroom for long, he knew.

He snapped on the light. The sheets were in disarray, half falling on the floor. He grabbed them and searched for something that could have been used to strangle Kelly. There was nothing.

He sank onto the edge of the mattress with a sigh, his hopes dashed. Even though her story sounded implausible, Michael had wanted to believe it. He'd wanted to be able to prove her sane. Now he felt as if he'd let her down.

His eyes fell to the floor. Something pink peeked out at him from under the bed. Michael lifted it up for closer inspection. It was a long dusky-pink scarf. There was a dark stain on one end. He smelled it to rule out certain substances such as ketchup and scratched it with his finger.

It was blood.

But whose blood?

He pushed that question aside. He had a bigger problem. Should he show the scarf to Kelly or keep it to himself? Which would be worse—thinking you might be losing your mind or knowing someone was trying to kill you?

Chapter Seven

Every little noise set her teeth on edge. Kelly paced from one end of the room to the next. Her nerves sizzled, and she felt ready to bolt, ready to scream. It was ridiculous. With over forty rooms to choose from she had to be locked in a small guest bedroom. Alone.

Alone except for a dog, and the golden retriever appeared to be asleep. She knew she should find that comforting. The dog's super hearing hadn't picked up anything. But she wouldn't relax until Michael was back safe and sound.

Outside the door, floorboards creaked in protest. The brass doorknob rotated slowly.

Her pulse raced.

"Michael? Is that you?"

There was no reply. The door rattled beneath a heavy hand.

She backed away. Her legs bumped into the mattress and she fell onto it. Her eyes frantically scanned the room for a weapon. The door wouldn't hold forever if an intruder tried to kick it down.

Boomer woke and whined in protest.

"Open the door!" Michael shouted.

Relief flooded through her. She raced to the door and turned the lock with a trembling hand. Yanking it open, she met Michael's gaze. His lips were compressed into a tight line.

"You scared me half to death," she complained. "Why didn't you answer me?"

"I said it was me more than once," he replied. "These doors must be thicker than they look." He handed her an armful of folded clothes. "I thought you might want something to change into."

"Thanks." He turned his back while she dressed. She continued to talk to him in an effort to keep her mind off the fact that she was standing naked behind him. "Well, what did you find?" She slipped the blouse over her head before he could answer and said, "Okay, I'm decent."

He immediately turned around.

He didn't answer right away. She watched his face, his solemn expression while he hesitated. Her heart plummeted. It wasn't going to be good news.

"I'm sorry," he said. "There was nothing."

She turned, keeping her agony to herself. It was true then. She was losing her mind. She thought back to the days with her mother living in the house, the mood swings, the crazy talk about voices in her head. Her mother had been paranoid to the extreme, actually believing people were trying to kill her. It all sounded familiar.

Frustrated, Kelly covered her face with a pillow and screamed into it. She was determined not to be locked away or put on drugs for the rest of her life. But worse than that was the possibility she could hurt another person, perhaps someone she loved.

Michael's hands covered her shoulders. He whispered into her hair. "Everything will be okay. Trust me. I won't let anything bad happen to you."

How could he stop it from happening? He couldn't climb into her head and fix what was wrong with her. No one could.

The urge to flee gripped her. She wanted to go somewhere no one would find her. In a mansion the size of Moore House it shouldn't be too hard a feat.

Acting on instinct, she spun around, knocking Michael's hands aside. Nothing was going to get in her way. Perhaps she would disappear into thin air like Elizabeth Barrington. The house just might open wide and swallow her whole. Kelly didn't care.

Michael tried to latch on to her again, but she fought him. She almost ripped his jersey in her haste to get away.

A long pink scarf fell to the floor.

Kelly grabbed it before Michael could.

His long fingers reached for it, but she snatched it up and studied it closely.

"Where did you find this? It belongs to Margo. Did you get this from my room? Is this what the man used to choke me?"

Michael nodded grimly.

"Why didn't you tell me?"

"I didn't know what to do. I didn't want to upset you," he replied.

"Upset me?" Her voice bounced off the walls. She lowered it and continued. "You let me think I was going crazy. Why would you do that?"

"Do you feel better now that you know the threat is real? Someone is trying to kill you, and we have no idea who or why."

Kelly nodded defiantly. "As a matter of fact, I do. I feel much better now. I'd rather fight a flesh-and-blood person than a mental disease any day of the week."

"Well, I'm glad you're so happy about this," Michael said sarcastically. "You said something about Margo? You've seen this scarf before?"

"Yes. I'm sure it belongs to Margo—the nice old lady who lives in what used to be the guest house. I told you I went to check on her before I got locked in the garage. Remember? She's Boomer's owner.'' When he nodded, she continued, ''How did somebody get her scarf? Dammit, Michael, do you think Margo's been hurt?''

''I don't know.'' He stepped outside the room. ''But I'm going to find out. The sun won't be up for another three hours.''

''I'm going with you.''

He didn't argue this time, and Kelly was relieved. She couldn't just sit around and twiddle her thumbs. If something bad had happened to her friend, Kelly wanted to know.

Boomer glanced at them but was clearly too relaxed to move. His head went back down and his eyes closed.

''What can you tell me about Margo?'' Michael asked as they were headed down the stairs.

''She bought the house three years ago. She's a sweet old lady. You know the type. She wants to feed everyone in sight. She worries about everyone and loves her dog as if he were a human child,'' Kelly replied, ''Margo is the type who would invite a stranger in off the street. She wouldn't question them or wonder if they were going to hurt her. She thinks everyone is as nice as she is.''

''Family?'' Michael asked, ''You mentioned family earlier.''

Kelly shrugged. She replayed every conversation she could remember having with Margo over a pot of tea and cookies. Margo had mentioned having grown children, but she didn't seem to visit with them very often. Kelly hadn't had the chance to meet them herself.

''I don't know their names. I don't have their phone numbers.'' She rubbed her forehead. ''I should have asked in case of an emergency. I just didn't think of it.''

''It's okay. I'm sure the lady is fine.''

Kelly had her doubts. She knew Margo well enough to believe the woman wouldn't leave her dog locked in the house by himself for more than an hour. She would have taken him with her on a walk.

Kelly climbed into the cab of her truck and Michael took the passenger seat. As they drove down the street, her headlights glided over something—something silver and metallic. Was it a car?

Her eyes wavered from the road and she glanced in the rearview mirror. "I saw something."

"What?"

"There's a car parked near the house. I think someone was sitting in it, watching us."

"I didn't see anything," Michael said. "Don't worry about it. We'll check it out on our way back."

When they reached Margo's house, Michael entered first. He stopped in the living room, motioning for Kelly to stay where she was and be quiet.

Who did he think he was? He assumed command of their invisible army, taking control as if it was his by right of birth.

She watched him move through the living room with silent, cautious footsteps. He walked through the house as if he knew what he was doing. Kelly watched in fascination.

Margo was nowhere to be found.

Michael knelt down on the kitchen floor.

Kelly drew closer. She stood above him as he scratched at a dark spot on the yellowed linoleum. He lifted his thumb nail to his nose and studied it closely.

"Is it blood?" Kelly was caught off guard by a dizzying rush to her head. "Who would want to hurt Margo? Everybody loves her."

"There could be a reasonable explanation for this. Margo could have cut herself and called someone to take her to the hospital. Or the blood could have come from the dog. There are hundreds of possible scenarios."

"I hope you're right."

"Well, there's no sense in borrowing trouble."

"How do you think the scarf got into my bedroom?"

Michael glanced up at her from his position near the blood. A grimace marred his handsome features. Her hand itched to stroke the furrowed lines from his forehead.

He sighed. "I don't want to scare you."

"Scare me?" Kelly threw up her hands. "How could you possibly scare me any more than I already am? You can't, okay? So go ahead. Say it."

"Okay." Michael stood, placing his large hands on his narrow hips. "Obviously, someone brought it into your room to strangle you with. That someone probably knows what happened to your friend, too."

Kelly was overwhelmed by his brutal honesty. Although, in his defense, she had asked for it. But hearing the words made everything real to her. Someone had invaded her room and tried to take her life. Who would do something like that?

A psychotic individual. Somebody like her mother.

Knowing that fact made her choices clearer. Kelly didn't want to take such a drastic step, but it was the only course left open to her.

"Okay." She looked directly at Michael. "I'll visit my mother with you."

A stunned expression swept through his eyes, and was gone in a blink. She hadn't truly grasped before what a good poker player he would make. He hid his emotions as easily as some people smiled.

He nodded. "We'll leave first thing in the morning. Right now I want to search the bedroom again. I might have missed something important."

He sounded like a cop, but she knew for a fact he wasn't. He'd told her he used to be a stockbroker. After making a small fortune, he had decided to write a book on legendary houses of the United States. That was what had brought him to her front door the first time.

"I'll help you if you want," she offered.

"Probably best if I do it alone."

"What do I do then while you're playing detective?" She scowled. "And don't you dare tell me to lock myself in your room. I'm tired of being scared. Now that I know I'm dealing with a flesh-and-blood individual, I can deal with it. Really."

"You're amazing." His dark eyes shone with a newfound respect for her. "At the risk of sounding flowery, I've got to tell you I'm in awe of you right now."

"Why?" She blushed, lowering her face as her cheeks began to burn. "I didn't do anything."

"On the contrary," Michael said. "You should be hiding under a blanket right now. No one would blame you. But instead you're here with me, helping me look for your missing neighbor. You are one hell of a woman, Ms. Hall."

You're not a woman. You're damaged goods. Who would want to marry something that looked like you?

Pain stabbed her from behind her eyelids. With a groan Kelly grabbed her head. What was the matter with her? Why did she keep hearing Michael's voice in her head? She heard him saying the nastiest things to her, but it wasn't real. Michael wouldn't say such hurtful things to her. Besides, she would have remembered being berated like that.

"Are you okay?" She heard the concern in his voice now. He grasped her by the arms and held her steady. "Tell me, what's wrong?"

A shocking revelation wrought a gasp from Kelly's trembling lips. She was hearing voices. Just like her mother. She was hearing Michael's voice in her head, hearing him yell awful words at her. It sounded as real as it did when he asked if she was okay.

Was this what it felt like to lose your mind?

"Kelly! Answer me, dammit!"

A lump rose to her throat. She didn't want him to know the truth. The way he looked at her would change, and she couldn't bear that. Of course, she knew she couldn't marry him now. She would not do to him what her mother had done to her father, forcing him through the wringer time and again.

She straightened. The pain faded as quickly as it had come upon her. It left her feeling exhausted.

"I'm fine," she said, barely audible.

"No, you're not." With two fingers he lifted her chin and stared deep into her eyes, searching for the truth. "Something's wrong with you, and I want to know what it is so I can help you. You can trust me."

"There's nothing wrong with me!" she insisted. "I have a headache. That's all."

"You need to see a doctor."

"No!" She stumbled backward, almost losing her footing. "I saw enough doctors to last a lifetime after my mother burned me, thank you very much. I can handle a little headache. I'm not sick!"

She fled from the room, from the house, into the night. She ran as fast as her legs could carry her, flying down the dark path at breakneck speed. In her mad dash it didn't occur to her to take her truck. Images of her mother returned to her, as vivid as if they had happened yesterday. She'd watched her mother descend into hell. Now it was going to happen to her.

A hand came out of nowhere and stopped her, as abruptly as a train would stop a car crossing its path. Michael spun her around. Her hair flew in all directions, the tangled strands whipping in front of her eyes. She jerked her head in an effort to clear her obstructed view, since her hands weren't free to accomplish the task.

Michael held her immobile in a tight embrace. She fought

him but he wouldn't release her. Like a parent trying to comfort an angry, frightened child, he wrapped his arms around her like steel manacles, while whispering reassuring words into her ear.

"Let me go!" she screamed.

"No," he said emphatically. "I'm not going to let you go. We'll stand here all day like this if we have to. You need me."

"I don't," she mumbled into his shirt. "I don't need anyone. I can take care of myself."

"Yeah, I used to say things like that, too. But I was wrong. I needed people just like everyone else in this miserable world."

There was a sad, lonely note in his voice that caught Kelly's attention. It reflected perfectly how she'd felt before he'd appeared on her doorstep.

"The reason we don't want to need people is because we're afraid they'll leave us or disappoint us," he continued. "Am I right?"

The fight went out of Kelly. She sagged against Michael's chest and put every ounce of remaining strength she had into not breaking down. She'd cried enough in front of him. If he thought she was unstable now, who could argue with him?

"I can't remember what my life was like before you," she said. "You're right. I do need you, and I hate it. I don't want to be weak."

"You aren't." He shook his head and smiled. "I don't want to need you, either, but I do. The question is where do we go from here?"

"I don't know." She shrugged. "I haven't allowed anyone to get this close to me in a long time. I don't know what comes next."

"I guess we play it by ear."

"Sounds good to me," Kelly said, "But I'm not going

to the doctor. I'm fine. You'll just have to take my word on that.''

"Fair enough. For now. But if you experience any more of these painful episodes, I want you to let me know immediately.'' Michael's eyes scanned the darkness surrounding them. "We have a lot of land to search. If Margo is dead—''

"She's not.'' Kelly cut him off. "Don't say that again. Don't even think it. We'll find her. We have to.''

He nodded. "We need to check your house first, from top to bottom. If the intruder is in there, hiding out somewhere, we'll find him.''

"I'm going to be with you every step of the way. Until we find out my house is safe, I'm sticking to you like glue. We can watch each other's backs.''

A small smile spread across Michael's mouth. He didn't seem to mind having her around. The funny thing was that she was getting used to having him around, too. Actually, it was more sad than funny. Michael didn't know it yet, but she was going to have to break their engagement. Regardless of whether she needed him or not. She was losing her mind, and Michael deserved better.

First they needed to find Margo.

The woman wasn't dead. Kelly felt the truth in her gut. Her neighbor was alive somewhere, waiting to be found.

MICHAEL INSISTED on driving her truck back to the house. He silently prayed that Paddy had moved his car. Their plans would come to a screeching halt if Kelly confronted the Irishman doing surveillance. The horizon was bathed in an orange glow welcoming a new day. Paddy's car would be easy to spot now. When the time came for her to know the truth, Michael wanted to be the one to tell her.

He drove through the open, wrought-iron gates. Moore House loomed up before them like a living entity, a monster that terrorized the present and swallowed the future. Michael wished the walls could talk—although he suspected they would reveal more mysteries than even he could handle.

He stopped the vehicle and turned to Kelly. Before he could say a word, she bolted from the truck, slamming the door behind her. Surprised, he watched her through the frosty windshield as she disappeared into the structure without a backward glance.

Michael remained where he was, staring up at the house with foreboding in his heart. There was something about the place, something beyond the obvious, something bad. Beyond the massive oak door lurked a secret, and Michael was determined to uncover it before Kelly could be hurt any more than she already had been.

With a rueful shake of his head, he pushed the driver's door open. His feet hit the soggy ground. He pulled his jacket tighter and raced for the only shelter available to him—Moore House.

Once inside, with the door firmly shut behind him, he called out for Kelly. He hoped she wasn't searching for clues on her own. Concern lit a fire under his feet. He ran from the foyer to the top of the stairs and called her name. There was no sign of her.

Michael went back downstairs, rushed into the parlor and found it empty. Fear claimed his common sense as stories filled his head. He remembered the woman Kelly told him about, in the 1920s. She'd vanished, never to be heard from again. What was the name? Barrington?

He cupped his hands around his mouth and shouted, "Kelly! Where are you?"

"I'm here," she replied from behind him. "You don't have to bellow. I was in the kitchen fixing us something hot to drink, something to warm us up."

He took the tray from her hands. He hated to admit it after she'd scared him half to death, but the drink smelled delicious. Hot cocoa. A vague memory stirred up warmth inside him. His mother had made him and his brother hot cocoa every time it snowed. She'd greeted them at the door with a smile when they came home from school. The sweet aroma filled the house now, evoking poignant memories. Michael mentally wiped them away.

Kelly ripped the sheet from the coffee table as if she were a magician attempting a trick. She smiled and motioned for him to set the tray down. The table was obviously an antique.

Michael placed the silver tray on it with extreme caution. A small splash of the hot liquid could mar the table's elegant beauty.

Kelly sat next to him on the sofa without uncovering it and gracefully poured the cocoa into two fragile china cups. She could have been a lady from the past offering her guests tea in the parlor on a lazy Sunday afternoon. She handed him one cup with a shy smile.

Michael squirmed a bit, feeling as if he was on a first date. So many times his job forced him to blend into awkward situations, live his disguise whether it was that of a drunken wino or a wealthy eccentric. Kelly Hall threw him off his game. Somehow she was interfering with his concentration.

He liked her.

He genuinely liked her.

He had broken the number-one rule by allowing her to get close. *Don't get personally involved.*

Of course this was different, had been different from the very beginning. This was personal. How was he supposed to hold on to his objectivity?

On top of that, a woman of contradictions was added to the mix. He couldn't figure her out. She was a frightened girl one second and a determined woman the next. She ran into his arms for safety, then stared through him with those extraordinary eyes as if she could see the real man behind the mask he wore.

"Cookie?"

Michael shook his head, reminding himself to focus on the current situation and not get lost in his thoughts.

Kelly nibbled on the chocolate chip cookie she'd offered him. She was so incredibly beautiful. How was he supposed to think straight around her?

She lifted the cookie to her delicate lips again. He took it from her and bit into the soft treat. He watched her face, labeling her expression as surprise. Did she feel it, too? Was she imagining what it would be like to kiss him?

He tossed the cookie onto the tray and leaned forward slowly, giving her time to escape.

She stared at him with wide eyes, but didn't look frightened. More like curious. Maybe even excited.

His lips brushed hers, a feathery touch like the wings of a butterfly. He kissed the corner of her mouth. Not wanting the other side to get jealous, he placed a kiss there, too. A sigh parted her lips.

It was the only invitation he needed.

He covered her mouth with his own and his tongue slipped inside, desperate to explore uncharted territory. Desire ignited a fire and it burned out of control, fueling their passion.

Their hands were everywhere, begging for tactile contact. Fingers lost themselves in hair, delving deep into silky strands. Palms smoothed down firm limbs and slipped around to the back, molding soft flesh and lean muscle. Hands pulled at clothing, nearly ripping the material.

Michael wasn't certain which of them pushed the other away first, but it felt like a draw to him. They both seemed to come to their senses at the same time, retiring to their separate corners of the couch, gasping for breath.

"I'm sorry," he said. "I didn't mean for that to happen."

"That was…" She looked away as if searching for the word she wanted in the air around them.

"Intense," he suggested. "Incredible? Wonderful? Better than chocolate chips?"

A reluctant smile touched her lips, barely curving them.

The light over their heads flickered.

"Great," she said. "I hope the power doesn't go off tonight. It can take days for the electric company to fix it. Being so far from town, we're low priority. Most of the time I don't mind a power outage. I use candles and go to bed early. But considering that we have a crazy person running around loose, I'd just as soon be able to see."

"I think we should catch up on our sleep so we'll be on our guard tonight."

Kelly nodded in agreement. She reached for the tray, prepared to lift it, but Michael stopped her with a gentle touch.

"Get it later. I'm beat. Let's go to bed."

They went to his bedroom, Kelly leading the way. She turned on a dim light as they entered. Once inside, she walked to the other side of the bed, her back to Michael, and stood motionless. He assumed she was nervous about sharing a bed with him. Boomer settled down at the foot of the bed.

Well, she could join the club. He wasn't going to get any sleep. But it wouldn't be thoughts of a killer on the loose keeping him awake. It would be the disturbing feel of the woman next to him. Every breath she took would pound nails into his good intentions.

IF A GENIE GRANTED HER one wish, she would want to know what Michael was thinking. Up until now he had been a perfect gentleman. But they hadn't shared a bed before. She wondered if the close proximity would change his behavior. Would he pull her into his arms as they slept? Did he want to make love to her?

A flush heated her cheeks. Excitement rolled through her in mighty waves. Would it be so bad if she made love to him? True, she couldn't marry him, but they could have one perfect experience to remember. It sounded like heaven to her.

Kelly climbed under the covers, careful not to make eye contact with Michael. Every pulse point she had throbbed to life. She shut her eyes, anxiously waiting for the bed to sag.

She heard Michael lock the door.

Her ears strained to pick up his every movement. She tried to picture what he was doing. A soft rustling sound made her think he was removing his clothes, even though she had kept hers on. She tensed under the covers, waiting for his next move.

Michael settled in beside her and sighed deeply.

He didn't try to touch her.

He didn't speak to her.

Kelly was surprised at her own disappointment. She tried to relax her limbs. She shifted around, trying to find a comfortable spot.

After what seemed like long torturous hours, she finally drifted off to sleep....

She was floating on air. In the back of her mind she registered the fact that someone was carrying her. A smile tilted her mouth. Michael was carrying her away with him. It had to be Michael's arms around her.

Who else could it be?

Chapter Eight

Michael?

Kelly woke with a start and glared at the clock. It was nearly noon. Her hand automatically reached out for him and found the other side of the bed vacant. Even though it was finally morning, her nightmare returned in a flash. The image of Michael dead in the closet sprang to mind. She jumped up, her eyes wide.

A startled gasp burst from her lips.

She inhaled deeply and screamed at the new terror.

Kelly was in her own bed, surrounded by at least twenty white candles. The candles, once tall and proud, had burned down almost to nothing. Someone had moved her to her own room while she slept, and placed each candle carefully to create a glowing semicircle around the bed.

"Where are you?" Michael yelled from somewhere in the bowels of the house.

Boomer barked, excited by the yelling.

"I'm in my bedroom!" She stood up on the bed, her eyes watching the closet door just in case someone was hiding inside. Her gaze alternately went to the bathroom, but that door was wide open and she could see inside.

Michael dashed into the master bedroom with a gun in his hand. The shock at seeing him with a weapon momentarily stunned her into silence. Since when did he have a gun?

He tucked the weapon into the back of his jeans and turned to her, taking inventory with his eyes. The heat of his gaze warmed her from the inside out. Those eyes saw everything. She wasn't sure if she liked the way he looked at her or not; it thrilled and frightened her at the same time.

"Are you all right?" Michael's hands encircled her waist. He lifted her off the bed, setting her down next to him. "What happened? Why are you in here and what's with all the candles?"

"I don't know. I woke up in here. I vaguely remember the feeling of being carried, but I thought it was a dream."

"That's not possible." He stared at her as though he thought she was lying or out of her mind. "I was asleep when you screamed, and my door was still locked from the inside. How did someone get into the room and carry you off without waking me? Even if they somehow managed to get by the locked door and were quiet enough not to wake us, what about Boomer?"

"I don't know," she repeated. "I can't explain any of this. I only know it happened. You can't argue with that. The proof is right in front of you, Michael."

"How do you explain the door still being locked then?" He asked the question with a tight jaw. She read the accusations in his eye. He *did* think she was crazy. He thought she'd returned to her room under her own steam and assembled the candles herself.

"I don't know." Kelly blinked her eyes rapidly, fighting back tears. His doubts hurt more than she thought anything could. For years she'd avoided getting too close to people, and now the person she'd opened her heart to didn't believe her. "I'm going to take a shower."

She tried to step past him, but Michael grabbed her elbow, restraining her.

"Don't be like this," he said.

"Be like what?" Her voice rose a notch. "I'm not being anything, Michael. I just want to take a blasted shower. Now leave me alone!"

"Fine," he said, releasing his hold on her. "I'll wait out here for you."

Michael sat on her bed with his back against the headboard and his long legs stretched out before him. He clasped his hands over his washboard abs, obviously prepared to wait it out.

"Suit yourself," she said. "I don't care."

"Obviously," he mumbled.

"What the hell is that supposed to mean?"

"You don't seem to care about anything. Not even yourself. You hide out from the world in this mausoleum, living a very lonely life." He gestured to the walls around them. "How long have you been here anyway?"

"Six years."

"I think that's long enough to lick your wounds." He sighed. "I'm not saying this to hurt you, but someone needs to give you a push in the right direction."

His words hurt, striking too close to the truth. Her father had been determined to keep her from living a life of isolation. Michael's words mirrored those her father had said to her so many times before his death. Tears pricked the backs of her eyes, but she was not going to cry in front of Michael. Not again.

Without a word, Kelly went into the bathroom and slammed the door behind her. She took a long, hot shower. The water washed away her tears but not the pain. Unfortunately, she didn't find the answers she needed in the shower stall.

MICHAEL'S EYES WERE closed when Kelly stepped out of the bathroom. He had almost fallen asleep twice while waiting for her. Women took a long time primping themselves as a rule, but Kelly had taken three times as long, and looked the same as she did when she went inside.

Not that he was complaining. He watched her move around the room, enjoying the view. She reminded him of an exotic doll, so tiny and beautiful with her golden hair and impossibly blue eyes. Her jeans fit like a second skin but didn't appear to be tight. They moved with her easily, the material breathing with her.

The sweater she'd chosen was white and appeared softer than cream. He was amazed at his own willpower. His hands itched to touch her. His body burned to imprint itself on hers. But somehow he managed to override those desires and concentrate on the task at hand.

"I need to search the house now," he said. "You can come with me or you can pick a room to isolate yourself in."

Isolate was probably not the right word for him to use, considering his earlier comments. Her eyes narrowed and her back stiffened. He knew before her compressed lips opened that she was going to refuse to join him.

"I need coffee. I'm going to make some. Do you have a problem with that?"

"No." He threw up his hands in surrender. "Do whatever you want. It's your house."

"Yes, it is."

"I'll let you know if I find anything." Michael headed for the door.

"Since when do you have a gun?" She stared at him— through him—and he got the cold feeling that she could see all of his deceptions, recognize every single lie he'd uttered since his arrival. "Why haven't I seen it before?"

He had to think of a reasonable explanation quickly.

"I didn't mention it because I was afraid you wouldn't

approve. I know how to use it," he assured her. "I took a class once. It's for protection."

"You were right about one thing. I don't like the idea of a gun in the house."

"I would offer to get rid of it, but you have admit if there was ever a situation calling for a responsible person to hold a weapon, it would be now."

She held her body rigidly, looking very much like a mother about to scold her naughty child. It was imperative he keep his gun. No matter what Kelly said, he was going to hold on to it. He had a bad feeling they were going to need it soon.

"Fine. Whatever. But I don't want to see it again."

He nodded. "Fair enough."

"I'll bring you a cup of coffee once I've made it. Where are you going to start your search?"

"Here," he said, glancing around her bedroom. "This is where all the activity appears to be centered."

"Okay." The anger was gone from her face, replaced by uncertainty. She was scared, but there was nothing he could say to reassure her. He had no idea what he would find, if anything.

After she left, Michael searched every inch of the master bedroom. He tapped on every wall and ran his hands along the edge of the molding. The windows were locked and seemed secure. If there was a secret passageway, he couldn't find it.

Michael dumped out Kelly's dresser drawers. He tipped each one over in case something was taped to the bottom. Under normal circumstances he wouldn't take the time to restore everything to its former position, but this was Kelly's house and he didn't want her any more upset than she already was.

He was about to give up and go to the next room when he spotted something from the corner of his eye; a small white triangle sticking out from under the vanity. He reached for it with clumsy fingers, missing it twice before he pulled it free. It was a photograph of an elderly woman with blood on her blouse. The pink scarf he'd found in Kelly's room—the scarf he suspected had been wrapped around her throat in an effort to strangle her—was on the woman's neck. Her eyes were wide open, staring straight ahead with a vacant gaze.

She was obviously dead.

Michael shoved the picture into his back pocket, uncertain whether he should show it to Kelly or not. She could identify the woman, but he already had a pretty good idea it was her missing neighbor. Seeing the picture might push Kelly over the edge, and he needed her in top form right now. She was a fighter deep down. He could see it in her eyes whenever she stood up to him.

On the other hand, because of her mother, she could be as fragile as a delicate glass sculpture. He needed to encourage her strength. She was a strong woman. She could handle anything as long as she didn't let her childhood insecurities take over.

Kelly entered with his coffee. "Careful," she warned him. "It's hot."

He accepted it with a smile he didn't feel. His mind was weighted down by a ton of worries. At the top of the list was the photograph. He couldn't get the poor old woman's lifeless features out of his mind, and he didn't even know her. Kelly's reaction would be a hundred times worse.

"Did you find anything?" She glanced around the room and he was glad he'd put everything back where he'd found it.

"Not yet," he said. "I'm going to go over the bathroom now."

"Need some help?"

"No. Only one person should search a crime scene for evidence. Extra people just trample the clues."

She frowned at him.

He'd said too much. He saw curiosity light a fire in her eyes.

"You can find out almost anything on the Internet," he said.

Michael set his coffee down and went into the bathroom. He searched every nook and crevice. His gaze strayed to the mirror. How had someone gotten into the bathroom to leave a message while Kelly was showering? Was it possible to write something on the mirror beforehand? Would it reveal itself once the bathroom filled with steam?

He thoroughly cleaned the mirror before writing his name on it with his index finger. He turned the hot water on. While he was waiting to see if it worked, he continued his search.

Michael lifted the toilet lid and found a spot of blood on the rim.

"What's that?" Kelly asked him from the open doorway.

He wished she hadn't seen it.

"Blood," he replied. "How often do you clean the toilet?"

"Every day," she said defensively. "I clean the bathroom and kitchen every single day."

"So you cleaned it today?"

"No." She rolled her eyes. "I didn't have time to get to it yet."

"But you cleaned it yesterday?"

"Well…" She shrugged. "I don't remember. I think I was too busy trying to convince you I wasn't losing my mind. I probably cleaned it the day before, though. Where do you think the blood came from?" she asked.

He knew where it had come from, but he couldn't share the information with Kelly.

"Back to work," he said. "I'm going to search the rest of the house now. You with me?"

"It will go faster if we split up."

Her suggestion was logical, but he couldn't allow it. There was a sinister shadow lurking in the wings. Kelly didn't realize how dangerous the situation could become. She could get hurt. The woman had become important to him. He had to make certain she was unharmed no matter what the cost.

"I don't think it's a good idea for us to split up," he said.

"But we could cover more ground," Kelly replied. "It makes the most sense."

"I don't like it."

"Well, I do," she insisted. "I'll search downstairs while you keep looking up here. I'm not helpless."

She was a stubborn woman.

He wanted to kiss her and wring her lovely neck at the same time.

"Okay." He gave in. "Do you know what you're looking for?"

"Mmm...clues?"

A reluctant smile touched his mouth. She had no idea what to look for, and she was probably better off for it. He certainly wasn't going to enlighten her. The more he thought about it, the more he liked her suggestion. She would be safer in the rooms below than she would be anywhere else in the house because he had already spent time searching downstairs. If there was anything important to find in those rooms, he would have gotten his hands on it by now.

"Yell if you find anything," he said.

"And you'll do the same?"

"Of course."

Not.

Her eyes met his with such trust, such innocence. He

would sacrifice almost anything to be able to tell her the truth. Being able to see the danger looming over her like the shadow of an ax was a heavy burden to bear. Sometimes he took a deep breath, the confession on his lips, but rigorous training and years of experience kept the secret locked deep inside of his mind and his heart.

Telling Kelly would be a big mistake.

He knew her well enough to know she would toss him out on his butt. She wouldn't want anything from him, least of all his help.

There wouldn't be anything Michael could do about it from outside the house. He needed to stay with her, by her side. If he had to be her fiancé for a while longer, then so be it. He'd played many parts in his lifetime, pretending to be engaged to the beautiful Kelly Hall wouldn't be a hardship.

"After we're finished," he said, "we'll compare notes."

Kelly nodded and stepped out of the room. Ill at ease, Michael watched her go downstairs. Maybe he shouldn't let her search alone. He didn't like the idea of her being out of his sight. Not even for a few seconds. Too many strange things had happened since his arrival at Moore House.

He couldn't search thoroughly with her hovering over him, however. If he found another piece of evidence like the picture of the dead neighbor, Kelly might see it, too. He was treading a fine line. He wanted her to be afraid enough to make her cautious, but he didn't want her scared out of her mind.

With a sigh, Michael moved on to the next room. The sooner he finished with his search, the sooner he would get back to Kelly.

IT TOOK KELLY half an hour to realize Michael had agreed to let her look for clues on her own because he knew she wouldn't find anything. Once the epiphany hit, she decided to raid the refrigerator. Fear had increased her appetite tenfold. She made herself a huge sandwich and a tall glass of iced tea.

It didn't escape her notice that food was missing. She had just made a fresh pitcher of iced tea two days ago, and now it was gone. Michael had probably finished it off. Being a man, it wouldn't occur to him to make more or to let her know so she could fix another pitcherful.

She sat down at the kitchen table and thought about offering to fix some food for Michael. But he had two hands. He could make it himself if he was hungry.

She was midway through her sandwich when the phone rang, startling her.

The telephone was mounted on the wall behind her, an old-fashioned faux wood box with a brass bell. She stood next to it and stared at it as if it were a poisonous snake. The thought of answering it filled her with dread. A sixth sense born out of necessity warned her not to accept the call, but curiosity got the better of her.

Elvin Grant's unmistakable nasal voice reached out to her. "My boss wants me to make one last offer to you," he said. "The price has been upped ten thousand dollars."

At first Elvin Grant had chilled her heart with a cold fear she hadn't experienced before. Not during her mother's psychotic episodes. Not even when Kelly had realized she would carry the scars on her arms for life.

The fear had slowly turned to anger. The man had no right to frighten her or threaten her. She took a deep breath, trying to rein in her temper. She had enough to deal with now without this nut making demands for his infamous "boss."

"This is the last time I'm going to tell you. I am not selling. I don't care what the price is. I am not selling my home! Got it?"

"That's not a wise decision," Elvin Grant snarled. "You may not live to regret it."

"Excuse me? Who the hell do you think you are? I'm going to call the police and report you!"

"No," he said. "You won't. Because you don't know who my boss is. The name I gave you on the signed check was just one of my boss's aliases. It could be anybody, and my boss would be extremely upset to see a faithful employee get into trouble with the law."

Kelly decided to try a different tack. "I don't live alone," she reminded him. "You met my fiancé, Michael. He wouldn't take your threats lightly. If you come here again, he'll deal with you."

"Who said anything about me going to your house? My boss employs other people besides myself. A small army could be put together, in fact. I doubt *Michael* could handle all of them by himself."

Kelly shivered. She didn't want to see Michael injured because of her. It was only a house. Part of her wanted to give in, sell it to the awful man's boss. It wasn't worth anyone's life. Besides, she was beginning to despise the place.

But deep in her stubborn heart she knew she couldn't sell no matter what. Moore House had been in her family for three generations. She was not going to be terrorized into giving up something this important to her. To her family.

"I'm not selling," she repeated in a less than certain voice. "Please leave us alone. If you kill me, you won't get the house, anyway."

"You're right," he said. "Maybe I should kill Michael instead. Maybe you would be more accepting of my offer then."

"No. You can't. Please."

"You're going to wind up just like your nutty mother," Grant said in a nasty little voice.

"No!" she cried. "Please go away. Leave us alone."

Michael grabbed the phone. She hadn't heard him enter the kitchen, but he was suddenly there, standing behind her. He lifted the receiver to his ear, his face stiff.

"Who is this?" His dark eyes settled on her face as he spoke harshly into the line. "Hello?"

A few moments later Michael hung the phone up.

"What did he say?" She asked the question although she was sure she didn't want to hear the answer. "Did he say something to you?"

"All I heard was a dial tone," Michael said. "Who was it? What did he want?"

"It was Elvin Grant."

"More threats?" Michael didn't wait for a reply. He swore beneath his breath and stormed to the other side of the room, as if he was going to explode and wanted distance between them so she wouldn't be hurt. His hands were balled into fists. The muscles in his back were solid rock.

"Yes," she said in a small voice, worried what his reaction might be. "His boss obviously wants this house very badly."

"Don't worry about him. I'll put a stop to it."

"How?" What did he think he was going to do— Threaten the man himself? Beat Elvin Grant up? "He promised there were more people on the payroll. If we could figure out who his boss is, we could end it."

Michael nodded absently, but she knew he hadn't heard her at all.

"Why did you come downstairs? Are you finished?" she asked.

"I wanted to check on you," he admitted. "I'm on my way up to the third floor now."

"You'll need the key to the attic then."

"It's not—" He stopped talking abruptly. When she glanced at him expectantly, waiting for him to finish his sentence, he said, "I mean, yes, I was going to ask you where the key's at."

"I'll get it for you."

Kelly hurried down the hallway to the study. Michael knew damn well where the key was kept. Why was he pretending he didn't? What was wrong with him?

She entered the study. A shocking sight was waiting to greet her. She screamed into her hands, muffling the sound.

An old rag doll with bright red hair and black button eyes swung from a rope over the mahogany desk. She recognized the doll as one from a box in the corner of the attic. It had belonged to her grandmother. A noose had been fashioned for it out of an old rope.

There was a note pinned to the front of the doll's dress. "You're next."

Her first inclination was to yell for Michael, but a niggling doubt stopped her. What if he had left the doll for her to find? It hadn't been in the room earlier when she'd searched it. What if Michael was behind all the strange events?

Her mind pored over the facts as she knew them, and her inner voice argued with itself. Logic and instinct went head-to-head in a violent battle.

Michael had sent her to the study even though he knew where the key was hidden. He'd had opportunity. But what about motive? She couldn't imagine why he would want to make her think she was losing her mind.

She knew nothing about him except for the few things he'd shared with her, and those could have been fictitious. As for what he hoped to gain—ten million dollars in diamonds was enough to tempt the most devout saint to temporarily lose his halo.

Kelly suspected Michael had lied to her about at least one thing: their wedding. She remembered the small pearls she'd held in her hand, the same pearls that had later vanished.

Michael could have taken them from her room easily enough.

She hated doubting him.

Michael was her last and only chance at having a family. If she lost him, her dreams would melt away forever. She wanted children, wanted a normal semblance of a life. But if she was losing her mind, a life with Michael would be impossible.

She needed the truth, no matter how awful it turned out to be. With a plan firmly in mind, she stepped out the study door. Covering her ears, she screamed as loudly as she could.

Immediately, footsteps rushed toward her.

She raced to meet them, running in the direction of the kitchen.

"What's wrong?" Michael grasped her shoulders, holding them steady. "Why did you scream?"

He appeared to be concerned.

She took a deep breath and tried hard not to overdo it.

"A doll...hanging...horrible." She lowered her eyes, hoping he wouldn't be able to read the deception in them. "The study. Please, come with me."

Kelly tugged on his hand.

She wanted to enter the study first and turn in time to see his expression. Would there be a cold familiarity in them when he saw the doll? Or would he be as shocked as she had been?

Unfortunately, it was Kelly who got the surprise.

The doll had vanished.

She turned on Michael, studying his unreadable face. He didn't blink. Part of her was glad the doll was gone. It meant Michael had nothing to do with trying to hurt her. He was in the clear.

Michael stared at her in total silence, and another horrible thought occurred to her. Michael was in the clear, unless...

Unless he had an accomplice.

Chapter Nine

Michael's eyes had been trained to pick out the smallest detail in his surroundings, but the study appeared unchanged to him. Compared to the library, the study was a compact space, rectangular with two small bookcases facing each other. A deep burgundy carpet lined the floor and the walls were covered with dark paneling that gave the room a sophisticated air. There were two Victorian arm chairs in opposite corners with floor lamps looming over them. The only other piece of furniture was the desk, a large polished wood surface, cluttered with papers and an assortment of odds and ends including an old-fashioned typewriter. Kelly's distraught gaze was fixed on his face as if she was waiting for him to say something. He didn't want to disappoint her. He just wished he knew what she wanted to hear.

He glanced down at his watch. He was supposed to have contacted Paddy fifteen minutes ago. If he didn't get to the phone soon, his colleague might come to the front door to check on him. Michael would really have some explaining to do then. It would be one big mess.

"There." Kelly pointed to the desk. "There was a doll hanging with a note pinned to it. It was a threat, but now it's gone. Are you going to tell me it was my imagination?"

No, he wasn't going to say that. He believed her. Somehow someone was moving around the house without being seen. Michael wanted to shout in frustration. How did they keep getting past him?

And why wasn't the dog barking?

"We need to figure out who is doing this and why," he said. "Is there anyone you can think of who would want to make you think you're crazy?"

"I lost contact with most people around here years ago. None of them would have any reason to hurt me."

Seeing her hug herself in that familiar gesture made him want to wrap his own arms around her, to protect and comfort her. But he had to keep his head on straight. He had to focus on the task at hand.

She added, "Wade would never do anything this horrible, and poor Margo is an elderly woman. She wouldn't have the strength to strangle me, nor would she want to."

Margo was also dead. However, Michael didn't want to enlighten Kelly on that point. She had enough to deal with already.

Kelly opened a small drawer on the side of the desk and pulled out a large old-fashioned key made of tarnished brass. She handed it to him, a strange expression in her eyes. She was suspicious of him again. This time he had no idea why. How did he keep screwing up without realizing it?

"Thank you," he said, taking the key. "I need to make a phone call to a friend back home first. He worries when he doesn't hear from me. Do you mind if I use the phone in here?"

"You live here. Why would I mind?" She snatched the key back from him before his fingers could tighten around it. "While you're making your call, I'm going to go up to the attic. It's rained a few times lately, and I want to check out the ceiling there before it has a chance to snow. I don't want my grandmother's things getting damaged."

He didn't like the idea of her going to the attic alone. What if the perpetrator was hiding out in there.

"Give me a second," he said. "I'll go with you."

"No need. I've been up there a few hundred times. I'll be fine. Make your call."

Kelly left the study and Michael didn't know what to do. His gaze darted between the telephone and the door. If he didn't call Paddy soon, the Irishman would definitely come looking for him.

Michael grabbed the phone and punched Paddy's cell phone number.

"It's about time," the man said. "I was starting to get nervous."

"I'm fine. Everything's under control."

"The girl? Does she suspect anything?"

"No," Michael replied. "I don't think so. She's been too busy dodging attacks. Someone tried to strangle her last night."

"Landis?"

"Could be." Michael sat on the edge of the desk. "The neighbor lady has turned up dead. I have a Polaroid of her in my pocket. The picture was left for Kelly to find, but luckily, I spotted it first. Whoever it is playing these games with Kelly wants her to think she's crazy. Landis isn't into notes and dolls. He hits fast. He would pop me and move on."

"Unless he knows about those diamonds you mentioned." Paddy chuckled. "That kind of dough would tempt a saint."

"Yeah. Maybe."

"Ten million? Isn't that what they're worth?"

Michael was almost a hundred percent certain he hadn't mentioned how much the diamonds were rumored to be. There was a hint of greed in Paddy's voice. Michael didn't like it.

"That's a lot of money, and it doesn't really belong to anyone anymore," his colleague added. "I looked into it just in case it was important, and the diamond company got the insurance on those jewels years ago. Do you have any idea what we could do with ten million and change?''

''Hey,'' Michael interrupted. ''Keep your eyes on the prize, man.''

''Right.'' Paddy's sigh traveled down the line. ''What if we just happened to find the jewels by accident? Who would we be hurting by keeping them?'' There was a long pause, followed by a confession. ''I haven't been doing too good lately, Tag. I have a dirty little monkey on my back.''

Michael's spine straightened in shock. ''Drugs?''

''No. Gambling,'' Paddy said. ''I fell off the wagon, Tag, and I can't seem to get back on. I'm sorry. I don't mean to lay all this on you. It's not your problem. It's just that Mary is counting on me to retire soon. We wanted to buy that cabin in Montana. It's our thirty-year-old dream. I can fish all day and Mary can work in her garden. She deserves to have that life.''

Michael opened his mouth but couldn't find the words. He hadn't expected to hear anything like this. Paddy and Mary were good people. Especially Mary. She had become a second mother to him when he'd worked in Chicago. He'd grown to love her and he would do nearly anything for her.

But in this instance, what could he do for them? The diamonds didn't belong to them—if they even existed. They were legend, not necessarily fact. The law hadn't been able to prove that Fuller had taken them. It could have been another jewel thief. Even if it had been Fuller, he could have buried them on the five hundred acres, half of which didn't belong to the Moore estate anymore, or he could have hidden them somewhere else entirely.

''I've been searching the house for clues to our killer's identity,'' Michael admitted. ''I haven't seen any sign of jewels. I've already been through practically every inch of this mausoleum. I'll continue the search, but I'm not promising anything. If I did find the diamonds, I would think Kelly has more claim to them than you or I do.''

"Just keep an open mind, Tag. That's all I'm asking."

"Fair enough." Michael changed the subject, hoping Paddy would put the jewels on the back burner for now. "Have you heard anything more about Landis's whereabouts?"

"There's still no sign of him. Our contact doesn't think he did the deed."

"Yeah," Michael said. "You're probably right. Still, we can't rule him out. Anything else?"

"Negative on that."

"Okay. I have to go now. Kelly is in the attic alone, and I don't want to leave her on her own for too long. Strange things have been happening."

"Gotcha. Call me later at the appointed time, and don't be late. You're giving me an ulcer." Paddy chuckled.

Michael tried to join in but it took more effort than he could muster. He was relieved to break the connection. Paddy's confession weighed heavy on Michael's shoulders.

He left the study and gazed up, wondering if Kelly had found her wedding dress yet. If he knew her, and he felt he did, she had gone up to the attic to find out if he was lying to her. It was a good thing he had returned the gown to its rightful place.

Perhaps finding it would rid her of her suspicions.

Maybe she would trust him.

He grimaced, feeling like the coldest bastard alive. He didn't deserve her trust. He certainly hadn't done anything to gain it. After this whole ordeal was over, he would be lucky if the blond angel ever spoke to him again.

THE KEY SLID EASILY into the lock at the top of the stairs leading to the third floor, like a warm knife through butter. Kelly pushed the attic door open and looked doubtfully inside. It had been a long time since she'd ventured into the claustrophobic rooms. There were three separate chambers, all tiny in size.

Choking dust, muted darkness and icky spiders kept her away. As a child she had played in the attic, trying on clothes and singing into her hairbrush as if it were a microphone. She wasn't as brave now. She hated the attic, but she had to know the truth.

She flicked on the one tiny hanging light and hurried across the floor. She opened the box where her grandmother's dress had been placed. A soft gasp burst from her parted lips. The dress was inside, but it was no longer wrapped securely to keep it from yellowing. Someone had tampered with it.

That didn't mean she was married.

It didn't mean Michael was lying to her.

Did it?

She lifted the dress carefully and studied the bodice closely. There were missing pearls. At least three. It wasn't irrefutable proof that Michael was lying. She needed more than this. Someone besides him could have taken the dress out and inadvertently knocked the pearls off.

Wade loved to drift through her house, looking for lost objects. He could have discovered the dress, studied it, not meaning any harm. Maybe he'd carried the gown to her bedroom to see it in a better light.

Hearing footsteps nearing, she returned her grandmother's wedding gown to its box. She turned in the direction of the door, waiting for Michael to poke his head inside.

Instead, the door slammed shut.

Kelly nearly jumped out of her skin. Pressing her hands to her mouth, she approached the door slowly. She willed herself to believe a stray breeze had sucked the door shut. God knew Moore House had its fair share of drafts.

Placing a shaking hand on the cold doorknob, she slowly rotated it.

She pulled the door open.

A hand shot through, grabbing her by the wrist.

She screamed as she was pulled through the doorway.

"It's okay," Michael said. "It's me. Relax. I came to make sure you were okay. You've been gone for quite a while."

"Why did you grab me like that?" she panted, trying to catch her breath.

"I didn't mean to," he replied. "I was worried about you wandering around up here all by yourself, considering the stuff that's been happening."

Kelly stepped into his arms. She was more than a little relieved to see it was Michael and not some awful intruder or a desperate ghost looking for a lost head or something. But it was more than that. Her emotions were riding high, swirling in constant chaos. However, there was one certainty she could count on. She loved being in Michael's arms.

She was surprised to realize she really did trust him. Her gut told her he was a good man incapable of hurting her. His feelings for her were real. He wanted to be with her. She could see it in his eyes.

She wanted him, too, in the worst possible way.

"I think we should go now," he said.

"What?" She stared at him in confusion. "Where?"

"To see your mother."

She took a step backward, leaving the safety of his embrace. Kelly knew it didn't make any sense, but she felt betrayed by him somehow.

"I know I agreed to go," she said, "but…"

"But nothing. You need to go. We both do. I think your mother may have some answers that we need." Michael stared deep into her eyes and said, "Trust me. I won't let her hurt you again."

She nodded slowly, believing him. "Let's go then," she said. "Before I change my mind."

With his arm wrapped tightly around her slender shoulders, they left the attic together. Kelly didn't say anything, but she felt another presence. She shivered, feeling a pair of terrible eyes on them.

Of course she was imagining it.

They were alone in the house.

THE KANSAS CITY INSTITUTION THAT Kelly's mother resided in looked much like other mental hospitals Michael had had occasion to visit. He knew what to expect. It didn't faze him a bit. Kelly, on the other hand, trembled next to him upon entering the facility.

The walls were washed in bright white. The linoleum had been white at one time, but now it was a dingy yellow. The staff wore white as if they wanted to blend into their surroundings and go unnoticed. Badges pinned to their uniforms listed names and job titles.

Michael approached the head nurse and requested a visit with Mona Hall. At first he feared the scowling woman would turn them away.

A few moans and a scream floated down the corridor to them.

Kelly appeared ready to bolt.

"This is Mona's daughter," Michael said. "She needs to see her mother. We both do."

The nurse nodded curtly. "She's in the solarium. She's always there in the afternoon. It's getting late. Visiting hours are nearly over. Be quick about it."

They had to sign in. Then they were given visitor passes to wear on their clothing in plain view of the armed security team. This was no ordinary institution. This place housed some of the most depraved and violent individuals in the

four-state area. Michael began to wonder if bringing Kelly
with him had been a good idea, after all.

He believed she needed to confront her deepest fear
needed to see that her mother wasn't going to hurt her again
but Michael wasn't a psychiatrist. He realized he could be
doing more harm than good.

At the solarium door, he turned to Kelly and said, "You
can wait in the car if you want. I won't think less of you."

"No," she said, her eyes glued to her mother's pale face
once she found her. "I want to do this."

With an inner strength that amazed him, Kelly took slow
steps to her mother's side.

Mona Hall was still a very attractive woman. Some might
even say pretty. Her blond hair was secured in a tight chi
gnon and she wore cream-colored silk pajamas, looking
more like queen of the manor than a psychotic patient. The
late-afternoon sun filtered through the windows.

"Mama," Kelly whispered. "Can you hear me?"

Mona's eyes, a lighter hue than Kelly's, swung upward
to slowly slide over them as if she was appraising a jewel
and finding it lacking.

"Who are you?" Her tone was as haughty as her ap
pearance.

"It's me, Mama. Kelly. Don't you recognize me?"

"Kelly?" The woman laughed. "Who are you trying to
fool? Are you one of those nuts that live here? You must
be new. My daughter is a little girl. She's living with her
father now." The woman returned her wistful gaze to the
solarium window, looking out with a tortured longing at the
garden outside. "My little girl has golden ponytails and
adorable freckles on her nose. She giggles a great deal.
miss that."

Mona's eyes glittered with unshed tears.

Kelly began to cry softly. The tears traced a path down
her face. She backed away and Michael silently cursed him

self for putting her through this. He had been ready to defend her from a physical attack. It hadn't occurred to him that this woman would bash Kelly mentally and emotionally.

He stepped forward.

"Ma'am, I need to ask you a few questions." He waited for Mona to look at him, then he continued. "You lived at a place called Moore House for fourteen years. There are rumors floating about that Moore House has hidden passages and secret doors. Do you know anything about them?"

"Of course," she said without hesitation. "My husband and I didn't want our little girl getting hurt, so we hid the map to the doors and tunnels in the guest house."

"There's a map?" Michael couldn't believe a map had been under their noses the whole time.

"It belonged to some jewel thief. He was a bit before my time," Mona said. "There were blueprints of all the buildings, geological surveys, pictures of his daughter."

Kelly took a step forward, joining the conversation again. "The man had a daughter? What happened to her?"

"She was a pretty little thing with dark hair and the biggest brown eyes you've ever seen. I saw a picture of her once. When her father died, she was only five years old. She got adopted by some prominent family in another state. Or so I heard." The woman frowned. "Now what was her name? Natalie, I think. Her name was Natalie."

"Thank you, ma'am," Michael said. "You've been very helpful."

Michael put a hand on Kelly's back, wanting to steer her toward the door, but she wasn't ready to leave yet. She stood frozen to the spot and stared at her mother's frail figure.

Mona glanced up again, looking slightly annoyed at finding her guests hadn't left.

"If you don't mind, I'd like to enjoy the sun before my afternoon tea. Was there something else you wanted?"

"I know you didn't mean to do it," Kelly whispered past the tears. It was important for her to forgive her mother, even if Mona didn't understand a word she was saying. "I couldn't see it before. I hated you. But you never meant to hurt me."

Kelly sank to her knees and circled her arms around Mona's small waist, hugging her tight.

Michael stepped forward, worried the woman might freak out at having someone she thought a total stranger embrace her. He wanted to be close in case. Kelly needed protection. It was his fault she was here. He had insisted she go with him. If anything bad happened to her—mentally or physically—he would hold himself responsible.

He stopped when he saw the look in Mona's eyes. She was touched, although confused by Kelly's gesture. Mona patted the golden head against her breast, smoothing Kelly's hair with a gentle touch.

Kelly mumbled a soft goodbye.

She raced out of the hospital with Michael on her heels. She didn't look back. Michael suspected she was aching to glance at her mother one last time, but she kept her gaze focused straight ahead.

Pride inflated his chest.

Kelly had taken a giant step toward a new life, although she probably didn't realize it yet.

BACK AT MOORE HOUSE, Kelly went straight to her room, holding on to her composure by a thin thread. Of all the things she had imagined happening at the hospital, forgiving her mother had not been one of them. The woman had burned her, scarred her for life, inside and out. But Kelly couldn't hate her mother anymore.

Mona Hall was sick. It wasn't her fault any more than it would have been had she developed cancer.

Kelly hadn't expected her mother to be stuck in the past, living in the hopes of seeing her little girl again. It was an awful tragedy all the way around. She prayed her mother would find some sort of peace.

Kelly entered her bedroom without a thought to a possible intruder or another awful message until she was walking through the doorway. Fortunately, there was nothing. Not a single thing out of place.

With a sigh of relief, she collapsed onto the bed and felt her tumultuous emotions wash over her. The bed sagged beside her and a hand stroked her hair. Familiar fingers rubbed her scalp. Before he spoke, before she saw him, she knew without a doubt it was Michael.

"I'm sorry," he said. "You probably hate me now for making you go through that. I wasn't thinking. I didn't know it was going to be like that."

"No." Kelly lifted her face. "I'm glad I did it. She's not the way I remember her at all. I was afraid of her. I had built her up in my head to be some sort of horrible monster. But she's not. She's a lonely, sick woman."

"I bet." Michael's tone was a bit hostile.

"I forgive her for what she did. I can't hold on to that anger anymore. It's not healthy."

"I agree with you there."

"I need some time to myself. Could you leave me alone for a while?"

"No," he said. He lifted her until she was sitting beside him. "I have to tell you something first. Then I'll go if you want me to."

"Okay."

"That was the most remarkable thing I have ever seen anyone do. You confronted your worst nightmare—your past and your mother. And you held together."

"I cried," she interrupted. "I wasn't exactly brave."

"Yes, you were. You *are* brave. You got in touch with your emotions. There's no shame in that." The muscle in his jaw jumped and he turned his eyes away from her. "There are some things in my life that I wish I'd cried over now. Instead, I played the tough guy. I locked my feelings away until I couldn't reach them anymore. There's nothing wrong with feeling."

"Tell me," she breathed. "Let me in, Michael. I want to know everything about you. I don't want you to hold anything back from me. It's too important."

"Know this," he said. One of his hands stroked her cheek. His eyes met hers steadily. "I am so in awe of you right now."

It was an incredible admission, and it caught Kelly off guard.

Tears filled her eyes, but this time they represented hope and light. She wanted Michael more than she ever had before. She wanted to make love to him, wanted to give him the one thing she hadn't given another living soul. Long ago she had made the decision to save herself for the faceless man of her dreams, a man she hoped to meet one day. Sometimes she'd felt silly for waiting.

Now she knew what she'd been waiting for, and it was more than worth it.

It was her turn to touch him. Kelly caressed his face, savoring the feel of the hard planes and the soft flesh. He had tiny wrinkles at the corners of his eyes that crinkled when he smiled. Her fingers lovingly touched them now, memorizing the moment, tucking it away in her mental scrapbook. She didn't want to ever forget what she was feeling at this moment.

She leaned closer and kissed him full on the mouth.

His lips were soft yet demanding, hardening for a brief moment.

Kelly straightened up. While holding his gaze, she reached for the hem of her sweater. A split second later it was off. She tossed it to the floor, her eyes still locked with his. She heard his breath catch and she saw the desire in his eyes. He wanted her as much as she wanted him.

"I should probably warn you," she said. "I haven't been with a man before."

"What do you mean?" His expression froze.

"I'm a virgin."

Her hands went to the hooks at the back of her bra.

Michael blinked at her in wonder. She had finally managed to stun him. She tensed for the rejection she feared would come after such a confession.

"Wow," he said, releasing the breath he had been holding. "I should probably tell you a few things too. I'm not who you think I am," he confessed.

She smiled, unhooking the bra clasps. "You are everything I've ever wanted."

"I've been with a lot of women," he said. It wasn't a boast, rather like an admission of guilt. "I just want you to know that. None of them made me feel like you do. If you don't ever believe another thing I say, believe that."

She moved to lower her bra, exposing her vulnerability to him.

Michael's hands covered hers, stopping her.

"This is an incredible gift you're offering me," he said. "But you should give it to a man who deserves it. I don't. I'm not a knight in shining armor, angel. I've done some bad things. If you knew, if you had any idea what my past is like, you wouldn't be here with me now."

"Yes, I would. Trust me. When I look deep into your eyes, I see the real you. The time for true confessions is past, Michael. Make love to me. That's all I want. Everything else is trivial."

He released her hands and she tossed her bra aside.

"Are you sure?" He asked the question even as his hands were betraying him, sliding up her body.

"Make love to me," she repeated.

Michael gently laid her next to him, and his clothes quickly joined hers on the floor.

Being with Michael was more incredible than Kelly had imagined it would be. He seemed to give her everything, sharing everything including his soul with her. It was a sensual dream. His hands, his mouth, his tongue traveled over her, exploring her flesh until she was ready to purr in delight.

After what seemed to be endless hours of amazing torture, Michael joined his body with hers. Brilliant colors swirled as Kelly was lifted higher than she'd ever been before.

In the past she had worried that she wouldn't know what to do, wouldn't be able to please a man. Michael took those concerns and blew them away like green mist.

His world became her world. There was the feel of his hair beneath her fingers and his hard muscles encased in smooth skin. All of her senses were being stimulated simultaneously, adding to her pleasure.

There was the sound of Michael's breathing, soft at first, then growing fast and hoarse as the two of them reached for the clouds.

There was the sight of Michael's incredible body as he moved over her and beneath her and within her. Not even the pain that accompanied his possession of her could mar the beauty of the moment.

There was the smell of lavender on his skin, from the soap he had used in the shower that morning. The sweet scent teased her nostrils. She couldn't get enough of it, of him.

There was the salty taste of his flesh on her tongue.

When she thought it couldn't get any better, Michael proved her wrong. He took them both to dizzying new heights, flying them closer to the sun. She couldn't take it. She was going to explode.

Kelly arched her back and dug her fingernails into his shoulders.

He didn't complain. He appeared to be lost in his own world, head thrown back and eyes closed. The thing that had brought them closer than any two people had a right to be was now tearing them away from each other, sending them on solo journeys of self-discovery.

Kelly cried out.

Michael collapsed against her, his damp forehead resting in the groove of her neck. His erratic breathing matched her own.

She was sure she wouldn't recover from this.

Her eyelids floated shut. Without a word they fell into a deep sleep in each other's arms. It was as it should be. Kelly relived the beautiful lovemaking in her dreams. Everything was perfect.

Then something was wrong.

Someone was trying to come between her and Michael, yelling at the top of their lungs.

"Fire!"

Chapter Ten

Michael's eyes flew open. He didn't move a muscle, barely breathing as he listened for the sound that had pulled him from a deep sleep. Part of him believed "Fire!" had been screamed in his dream, a mere apparition that faded in the light of reality.

So he waited and listened.

"Fire! There's a fire. Get out!"

The desperate voice didn't come from his imagination. Paddy—he was certain it was Paddy—yelled from somewhere down on the first level, trying to wake them before they burned to death. Paddy was probably trying to control the flames by himself until help could arrive.

Michael threw back the covers and jumped to his feet. He ran to the door, testing it by placing his palms flat against it. The door was cold; there wasn't any telltale warmth in the wood. If there was a fire, it wasn't anywhere near the bedroom.

He opened the door and stepped into the hallway, sniffing the air. There was definitely an acrid smell of smoke in it; the house was on fire. Michael raced back into the master bedroom, knowing every second counted. He struggled into his clothes. The house was big, but that didn't mean they had forever to make their escape.

Michael took a blanket to the bathroom. Tossing it into

the tub, he turned the water on full blast. He didn't take time to turn the water off. Instead, he pulled the dripping blanket from the tub and returned to Kelly's side.

"There's a fire," he shouted, shaking her awake. "We have to get out!"

"Fire? Are you sure?"

"I could smell smoke in the hallway. I'm sure enough. Better safe than sorry." He threw her clothes at her. "Get dressed."

He lifted Kelly high into his arms once she was fully clothed. "I can walk," she yelled back. "Put me down."

Michael set her on her feet but grabbed her hand, fearing he could lose her if the smoke was too heavy downstairs. They held the wet blanket over their heads and stepped into the hallway. The smell of smoke was heavier now, more insistent.

They stumbled forward.

Michael wrapped an arm around Kelly's waist as they descended the stairs. A black fog of smoke enveloped them. Oxygen became a precious and rare treasure. Michael would have traded ten bags of diamonds for one breath of clean, fresh air. He covered his mouth and nose with an edge of the blanket.

He took a tentative breath and choked.

It wasn't working. A wave of dizziness crashed over him, almost knocking him from his feet. The front door was too far away. They weren't going to make it.

Kelly stumbled, and his arm tightened around her in an effort to keep her on her feet. They made it to the bottom of the staircase. Michael looked in the direction of the front door, but he couldn't see a damn thing with his eyes burning from the smoke.

Kelly swayed and slumped forward, obviously losing consciousness. She would have hit the floor if he hadn't grabbed her more tightly. He let the blanket go and swung her up in his arms for the second time. The most intelligent thing he could do was to get down on the floor and crawl to the door, he knew, but he had to get Kelly out of the house. Desperation pushed him. For all he could tell she wasn't breathing.

He staggered forward. She didn't weigh much more than a feather, but he was feeling weak and nauseous himself. His limbs had turned to molasses. His throat was raw and his lungs ached, scorched by the heat.

They weren't going to make it to the door. At least Kelly was out cold and wouldn't suffer. Michael didn't care about himself, only the sweet lady in his arms. She had to live. Paddy would have phoned out to report the blaze. Where were the firemen?

Flames crackled somewhere in the background. Michael didn't have the time or the inclination to look for their source. He only knew the fire was closer than ever before.

His arms strained under Kelly's weight. He went down on one knee, striking the bone hard against the wood floor. Pain shot up his thigh. Desperate to breathe, he turned his head, pushing his face into Kelly's hair. Smoke was everywhere. He couldn't get away from it.

Grunting, he used his last drop of strength to stand.

His life flashed through his mind like a series of snapshots. *What a waste.* From the sadness of losing one person after another, to his current situation, he saw his life laid out like a giant map, going nowhere.

He gazed down at Kelly's angelic face and felt the pang of true remorse. He should have told her the truth. He vowed that if they made it out of the house alive, he would tell her everything, hold nothing back. Then once he knew she was safe, he would let her choose. If she told him to leave and never return, he would do that. Even if it killed him inside.

Perhaps leaving would be for the best. He was a lost cause when it came to relationships.

The truth was Michael Taggert didn't know how to love. No one had taught him, although a few had tried. For some reason he was cold inside. His heart and soul had turned black long ago, long before he'd seen Kelly's loving blue eyes.

As if in answer to his prayer, the front door swung open and firemen poured in. The first one through the door took Kelly from Michael's arm, ignoring his faint protests. The second fireman grabbed Michael by the arm and half dragged, half carried him outside into the frigid cold.

Blessed oxygen filled his lungs. The fresh air brought on a horrible coughing spell. Michael's body shook uncontrollably.

When they reached the ambulance, a paramedic slapped an oxygen mask onto Michael's face. A few more coughs racked his body, but he didn't care. He was in better shape than Kelly. He watched the paramedics work on her, using a round of CPR to revive her.

She didn't appear to be responding.

Michael offered a silent prayer to the heavens, begging for his angel's life. In a short time she had become the most important thing on earth to him. He didn't care what happened to him in the future; he just wanted Kelly to live. She was too good, too pure to die so young.

He stood at the foot of the gurney, willing her to live, and everything fell into perspective. Nothing seemed as important as the woman now fighting for her life.

A violent cough burst from her, and tears filled Michael's eyes. She was alive.

Moments later Kelly opened her eyes and glanced around. Her gaze landed on him and a small smile touched her mouth. She held a shaking hand out to him. He took it without hesitation, holding it gently between his palms. He swallowed the lump in his throat, fighting the urge to drop his head against her chest and cry like a baby.

"She has to go to the hospital," the paramedic said. "The sooner the better. You should get checked out, too."

"No." Kelly shook her head. Her hand frantically pulled

at his. "Please, I don't want to go to the hospital. I hate hospitals."

"I'll be with you," he said.

"You won't leave?" Her eyes, wide and trusting, latched on to his face.

"I'll be with you," he repeated.

She settled back, seemingly reassured.

Michael wished he could relax. He had a terrible feeling that the fire hadn't been an accident. Someone was trying to kill Kelly, him—or both of them together. There was a strong possibility it was Landis. But it could be any number of people, depending on which of them was the real target. Michael had a long list of enemies, and Kelly living in a house rumored to hold diamonds didn't put her out of danger.

The paramedics loaded Kelly into the ambulance, and her eyes widened again in barely restrained fear. Michael climbed beside her, hoping his presence would reassure her.

As the doors swung shut, he caught a glimpse of Paddy telling the firemen he was on his way to visit a friend when he'd seen the fire and stopped to help. The Irishman shrugged to let Michael know he had no idea what had happened. Paddy would probably follow them to the hospital. The two of them would find time to talk privately somehow.

Michael didn't want Kelly to see them together, not until he had an opportunity to tell her the truth. He was going to keep his promise. No need to tempt fate. He would tell her everything just as soon as he got the chance.

HOSPITALS WERE NOT ON Kelly's list of favorite places. She hated everything about them, from their awful sterile smell to their bright lighting. She had spent too many wasted days in the hospital after her mother had doused her with scalding water. Nightmares had followed her into sleep every night during that horrible period.

But this time was different, she reminded herself. Michael was with her. He would hold her hand and watch over her while she slept. Nothing bad would be able to harm her. Michael would guard her well. She trusted him. He wouldn't let her down.

The kind nurses settled her into a private room. One of them checked her vitals, noted the information on a chart and left her alone with Michael. With a relieved sigh, Kelly slid beneath the covers. No one had noticed her scars, or at least hadn't commented on them. She hadn't seen a single look of pity cross any of the nurses' faces, and she'd been watching, too. Maybe Michael was right. Perhaps the scars weren't as bad as she thought they were.

Michael sat next to her on the bed. "Can I get you anything? Water? Something to eat?"

"My throat hurts like the devil," she said. "Some ice chips might be soothing. The nurse told me they have an ice machine around the corner."

"I'll get you some then."

Michael left and the room seemed to shrink in on her.

Her mind raced in circles, going over every aspect of their escape from the fire. Michael had saved her life. She owed him so much. There was no way she could ever repay him.

Her eyes went to the door, and she hugged herself in nervous anticipation of his return. Why was it taking him so long? He could have gotten lost. Maybe she should buzz for the nurse after all, and ask the woman if she had seen Michael turn the wrong way.

Before she could press the red button, a nurse walked in with a tray.

"Hello. I'm Regina. The doctor wanted me to give you a little shot to relax you."

Kelly tensed. "Did you see my fiancé? He went to get me some ice. He's been gone a long time."

"Is he a gorgeous fella with dark hair and a brooding

stare?'' The nurse smiled with a look of pure envy on her pretty, oval-shaped face.

"Yes," Kelly said. "He's wearing a leather jacket."

"I saw him," the nurse confirmed, "but he wasn't anywhere near the ice machine. I saw him talking to some old, hefty looking guy with a nice smile. They're down the hall. Maybe he was talking to your daddy. They both looked kind of upset."

"My father's dead."

"Oh, I'm sorry." The nurse gave her the shot before Kelly could protest. The sting of the needle made her wince. "Would you like me to get him for you?"

"No. I'm sure he'll be back any minute." The nurse headed for the door, but Kelly stopped her again. "You say the man my fiancé was talking to is heavyset? Are you sure he's not real tall and skinny?"

"Positive. He reminds me of an uncle I used to have. He's, uh, stocky. Definitely not skinny. Anything else I can do for you?"

"No. Thank you."

At least Kelly knew Michael wasn't with Elvin Grant, the skinny creep who wanted her house.

Kelly started to feel strange, as if she was floating up to the ceiling. She wanted to stay awake long enough to ask Michael who he'd been talking to. As far as she knew Michael didn't have any friends in town. She was probably overreacting. The other man must be a cop or a fireman, and Michael was finding out about the damage to her house.

Her house. She thought about Moore House and how long it had been in her family. She wondered how much damage had been done by the fire. Hopefully it could be repaired. She had quite a bit of money in the bank, an inheritance left by her grandfather to her dad. Her father hadn't had expensive tastes. And neither did she. The money was safe, waiting for a rainy day.

She could hire Wade to fix the house.

Wade was a genius. He couldn't read a blueprint, but he could fix anything. With his help, and her inheritance, perhaps she and Michael could restore Moore House to its original beauty.

Michael pulled up a chair beside her bed and took a seat. She opened her mouth, wanting to ask him about the house and about his friend. Her throat ached. Her vocal cords refused to work.

Her eyes drifted shut.

She floated away on a soft cloud.

MICHAEL'S MEETING WITH Paddy had been cut short by a well-meaning nurse. She'd informed him that Kelly was asking for him, so he'd returned to her side without hesitation. Paddy was going to nose around Moore House, hopefully without being seen. If he found anything, he promised to have the hospital page Michael right away.

Michael wanted to know who was trying to kill Kelly. Saving her was his first priority now. He would protect her with his life.

The friendly nurse poked her head in. "You wanted to speak to the fireman in charge of the investigation, right? He's in the waiting room."

Michael glanced at Kelly. He didn't want her to wake up in the hospital alone. The fire was enough of a trauma for her to suffer.

"She'll be out for hours," the nurse assured him.

He reluctantly left the room and strode down the hallway to the lounge. The fire chief stuck out his meaty hand and shook Michael's firmly. He was a pleasant man with sparkling brown eyes and a friendly demeanor.

"I'm Chief Truman. I was told you have some questions about the fire at Moore House."

"Yes, sir."

"Are you the owner?"

"No, sir," Michael said. "I'm a friend of the owner's. Can you tell me how the fire started?"

"Well…" The fire chief scratched his gray head as he spoke. "At first I thought it was probably an electrical fire, because it's an old house. But the fire originated in the kitchen. The stove had been left on. There appeared to be a greasy rag close to it."

"You think it was deliberate?"

"We are working under that assumption at this time, but we haven't ruled out an accidental fire."

Michael nodded, thinking back to earlier that night. He and Kelly had eaten sandwiches for supper. Neither of them had used the oven. He went over all the possible scenarios and came up with a single name.

Wade Carpenter. The man let himself into Kelly's home whenever the urge took him. He was a carpenter. Maybe he worked on cars, as well. He could have turned on the stove, left an oily rag next to the burner and forgotten about them both. Although Wade had returned the key Kelly had given him, he could have made a copy.

It could have been an accident. The man was mildly retarded, after all. Even the brightest of people could be forgetful at times. Michael wanted to give Wade the benefit of the doubt because he was a friend of Kelly's, but his gut told him the fire had been set on purpose to kill either one or both of them. The perpetrator hadn't "accidentally" strangled Kelly. He wouldn't leave threats and try to frighten her without realizing what he was doing. If it was Wade Carpenter, the man wasn't as clueless as he pretended to be.

"How far did the fire spread?" Michael asked.

"We managed to contain it to the kitchen. There is smoke and water damage in several rooms, however."

"Thank you." Michael shook the man's hand for the second time. "If I need to know anything else, I'll call you."

"Glad to be of service."

Chief Truman walked away.

Michael went to a pay phone and called Paddy. He told the Irishman everything the chief had told him. Then he asked if Paddy had anything new to report.

"Not a thing," his colleague replied quickly.

"I forgot to thank you for saving our lives tonight."

"What do you mean?"

"I was sleeping like the dead," Michael admitted. "If you hadn't yelled 'fire,' I wouldn't have woken in time to get Kelly and myself out. You saved our butts. I owe you a big one."

Silence followed his statement.

"Tag," Paddy said at last, "I didn't yell anything. I didn't even know about the fire until the fire department and the ambulance arrived."

"What?" Michael clearly remembered the masculine voice shouting from somewhere in the house. "I was sure it was you."

"Well, it wasn't." There was a hearty chuckle. "Hey, maybe you got yourself one of those guardian angels."

"Yeah." Michael dismissed the thought. "I'm going to tell Kelly the truth when she wakes up about who I am and why I'm actually here."

"Are you crazy? Are you going soft on me or what? The girl almost dies so you're going to tell her everything? That's nuts."

Michael didn't feel like discussing the issue further. He was going to tell her. There wasn't anything Paddy could do to stop him. He said goodbye and disconnected the call before Paddy could protest again.

He marched to Kelly's room, desperately wanting to lighten the heavy burden that weighed down his soul. But she was still fast asleep.

So he decided to take a walk, get some coffee, plan his words carefully. If he told her in just the right way, perhaps she wouldn't hate him for it. She was an understanding person. Surely she would be able to see he didn't have a choice in the matter.

There would be plenty of time to tell Kelly later. He stuffed his hands deep into the pockets of his jeans and whistled as he walked away from her room.

A NOISY CLANG followed a muttered oath.

Kelly's eyes popped open. It was morning—the day after the fire. Feeling groggy, she struggled to sit up. Her head swam dizzily. So this was what it was like to be drugged. It was an oddly familiar sensation. Loud voices went off like dynamite in her brain.

Michael's voice intruded, but it was coming from inside her head.

Me? Marry you?

Who would want you?

Searing hot pain ripped through her skull. She cried out, holding her head tight between her trembling hands. She didn't understand where the voices were coming from.

She didn't care. They hurt. She only wanted them to stop before her head exploded.

You're nothing but a screwed-up prude!

"Are you okay? Should I get the doctor?"

Kelly forced her eyes open and the pain evaporated as quickly as it had come. Wade stood over her. Worry had etched deep lines in his forehead. He held a huge box in his hands. Funny, she thought, how most people brought flowers to the sick, but Wade brought an old box.

"No. I'm fine. I'm sorry if I scared you. I just had a headache."

Wade nodded. He set the box on her lap and began to open the flaps as he explained its presence.

"I found something I think you should look at."

She recognized the box. It was Wade's lost-and-found box, his private collection. She didn't feel like company, but she didn't want to hurt Wade's feelings. He was a bit sensitive when it came to his hobby. His co-workers poked fun at him. They tormented the poor man over his precious finds. Once he had even been jumped by a big bruiser of a man over a baseball cap that Wade had "found" in the man's locker.

Wade didn't understand the concept of things having to be actually lost before he could find them.

"I found this at your house," Wade said. "I don't want you to be mad at me."

"Why would I be mad?"

"Because I took it from Michael's room." Hands tucked in his pockets, Wade lowered his head and kicked at the floor with his big shoe. He refused to meet her eyes. "Michael was mean to me. I don't like him. I don't want him to hurt you."

"Michael saved my life tonight, Wade. There was a fire at the house. Did you know about that?"

"Uh…yeah. I—I was there. I was walking around outside when the fire trucks pulled up. I saw you. I was scared you were dead."

"Why didn't you say something to me? Were you hiding?"

"Yeah." Wade nodded. "Michael's a mean man. I didn't want him to see me. He hates me."

Kelly wasn't sure what Wade meant by the statement. He'd repeated it as if it was fact. Wade hadn't lied to her in the past. Why would he start now?

"How was Michael mean to you, Wade?"

"He calls me names when we're alone. He told me to get lost. He told me you didn't want me around 'cause I was dumb. And he took the key you gave me."

She felt the color drain from her face. Michael didn't speak like that around her. She couldn't imagine him being so cruel. Taking the key from Wade was ridiculous. Michael had no right to do such a thing.

"You know that isn't true. I enjoy having you around. I gave you the key. Remember?"

"Yeah. He's a liar." Wade's worried gaze traveled to the door. "Is he here? I don't want to see him."

"I don't know where he is, Wade. I just woke up."

"I need to go." Wade backed up fast, leaving the box on her lap. "I trust you. You can keep my things. Don't lose them."

"Wait, Wade."

It was too late. He was gone in a flash.

Even though he had given her permission to go through his stuff, Kelly felt like an interloper as she opened the box. She pulled out items a handful at a time, glanced at them and set them aside. If she had ever imagined what Wade's lost-and-found box would be like, this would be it. There was nothing terribly exciting.

Wade had collected quite an array of odds and ends. There was an assortment of change, old pencils, paper clips and pieces of scratch paper. She pulled out a small box of rocks, a couple of cigarette butts and a snapshot of a loving couple, complete strangers to Kelly.

Her hand settled on what appeared to be a thin, black wallet. She flipped it open and took a long, painful look at it. There was a badge and an identification card with a small photo.

The badge belonged to a CIA agent.

Michael Taggert.

Chapter Eleven

"Is something wrong?" Michael asked later that morning. He turned the steering wheel slowly and headed down the dirt road that would eventually take them to the wrought-iron gates separating Moore House from the rest of the world. "You haven't said a word since we left the hospital."

Kelly's fists curled in her lap, but she remained stubbornly mute.

"If you're worried about the house not being safe, we can go somewhere else. A hotel maybe."

Michael turned the car into the gravel driveway, stopping near the porch. He glanced up at the sky through the windshield, scanning the dark clouds there. A few snowflakes began to drift down, dissolving as they touched the glass.

"I think the weatherman's finally hit the mark," he said. "I guess he had to be right eventually. He's been running around like Chicken Little, crying snow every day."

Kelly didn't bother to look at him.

Michael turned to her. The silence had gone on long enough. He didn't know what he was going to say. Somehow, he hoped words of wisdom would spill from his lips.

Before he could utter a single syllable, Kelly sprang from the car like a jack-in-the-box. On quick feet, she disappeared into the house, not giving him time to think, much less speak.

The car's engine was still humming, so he switched it off and pocketed the keys. Following Kelly's lead, he entered Moore House. From outside the structure appeared massive in height and width, but inside it was a whole different story. The walls seemed too close together for his comfort. The air was old, stale, as if he was breathing the same air John Moore, the original owner, had breathed over a hundred years ago.

Michael didn't have to search the house to find Kelly.

She stood just inside the door, her stiff back to him.

"Kelly." He squeezed her trembling shoulders, hoping to reassure her without speaking. Something was wrong. Why wouldn't she confide in him?

She spun around, knocking his hands away.

"Why the hell didn't you tell me? Was this all a game to you?" She shoved her palms against his chest, forcing him to take a step backward. "You never intended to marry me, did you?"

"Kelly, if I did something to upset you—"

"Did something?" She interrupted. "*If* you did something? You lied to me!"

"What?" The bottom dropped out of his stomach. He had a sick feeling he knew exactly what she was shouting about. "What did I lie to you about?"

"The jig is up. You can stop pretending." She laughed, but there was no humor in it. "Why are you really here? Are you looking for buried treasure? Is that it? Are you just another stupid fortune hunter?"

"No." Fear slammed his heart into fourth gear. He had wanted to confess before she'd had the chance to figure things out on her own. "I'm not here to steal anything from you."

"Then why are you here? Are you investigating me?"

She withdrew an item from her purse and dropped it onto the floor near his feet as if it was a piece of garbage. It bounced off the toe of his sneaker before coming to rest nearby. He recognized the object on sight. He'd had an intimate knowledge of it for years.

She'd found his badge.

"I can explain," he said.

"Oh, I can't wait to hear this." Counting on her fingers, she listed all the ways he had wronged her. "You've used me. You've lied to me. You've almost gotten me killed. No one tried to hurt me until you came onto the scene. Coincidence? Somehow I doubt it."

"That's not exactly true." He sighed and rubbed a hand over his tired eyes. "Can we sit down? This is going to take a while."

Without a word, Kelly spun around and headed for the parlor. She took a seat on the far end of the sofa, her arms crossed in front of her chest, her eyes averted. She wouldn't even look at him. Michael wasn't so sure she would forgive him after she heard the truth. But he had to try. They'd shared an extraordinary night in each other's arms. He wasn't quite sure if they could have anything beyond the here and now, but the possibility of something wonderful happening between them was worth a fight.

He sat on the other end of the sofa, silently praying she would listen to the whole sordid story before flying off the handle again.

"I need to start from the beginning," he said. She waved him on, still refusing to look at him. He continued, "I told you about my brother. What I didn't tell you was that Jimmy was my twin."

Michael opened his wallet and withdrew a picture of himself with Jimmy. The two boys stood side by side, each with an arm slung over the other's shoulders. The photo had been taken on their tenth birthday. It was the only picture Michael had of his brother—the only one he would ever have now.

Her eyes reluctantly fell to the photograph and she gasped. ''Oh, my God. The resemblance is remarkable.''

''Looking at him was like looking into a mirror,'' Michael said, ''As I mentioned before, Jimmy and I were raised separately. I didn't see him for years. Then one day he showed up at my door, out of the blue. We talked for a while, but it didn't go very well. Jimmy wasn't doing anything productive with his life. He hated me, I think, because I seemed to have it together. I think that's why he did it.''

''Did what?'' Kelly's eyes locked with his. ''Tell me the rest. What did he do?

''He borrowed my identity,'' Michael said. ''I'm not the man you got engaged to. You agreed to marry my brother Jimmy while he was using my name.''

He saw her shocked expression but forced himself to continue. ''I know this is hard to understand. Please bear with me while I try to explain. Jimmy conned women for a living. He convinced them he loved them, proposed to them. Even occasionally married them, all with the support of my name. Then he took them for every cent he could get.''

''You're saying he just wanted my money?'' Pain filled her blue eyes. She turned away. Bitterness dripped from her voice. ''Of course. What else would he want?''

''Don't do that.'' Michael touched her fingers briefly moving closer to her. ''I met a few of the women my brother conned. Every single one of them felt small because of it. They blamed themselves, felt stupid. Don't do that to yourself. You are worth ten of Jimmy.''

''Why would somebody lie like that for money? It's disgusting.''

''Angel, I've seen people do a lot worse in the name of the almighty dollar.'' Michael moved closer still and tipped up her chin, turning her face so he could look her in the eye. "Jimmy was a fool. You are incredibly beautiful and strong. You're intelligent. Any sane man would thank his lucky stars to have a woman like you in his life."

"Don't try to sweet-talk me, and don't call me angel." She turned her head, escaping his grip. "I'm not interested in your lines. You are just as much a liar as your brother was."

"True," Michael said. "I apologize for last night. I shouldn't have made love to you while you were still in the dark about my identity. I shouldn't have let you down. Maybe if I'd been guarding you instead of losing myself in you, we could have prevented the fire. Maybe I would have even caught the maniac behind all of this."

"You didn't make love to me," she denied hotly. "You used me. You had an itch to scratch, and I was convenient."

"Don't say that."

"Why not? It's true."

"No, it isn't." He grabbed her shoulders and lifted her to her feet. He had to make her understand. "I care about you."

"You bastard!" She practically spat the words from her compressed lips as she slapped him. Michael's head snapped back, and tiny needles seemed to sting his cheek. He released her.

His own hand went to his face, testing the injured area. He opened and closed his jaw, making certain nothing had been knocked out of position.

"Don't you dare tell me you feel something for me!" Her face burned red. "Don't insult me like that."

"Okay. I won't... Why don't we get back to the facts then?" he suggested. "I'm sure you have more questions. What else do you want to know about Jimmy and the situation?"

"If what you say is true, where is this brother of yours?

Why isn't he here? And how did you know he was conning me in the first place?''

Michael sighed. "Well, it all started when I found out I was on the top of a hired killer's hit list. Zu Landis killed some of our top agents. He moved me to the top of the list after I tried to trap him. The agency wanted me to travel, leave a trail for the assassin to follow. Then other agents, the ones that were going to follow me, would swoop down and bag the guy. One problem, though. My brother was using my name again.''

Kelly blinked at him, looking a bit seasick.

"I tracked Jimmy to Tinkerton," Michael said. "I told my superiors I needed a few days of personal time to take care of a problem. I came here one night to confront Jimmy, to scare him with the possibility of being mistaken for me by a killer. But I'd arrived too late.''

He watched the color drain from Kelly's face as she made the connection.

"I found Jimmy in the closet," she said. "He was dead. Then I ran down the hallway and you were there. It was you, right? Then I fainted, I think.''

"Yes," he admitted. "And I caught you. I carried you to your room, and I found Jimmy on the floor in front of the closet. My brother was dead, and you were out cold on the bed. I had to make a quick decision. Either I could tell you everything and risk you forcing me out before I could find the killer, or I could play the part my brother had conceived. I had no idea if you would help me or not.''

"Who killed him?" Kelly asked, her mouth barely moving. Her brow creased. "The assassin? This Zu Landis person?''

"He's my number one suspect. That's the problem. I had to stay here, pretend to be the Michael Taggert you knew in order to flush out the killer. I'm afraid the person responsible for my brother's death is still around somewhere.

He could be close by, watching the house, watching us. If it's Landis he probably knows that the man he murdered wasn't his intended target and he's coming back to finish the job.''

Kelly stood slowly. She went to the old stone fireplace and turned around, but she didn't look directly at him. Her eyes were on the wall as if she could see through it.

"I can't believe this," she said, hugging herself. "Your brother was killed in my home. Someone was murdered while I slept not more than ten feet away."

"You weren't asleep. You were drugged. I found the vial," he explained. "Jimmy gave you something to knock you out, probably so he could search the house and take what he wanted before you woke up. He was planning on making a clean getaway. He would have probably succeeded if it hadn't been for the intruder."

"The jewels," she said. "Do you think your brother was looking for the jewels?"

"I don't know." Michael shrugged. "Did Jimmy seem a little too interested in the legend?"

"He mentioned it a few times. Asked questions." She laughed derisively. "I thought he was interested in me. It was flattering. He even dropped the idea of writing the book because he said he didn't want to upset me. Of course, now I know he never had any intention of writing a book in the first place. That was just a ploy to get close to me."

"Did you love him?" Michael leaned a bit closer, waiting for her to answer.

"I thought I did," she admitted with a deep frown. "But I didn't know him, did I? He was pretending to be someone else." Her eyes narrowed on Michael's face. "Like you. He was playing a game with me. There were times when I caught a glimpse of the real man, his selfish nature, but he covered it quickly enough. He would focus on me, my needs, like no one else ever had. I thought he was an incredible man.''

"How long did he live with you?''

"A couple weeks.'' She shrugged. "I let him move in because the motel was costing him a fortune and he was constantly complaining about it. Like he said, we were about to be married. Why shouldn't he move in with me?'' Looking away from Michael, she said, "At least I didn't sleep with him. I have that to be grateful for, but I still feel like such a fool.''

"Well, you're not.'' Michael took a chance; he went to her and tried to take her into his arms. She didn't have to hug herself anymore for comfort. He wanted to make her understand that. He was with her now, ready and willing to embrace her whenever she needed it. He added, "My brother was an expert. He could trick anyone into believing him.''

"Don't act as if you're on my side.'' She stepped away, reading his intentions and spurning him. "You must have thought I was a fool, too, because I fell for your line. You came in here and turned my life upside down without a moment's hesitation. You are a vile, low-down, sneaky son of a—''

"Hey,'' he interrupted, holding up a finger. "I've been the only thing standing between you and a killer. Let's not forget that.''

"Says you.'' Kelly paced to the other side of the room. "You could be running another scam on me right now. I think you should leave.'' She headed for the front door, determined to get rid of him.

"I'm not going anywhere until I find my brother's murderer.''

"That's what you think,'' she said. "I'll call the sheriff and have him throw your butt out if I have to. You have no right to be in my home. You weren't invited.''

Kelly walked over to the phone on the table near the parlor door and picked up the receiver, but she didn't get the chance to use the phone. Michael quickly snatched it from her fingers.

"I hardly knew my brother," he said. "But deep down I know there was good in him. I have to find his killer." His dark eyes purposely drifted to the winding staircases. "And you can't stay here alone right now. It's too dangerous."

"I think I need protection from you more than I do from some phantom killer. For all I know you were the one who tried to strangle me."

"You don't believe that." His voice softened as he approached her. "Come on. Let me stay a little longer. I believe the so-called phantom killer is lingering nearby, watching you and me and this house. I can catch him if you give me the chance. Then I'll leave you to your life. Sound fair?"

She shrugged her shoulders, grudgingly giving him permission to stay. "Do what you want. I don't care. But don't think you're going to weasel your way back into my bed. I hate you more than I've ever hated anyone in my entire life."

"That's probably for the best," Michael said.

"You betrayed me in the worst possible way. I won't forget it. There isn't anything you could say or do to make this all right."

He nodded in agreement.

"So," he asked, "where did you find my badge?"

"Wade found it, and don't you dare go after him. He meant well. He was trying to protect me."

"I hope so," Michael said. "I hope you're right about him."

"I am," she said with confidence. "You'll see. Anyway," she added, "I trust him a lot more than I trust you at the moment."

Michael folded his arms over his chest. He wanted to

reach out to her, ease her pain, but she wasn't ready to open her heart to him. Perhaps she never would be.

"I hope someday you'll be able to understand why all this subterfuge was necessary. I wanted to protect you from the truth about Jimmy and I figured the less you knew about the murder, the safer you would be."

"Who do you think you are? Who gave you the right to make decisions for me?" A horrible thought occurred to her. "Am I married to Jimmy? Was that part a dream?"

"No, it wasn't a dream, but the marriage isn't legal. If it was, you'd be married to me, not to Jimmy. He used my name, remember?"

Her cheeks burned hot-pink.

Unable to resist, Michael reached for her. She dodged his embrace, walking in a wide circle around him.

"What happened to the body?" she asked.

"A friend of mine took it to a morgue in Kansas City, and a forensic team from the home office was sent to do an autopsy. Jimmy was bludgeoned to death."

"What about the crime scene?" She hesitated before asking, "Did you clean it up? The blood and everything?"

"Yes." Her bathroom, the way it had appeared that night, came to life in his mind. He hated thinking about it. But she deserved answers. "I gathered the evidence before I destroyed it. The agency has given me free rein just in case Landis is behind it. They want him put away before he can kill any other agents."

"How many has he killed so far?"

"More than one." It was a lame answer, but he couldn't tell her. "It's classified."

"Oh. Right…" Kelly stepped out of the parlor and glanced up at the staircase. "The wallpaper will have to be replaced," she murmured distractedly. "It reeks in here."

If she felt more comfortable changing the subject, Michael wasn't going to stop her. "The fire chief told me the kitchen is a total mess," he answered.

"The kitchen!"

Her mouth fell open in horror. Kelly's feet pounded against the marble as she raced across the foyer. She shoved the kitchen door open and froze like one of the statues in the foyer.

The kitchen was indeed a mess. The cabinets were gone, nothing but charred ashes on the floor. The stove and refrigerator were done for, too. In fact, Michael didn't see a solitary item they could salvage.

Kelly stood immobile, her eyes blazing with fury.

"I can't believe it," she said quietly. "Wade and I put hours of work into remodeling this room. We put in new cabinets and appliances. It's destroyed."

"It can be fixed again," Michael said, trying to get her to focus on the bright side. "At least it's the only room with this much damage."

"And at least no one was killed," she said.

"That's right." He wrapped an arm around her waist from behind and whispered in her ear. Making love to her and then almost losing her in a fire weighed down on his already overloaded emotional state. He couldn't restrain himself from touching her every chance he got. His body ached to possess her again. "We both got out safely. I don't mind telling you, you had me scared."

"Why is that?" She stood stiff in his arms.

"I thought you were going to die."

"And that would have mattered to you?"

"You matter to me," he admitted.

"If that were so—" she shoved his arm away and turned hostile eyes on him "—you would have trusted me with the truth."

"I wanted to."

"What stopped you? You could have told me if you'd

really wanted to. You made the decision. Now you can live with the consequences.''

He wanted to say more. He wanted to tell her how his heart beat harder every time he thought of her. In truth, he hadn't felt like this about a woman in a very long time. But it wouldn't be fair to Kelly to share his growing feelings with her. In the end he was going to return to his job, a profession that didn't have a good track record when it came to relationships.

The agency trained their people to lie convincingly. In certain situations a lie could save a life. However, a lasting relationship needed trust, honesty and open communication. The agency was against all three when it came to their people. The less others knew about the CIA and its workings, the easier it was to continue with business as usual.

''I'm sorry I hurt you,'' Michael said. ''Whether you believe it or not, you've become a very important part of my life.''

Kelly glared at him, ''My house almost burned to the ground. Then I find out I'm sharing my bed with a liar. Excuse me if I don't believe your pretty words now.''

He hated the look of betrayal in her eyes, but it was probably for the best if she loathed the sight of him. Kelly wasn't going to move away from Moore House, from her safe haven. She wouldn't put up with being practically abandoned as he went off to other countries to work a mission. He couldn't see her standing beside him at a dinner party or skiing in Aspen.

She would always believe other people were staring at her scars, feeling sorry for her.

She didn't know how beautiful she was.

''I want to introduce you to my friend Paddy. He's been working on the case with me. I realize you don't have any reason to trust me, but maybe you'll believe him if he tells you my hands were tied. I wanted to tell you, but I couldn't.

He's probably down the road in a gray sedan as we speak. I'll just wave him in.''

"I saw him on the way to Margo's, didn't I?''

The lady had a mind like a steel trap. Hard to get one by her.

"Yes. Again, I apologize. If there was any way I could have told you the truth from the beginning, I would have.''

Kelly nodded, but her eyes were clouded with bitterness. He wasn't reaching her yet. She had a lot to digest. Hopefully he would be forgiven tomorrow. Or the next day. Hell, he would be happy if she forgave him at some point this side of eternity.

"I want to search Margo's house," he added. "Your mother mentioned something about plans to this place and other things being hidden there.''

"I think Margo would have noticed them by now," Kelly said. "Her home isn't that big.''

"Still, I'm going to search there.''

"Fine. I want to go with you.'' She gasped. "Oh no. I forgot about Boomer. Where is he? Did he get out?''

"I don't know where he is at the moment, but Paddy saw him last night. He was fine. Don't worry.''

"Thank God. I wouldn't want to have to explain his death to Margo.'' She gestured to the doorway. "Well, what are we waiting for?''

She lifted a chin in that stubborn tilt. There was nothing he could say to convince her to stay behind. It would be a waste of energy and time.

"You want to help me search your neighbor's house?''

"Yes," she said. "Now that I know you're a secret agent and that a murder took place in my home, I want to help you catch the guy. Two heads are better than one, and the sooner we find out the killer's identity, the sooner you can leave.''

Her aim was clear and true. The barbed arrow hit Mi-

chael's heart, dead center. She wanted to see the back
of him.

He hid the hurt from her watchful gaze, assuring himself
it was for the best. He would be leaving soon, anyway. At
least he wouldn't hurt her when he left, if she already
wanted him gone.

Michael motioned for her to exit the kitchen ahead of
him.

Kelly walked out, spine rigidly straight. If he lived to be
a hundred, he wouldn't meet another woman like Kelly Hall.
He had the feeling she was going to be one of his deepest,
darkest regrets.

THE SNOW WAS FALLING more heavily now. Kelly snuggled
into her jacket and climbed into her truck before Michael
could offer to drive. She gunned the engine as he jumped
inside. He barely had time to shut his door before they were
flying down the road in the direction of Margo's house.
Kelly glanced into her rearview mirror, spotting the gray
sedan with his friend inside.

"How long has he been watching my house?"

"A couple weeks," Michael said with seeming reluc-
tance. "He's the one who tracked Jimmy down for me. Then
he notified me and waited for my arrival. When we found
Jimmy dead, he went into surveillance mode. He's been
watching the house to make sure no one sneaks up on us in
the dead of night."

"Did it occur to him that maybe he should warn me about
Jimmy rather than watch from the bushes?"

"I hired him to watch. I didn't want him to approach you
or Jimmy. Especially with Landis on the loose." Michael
explained, "The agency doesn't usually allow civilians to
help them out, but I couldn't have an agent contacting me
here. Paddy is less suspicious than a dark suit. If you'd seen
him, if someone else had stopped to question his presence,

he would have said he was working on a missing person's case or maybe a cheating lover.'' He shrugged. ''Paddy has been my go-between with the agency, but he's taking his orders directly from me. It was my call for him not to alert you.''

Kelly mulled the situation over. No matter how many times Michael insisted he'd lied for her own good, she couldn't get past the hurt and betrayal. He could have told her if he'd really wanted to.

Now it all made sense—the changes in him, the way he'd looked at her.

She should have stayed behind and let him search Margo's house alone. She wanted to cry her eyes out for a few hours. Jimmy had been faking his love for her. Michael had made love to her, but he didn't have any real feelings for her. He'd been playing a dangerous game to catch a killer, and using her to do it.

Her feelings for him churned in sickening circles. Part of her wanted to wring his neck. The other part wanted to demand to know if anything he'd told her was true. Had everything been a lie?

Who would want to chain himself to something that looks like you?

Her memory returned with a thunderous flash. She remembered Jimmy standing over her after drugging her glass of champagne. He'd confessed to using her, then had laughed about it. He'd laughed at her right to her face when she'd been in no position to defend herself. She'd lain there helplessly as he tore her world asunder.

She looks like an angel.

She remembered bits and pieces of Michael's arrival, as well. Michael had told somebody, probably his partner, that she resembled an angel.

''Watch out!''

Michael's shout brought her crashing back to the present,

to find him wrestling the steering wheel from her grasp. The truck was heading into the ditch. Michael forced it onto the road again as her foot slammed down on the brakes.

The wheels squealed, sending a cloud of dust into the air.

"Are you trying to kill us?" Michael cried.

"No," she said. "I just remembered the night Jimmy drugged me. I was seeing it as if it was happening again."

Michael stared at her, his dark eyes huge. "Great. Tell me. Did you see anything that could help me find Jimmy's killer?"

"No," she repeated. "At least I don't think so. Jimmy was saying horrible things to me."

"Like what?"

"How nobody would ever want a girl like me. He told me my scars were hideous and he had to pretend I was somebody else every time he kissed me."

Michael swore viciously beneath his breath, but she heard every word.

She ignored his outburst and closed her eyes, trying to remember as much as she possibly could. "He was running around the room like a chicken with its head cut off. I don't know why. It was as if he was looking for something. He disappeared into the bathroom for a long time." She sighed. "That's it. That's all I can remember."

"And you didn't see anyone else?"

She shook her head. Jimmy had been the only person in the room with her when she'd lost consciousness. She was sure of it.

"I heard someone call me angel. Was that you?"

"Yeah." Michael turned to stare out the window while he answered her. She wasn't able to read his expression. "I told Paddy you looked like an angel in that stunning white dress you were wearing. I wouldn't have been surprised to see wings attached to your spine."

"That one word floated into my dreams. I remember feeling safe.'' She rolled her eyes. ''If only I'd known what was really happening around me.''

''Well,'' Michael said, ''let's get this over with.''

They went into Margo's house without knocking. Kelly didn't feel right about it, but she followed Michael's lead. He searched the place thoroughly. She was amazed at some of the places he looked. He turned over drawers to expose the bottoms. He felt the top of every door, running his fingers along the ridges. He even went through the refrigerator and stared into each individual ice cube as if something important might be hidden inside.

Kelly watched in stunned silence.

Eventually her mind wandered, and she became lost in thought. She saw her dreams swirling down the drain. Gone were the future children she'd hoped to have. Just last week she'd been happy, ready to marry and start a family. Now she was left with nothing but could-have-been.

Michael dumped a second ice tray and started to crush each cube.

''What are you looking for?'' She had to ask. ''Aren't we supposed to be searching for maps or something? I doubt they're small enough to fit into ice.''

''I don't want to leave a single stone unturned,'' he replied briskly. ''If there is a clue here as to exactly what happened to Margo and who did it to her, I want to find it.''

''What do you mean 'who did it to her'? We don't know for sure anything happened to her.''

''Actually, we do.'' Michael left the icy mess on the countertop to stand beside Kelly and look into her eyes. ''I didn't tell you about this before, because I didn't want to scare you. But I see how I hurt you with my lies and my silence. So I want to tell you everything now.''

''Everything?'' Fear clutched her throat.

"I found a picture of Margo. I'm sorry, Kelly, but your neighbor is dead."

Kelly gasped. "No! Not Margo. She was so kind."

"I know. I am sorry. If there was anything I could do to change it, to spare you this, I would."

"But why?" she asked. "Who would do something like that to a nice old lady?"

"I think Margo was just in the wrong place at the wrong time." Michael took Kelly by the shoulders as if he needed to hold her steady—keep her from bolting. "Maybe the killer needed somewhere to hide. Or perhaps he knew about the diamonds and wanted the plans. That could be why I haven't found them yet. They might not be here anymore."

Kelly shook her head in disbelief. What was happening? She had lived at Moore House for years without any trouble. Now, all of a sudden, people were being killed all around her.

Her gaze focused on Michael. Things had been normal until he and his brother had come into the picture. She realized she had only Michael's word for any of this. What if his badge was a fake and the whole thing was a setup? They could be trying to drive her away from Moore House so they could search for the missing jewels.

Suspicion reared its ugly head once again. She had a choice. She could believe in him, accept his protection. Or she could find a way to get rid of him. The police might be interested in hearing a murder had been covered up in their jurisdiction.

"I found it!"

Michael's yell caught her attention. He was bent down, peering under the kitchen sink. He had a roll of papers in his hand.

"What is it?"

Michael's happy grin lit up his dark eyes. He spread the papers out on the table in front of her.

''Don't you recognize it? It's a few crude drawings of Moore House. Maps, if you will.'' He bent his dark head and studied them for a moment. ''Look. Here.'' He pointed at a corner with his finger. ''According to this, there is an opening in the study somewhere along the wall. If I can just figure out how it opens...''

''The map doesn't tell you?''

''No, angel.'' Michael smiled at her. He grabbed the papers, holding them against his chest. ''Let's get back to the house and check it out. If I'm right, we'll find a secret door in your bedroom, as well.''

Kelly shivered at his prediction.

If he was right, anyone could enter her bedroom as she slept and—

It was too horrible to even think about.

Chapter Twelve

Back in the study at Moore House, Kelly was feeling like a fool. She ran her hands down one side of the bookcase, groping for something that shouldn't be there, while Michael repeated the action on the other side. Nothing happened. Splinters would be her only reward if she kept this up much longer.

She wasn't surprised. She didn't expect a magic door to suddenly burst open. Regardless of what Michael insisted the papers hinted at, there weren't any secret passages in her house. She would have found them by now if there were.

"My mother is in the hospital for a reason, you know," Kelly said. "I can't believe you took her seriously when she talked about hidden passages. There aren't any."

"I don't get it," Michael said. He went to the desk and lifted the paper with the study drawn on it. "According to this, the door should be right here." He gestured to the bookcase.

"Hey," he exclaimed, "I saw a movie once. The mechanism to spring the door was dressed up like a book. It was made of wood or something and when it was pulled out, the door opened."

She sighed in frustration. There wasn't any use in arguing with him. He'd made up his mind. Since she couldn't convince him, she decided to help him. Together, they moved each book out an inch or two. When nothing happened, they went to the next book. On and on.

Kelly heard the front door slam. Someone had come inside, probably Wade.

"Kell? Are you here?"

It *was* Wade.

Relief swept over Kelly, easing the tension, until she saw the look on Michael's face. He didn't like or trust her friend. She gave Michael a reproachful glare, hoping he wouldn't attack Wade the second he saw him. She was certain Michael wouldn't hurt Wade physically—he wasn't that type of person—but even a verbal assault could scar her sensitive friend for life.

"I'll handle him," she said. "You can finish looking for your mysterious door."

"Maybe you should ask your buddy Wade if he knows where the entrance to the passages are. He hangs out here often enough. He probably knows more about this place than you do."

"I doubt that."

Michael's attitude left a lot to be desired. Wade was a good person. At least he didn't lie to her. When it came to Wade Carpenter, what you saw was what you got. He couldn't deceive someone if his life depended on it.

"You are far too trusting," Michael said, reminding her of the way his brother had gotten into her house and through her defenses. She wanted to wipe that smug look from his face, but she didn't have time. She had a guest waiting for her.

Kelly hurried to find Wade.

He was in the kitchen, surveying the damage with damp eyes. She knew exactly what was going through his mind. They had worked so hard on the room. In fact, the only room they had put more time and effort into was the master bath.

She reached up to place a hand on Wade's solid shoulder.

He glanced down at her, smiling through the sadness. "I'm sorry, Kell."

"What are you apologizing for? It's not your fault."

Wade shrugged without further comment.

His eyes widened and he lowered his voice to ask her a question. "Michael here?"

"Yes, Wade. He's here. But don't worry. Michael is not a bad guy." At his expression of disbelief, she added, "He works for the government. He's trying to catch a killer, and he's not the man who treated you badly. That was his twin brother, Jimmy."

"There are two of them?"

"There were two of them," she said. Was she giving Wade too much information? Michael was undercover, after all, and Wade wasn't known for being able to keep secrets. On the other hand, who was he going to tell? Most people treated him like a fool. They wouldn't listen to him if he said the sky was blue. "Michael's brother was killed in this house. Michael is pretending to be his brother right now, though, so we need to keep quiet about it."

"I don't like him," Wade announced. He folded his arms like a petulant child. He struck his head against the wall. "I wish he'd go away."

"If you got to know him, you would like him. He's a great guy." She smiled, hoping her true feelings didn't shine through. She still hadn't forgiven Michael for lying to her, and she doubted she ever would. "Do you think I would lie to you?"

"No. Never. Friends don't lie."

Kelly swallowed hard, mentally numbering all the lies Michael had told her since his arrival. Each and every one for her own good, of course. Wade had a nice, unrealistic view of the world.

"Your box is in the back of Michael's car."

Wade gasped. "Michael's car? Did he see it?"

"Relax. Michael didn't look in the box. You trusted me with it, and I wouldn't betray you like that." She paused, knowing he wasn't going to like her next suggestion. "But I think you should show him the contents of the box yourself."

"No!"

Kelly was startled by Wade's reaction. She hadn't heard him shout before.

"Wade, Michael is like a cop. There might be something in that box that can help him figure out who killed his brother."

"I don't care." Wade pouted, sticking out his lower lip. "I don't like him. He's mean."

"Someone is trying to hurt me, Wade. Do you care about that?"

"Yeah. I like you, Kell." His expression changed in an instant, filling her with regret. Wade took everything to heart. She had to be gentle with him. "Who wants to hurt you? Michael?" he asked.

"No, Wade. Michael is trying to help me. He wants to catch the bad guys before they *can* hurt me."

"Okay." Wade headed for the front door. "I'll get the box. You can let him see it." He stopped abruptly. "I'm not in trouble, right? Bobby Watts says if I keep finding stuff the cops are gonna lock me away somewhere and throw away the key."

"Bobby Watts is an idiot. Why do you listen to him? I promise that showing Michael the box won't get you into any trouble. Do you trust me?"

"Yeah. I guess."

Wade left to retrieve the box and Kelly raced to the study to retrieve Michael. This could be the breakthrough they needed.

MICHAEL AND KELLY WERE standing in the doorway when Wade brought the box inside. Michael remembered how Kelly had struggled with that same carton that very morning as they left the hospital. He'd offered to help her, but she hadn't wanted him anywhere near the box. Now he knew why. She had been protecting her good friend Wade.

The man was a muscular ox. He could probably bench-press his own body weight. Michael thought about the night Kelly had been attacked in her room. Wade would have snapped her neck like a flimsy stick. He couldn't be the person they were tracking.

On the other hand, Michael still didn't trust him. For all they knew Wade could be working with Jimmy's killer.

Wade reluctantly set the box on a side table in front of Michael. "Here," he said.

Kelly poked Michael in the ribs with two fingers, reminding him in her subtle way to be nice.

"Thank you," Michael murmured, forcing out the words.

He opened the box and peeked inside. What a collection of junk! He didn't know where to begin. There were rocks, marbles, a clothespin and numerous other miscellaneous items. There wasn't anything in here that could possibly help him figure out the identity of his brother's killer.

And that was when he saw it.

Glittering at the bottom of the box like fool's gold, it sparkled in the light and instantly caught his attention. Michael carefully plucked the chain from the carton. He held it up to the light. A round black charm hung from an expensive gold chain. There was something engraved into the charm. He had seen this necklace many times before, in photographs, but this was the first time he'd seen it in person. He held it up and studied the engraving with a sense of awe.

"Does it mean something?" Kelly asked, "It's a strange design."

"It's not a design," he corrected her. "It's Arabic for Zu."

"Who?"

He glanced from her to Wade. Michael didn't want to talk about Zu Landis in front of Wade. He waited, staring at Kelly until she made the connection between the name and the assassin he'd mentioned before.

Her mouth formed a pretty O as she remembered the conversation. She took the necklace from his hand, carefully, as if she feared it would crumble into dust.

"What does it mean?" She asked the question with a fearful frown.

"Well…" He chose his words carefully. "If Landis isn't here now, he was at one time. This is the proof." He took the chain from her and held it high. "He killed my brother. He must have."

With huge eyes she glanced around her. She hugged herself, looking as if she was going to jump out of her skin at any second.

"Do you think he's still here? Could he be watching us right now?"

"I don't think so." Michael's hand went to her spine, stroking her back in an effort to comfort her. Wade's jealous scowl did not go unnoticed by him. "Landis is a professional. If he saw I was alive, it would take him all of two seconds to remedy the situation."

Kelly shivered, and Michael cursed his choice of words. She was frightened enough without him compounding the emotion.

"What do we do now?"

Before he could reply, the front door swung open after a heavy knock. The door was unlocked. Paddy entered with a broad grin on his face. His warm eyes immediately went to Kelly. He stuck out a meaty hand with all of the grace of a charging bull.

"You must be Kelly Hall," Paddy said. "It is a pleasure to meet you at last, my dear. I work with Tag here."

"Tag?" She stared at Paddy as if she didn't understand English anymore.

"Taggert. I call him Tag for short. We go way back. When he hired me to find his brother, I was afraid I would discover the man conning a sweet young lady like yourself."

She frowned. "You didn't seem to mind enough to warn me. You could have saved me a great deal of trouble."

"Hold on there," Paddy said. "Tag was paying me to do a job. He specifically told me to hang back, so I did. It's not like I was enjoying watching that boy play games with you."

"I already explained this to you," Michael interjected. "Let's not rehash it in front of your guest."

Paddy turned to Wade and stuck his hand out again. "It's nice to finally meet you, Wade."

Wade glanced from Paddy to Kelly.

She nodded.

Wade shook Paddy's hand, pumping it hard. Paddy winced a bit, but the smile didn't leave his face.

"I find things," Wade said.

"That's nice," Paddy replied.

"Wade found this," Michael said, lifting the necklace high for Paddy's inspection.

The investigator whistled between his teeth. "My word. Just exactly where did he find that?"

All eyes turned to Wade.

Michael couldn't believe he hadn't thought to ask the question himself. Of course, he really hadn't had time to get over the shock of seeing the thing up close and personal yet. The clasp was broken. If it hadn't given out, the chain would be looped around Landis's neck.

Wade seemed to wilt under the intense curiosity of the trio. "I don't remember. I don't want to get into trouble."

"You aren't in trouble," Kelly assured him. "It's just important that we know everything you can tell us. Are you certain you don't remember where you found the chain? I won't get mad, Wade. None of us will."

"I found it in your bedroom," he admitted with a sigh. His shoulders sagged beneath the weight of his confession. "I'm sorry I took it. It was in your bedroom, and I know that was bad."

"It's okay, Wade." Kelly patted him on the arm. "Where in the bedroom did you find it?"

"On the floor in front of the bathroom door. If something's on the floor, it's lost. Right, Kell? It was lost."

"Okay." Michael asked, "Do you remember when you found it? What day?"

He shook his head, refusing to meet Michael's eyes.

"Wade doesn't understand the passing of time the way we do," Kelly murmured. She turned back to Wade and asked, "Did you find anything else that day, the same day?"

Wade appeared to be thinking hard, trying to remember for Kelly's sake. The man was so besotted with her it was ridiculous. Michael knew he shouldn't be jealous. First of all, he himself had no right to Kelly; she'd made her feelings clear enough. Secondly, Kelly wasn't interested in Wade.

But it burned all the same.

Michael followed Kelly with his eyes. The memory of her entwined in his arms surfaced. He had to concentrate hard to make it fade. He wanted her even now when he should be concentrating on finding his brother's killer. Wade's words skittered by his ears instead of into them.

Paddy and Kelly both looked in his direction. Neither of them spoke. They were waiting for something, he realized—some sort of reaction from him.

"Sorry. What?"

Paddy chuckled. The old Irishman was too familiar with Michael and his expressions. He knew what—or rather who—was on Michael's mind.

Hands on hips, Kelly asked, "Weren't you listening?"

"Sorry. I was going over something in my head."

It was close enough to the truth.

"Wade says he didn't find anything else at that time, but he did find something interesting last night after the fire was put out."

"What?" Michael searched the faces of everyone there. "Well?"

Wade pulled a silver lighter from one of his overall pockets. He handed it to Michael. There were initials on the lighter: E.G.

"Elvin Grant," Michael said without hesitation. "Elvin Grant could have started the fire. I knew that bastard was involved in this somehow."

"But his boss wants the house," Kelly reminded them. "Why would he burn down the place if his boss wants to live here?"

"Maybe the boss doesn't want to live here," Paddy interjected.

"Maybe they want the diamonds," Michael said.

"Diamonds?" Wade frowned.

Kelly explained, "Some people think there are diamonds hidden in the house. There aren't. Some folks are just plain silly."

"Yeah." Wade nodded as if in full agreement. "They sure are."

"Yeah," Paddy confirmed, but his eyes held no humor. He looked directly at Michael. "It would be funny, though, if those diamonds should happen to turn up." He turned to Kelly. "You could be sitting on a fortune and not know it."

"I have enough money to keep the house running and

food on the table for decades to come,'' she said. ''I don't need diamonds. I just need some peace and quiet.''

Paddy's probing gaze returned to Michael.

Michael could practically read his colleague's mind. He wanted to search for the missing jewels. Michael shook his head slowly but didn't say a word.

''Can I go now?'' Wade asked the question while he was picking up the box.

''Sure,'' Michael replied. ''But the necklace and the lighter stay. They're evidence now.''

Wade nodded but didn't seem too sure about what Michael was getting at. Kelly insisted on walking her friend to the front door. While she was out of hearing, Michael told Paddy about the drawings of the house and the secret door they couldn't find. Paddy went to the study to check it out for himself.

Kelly returned a moment later. ''Where did your friend go?''

''He's in the study.''

She rolled her beautiful eyes. Michael knew what she thought about the idea of hidden passages in her home. She didn't need to spell it out.

''I wanted a second alone with you,'' he said.

Immediately, her shoulders tensed. She stood straighter, as if preparing for an attack. Her arms went around herself in that damn protective gesture he was coming to despise. She was trying to erect an invisible wall between them.

''None of this worked out the way I planned.''

''Planned?'' She appeared to be startled by his choice of words. At least he had her complete attention now. Curiosity would keep her standing in one place long enough for him to say what he had to say.

''After we made love, I wanted to wake up next to you, wrapped around you.''

She blushed furiously. The pink tinge encouraged him to

go on. He moved closer to her and lowered his voice lest Paddy overhear.

"I was going to get up early and make a fantastic breakfast. Then I was going to serve it to you in bed."

"In bed?"

"That's right. I just wanted you to know that night meant something to me. But I never got the chance because of the fire, and then you found out the truth about me."

With that Michael headed for the study, but Kelly had other ideas. She grabbed his forearm. Her slender fingers closed around his flesh, burning his skin through the thin fabric of his shirt.

"What, uh, what did that night mean to you? Was it supposed to be a one-night stand, a fling? Was it the beginning of an affair? Or something—more?"

Her eyes were trained on his face. She wouldn't miss the slightest hint of excitement or disappointment. He had to be careful. He didn't want to hurt her, but he couldn't give her false hope, either.

The truth was Michael wanted more than one night with her. However, in his current line of work, he couldn't promise her there was going to be a tomorrow for them. What could he possibly say to her?

His hands slid over her shoulders, clasping them lightly. He wasn't going to let her go until he was finished.

"You are an incredible woman. I've honestly never felt like this about anyone before."

"But," she interjected, "you need to go your own way once this is finished. You're probably anxious to get back to your life, your home, your job."

She couldn't be further from the truth. He lived in a small one-bedroom apartment in Washington, D.C., sparsely furnished. He could afford something better, but what was the point? He was rarely at home. His apartment was a pit stop between operations.

As far as his job was concerned, he had grown to hate it. Every time he went out into the field, it got harder to lie. It was a young man's game. Although he was only thirty-three, he felt as if he was going on fifty.

If he continued on in his current situation, he would probably wind up dead. Agents were killed in the line of duty every day.

Those who lived to see retirement more often than not found themselves alone. They had angry children and bitter wives. Michael didn't want to wind up an eighty-year-old man in a retirement home dreaming of what might have been had he chosen a different path.

Now, looking into Kelly's expressive blue eyes, which were clouded with pain and doubt, he wanted to promise her forever. He wanted to hang up his gun, hand in his badge and live a long life with her.

But what did he have to offer her?

He'd opened his mouth to tell her how he genuinely felt about her when Paddy's voice called down the hallway to them. "I found something! Come in here."

Exchanging surprised glances, Michael and Kelly headed in that direction.

"Did you find the door?" Michael asked as they entered the study.

"Uh...no," Paddy said. "But I think this paper was turned the wrong way. Look. See what I mean?"

Michael laid the blueprints on the table and studied it. The words would have been written upside down, though, if Paddy was correct. His eyes went to the bookcase on the other wall. Could it be possible they had just been looking in the wrong place?

THE DOG YELPED FROM somewhere in the house. Without a word to Michael, Kelly left the study. She followed the dog's soft barking. She hadn't seen Boomer since the fire and was worried sick about him. At least he was alive. Maybe he had gotten locked in one of the rooms, poor thing. He was probably scared and hungry.

The barks led her to her own bedroom.

Kelly raced toward the sound.

She shoved the door open and stepped inside in time to see someone disappear into her closet. She stared, disbelieving, at the vanishing figure. She wanted to run, wanted to scream, but was frozen to the spot.

Boomer yelped happily and followed his tail in a circle, then raced toward the closet door.

"Boomer, no," she whispered with frantic urgency, but the dog was gone. He had disappeared inside.

Kelly grabbed a weapon, a heavy clock carved of marble. If there was an intruder and she wasn't losing her mind, she could use it to hit the person over the head. She left the bedroom door open, hoping the two men downstairs would hear her if she screamed for help.

She edged closer to the closet.

Every step she took led her nearer to the edge of terror.

Her heart took up residence in her throat, blocking her oxygen. She couldn't breathe. She couldn't think. Her entire body shook with fear.

Kelly stepped in front of the closet, marble clock raised high above her head.

There was nobody in the closet, but there was another opening. Part of the wall had been moved to reveal a dark abyss.

Michael was right! There were secret passages in her house. This was how the guy who'd tried to strangle her had gotten into her room in the first place. This was why she had seen two flashes of light that night. The man had escaped back into the passageway just before Michael had come racing down the hallway to see if she was all right.

Boomer barked from somewhere deep in the black corridor.

Kelly entered the dark space carefully and called for the dog in a barely audible whisper. The bad guy could still be around, hovering nearby, ready to attack her.

The secret door shut behind her.

She didn't have time to stop it.

She was plunged into inky blackness and screamed.

Chapter Thirteen

"I think I've got something," Paddy said. He grunted with the exertion it took to reach up high, struggling on the tips of his worn leather shoes. He swayed and grabbed on to the bookshelf with his free hand. "It feels like a small metal piece buried in this groove of wood here. Just a second. I think I can...yes."

The bookcase opened, revealing a door-size black hole. It gaped wide, yawning before them, leading into the unknown.

Michael turned to note Kelly's expression, but she was gone.

Just then a scream echoed from the passageway, sounding faint and far-off.

"Kelly?" Michael pushed Paddy out of the way and raced into the dark tunnel without giving the lack of light a thought. Fear for Kelly's safety had adrenaline pumping through his veins.

Michael grabbed the lighter from his jeans pocket once he remembered it and clicked it on. The small flame barely lit the pitch-black passageway, just enough to reveal a dirty wood floor and unfinished walls. Spiderwebs hung down from the ceiling beams. He stepped farther into the black abyss, leaving the security of the study behind. He was in a hurry to find Kelly, but placed his feet with care. The floorboards could have rotted in places. Since Kelly hadn't known about the passageways, he doubted anyone was repairing damage done by time and bad weather.

He held the lighter high and yelled Kelly's name.

KELLY'S FISTS WERE bruised from banging against the hidden door. It wouldn't budge an inch. She suspected there should be a latch or something to spring the damn thing open again, but her groping fingers couldn't find anything in the dark. She was trapped. Without a light it was going to be extremely difficult to find another way out. But she had to try. She started to feel her way along the narrow passage. .

"Kelly!"

Michael's voice reached her in the darkness. All of her doubts about him fled as if with an outgoing tide. She longed to find a refuge in his arms, a safe spot that would be hers forever. In her twenty-four years she hadn't found anyone besides her father whom she could count on, but Michael was there for her every time she needed him.

But he had lied to her. Could she ever trust him again?

"Michael! I'm here," Kelly shouted. "There's a secret door into my bedroom closet. Follow my voice."

She didn't have to wait long before a tiny dot of light floated toward her. At first she thought she was imagining it, but the flickering glow drew closer and grew brighter.

Michael was holding Elvin Grant's lighter in his hand. When he reached her, he grabbed her with his free arm, pulling her into the safety of his embrace. She reveled in the feeling. Kelly didn't want him to let her go. Not ever.

Tingles of familiar electricity shot through her body. The warmth of his hand sliding down her back fueled the desire in her veins. She wished she could melt in his arms. If there hadn't been a fire the other night, what would their relationship be like? Would he have made love to her again? Would he have whispered loving words in her ears?

More importantly, would Michael have confessed before Wade had had the chance to show her his badge?

The truth might have affected her differently if it had come from Michael's lips first. She would have known he trusted her.

But there *had* been a fire. She had been rushed to the hospital and Wade had tumbled her world upside down for her.

"I saw someone," Kelly said, pulling out of Michael's hold. "I didn't get a real good look at him—I just saw a foot, maybe part of a leg. Whoever it was disappeared into the closet. For the first time since all this started I didn't have to wonder if I was imagining it."

"You should have yelled for me." Michael shook his head worriedly. "Chasing criminals is a dangerous business. Leave it to the professionals."

"I didn't chase him." She glanced up at Michael's handsome face, memorizing every inch of it in the dim light. She'd gotten used to having him around. "Boomer ran into the passage, and I was worried he might get hurt. I was chasing *him.* Unfortunately, the door swung shut behind me. I got locked in." She frowned, realizing something. "How did you get in here?"

"Paddy and I found the door in the study." Michael grinned smugly. "Persistence pays off."

"There really are secret doors and passageways throughout Moore House," she said in awe.

"Obviously," he replied in a dry voice.

Boomer barked, making them both jump.

"Boomer!" Kelly laughed. "You silly dog. You scared me half to death."

She bent over and petted his golden fur. He didn't appear to be hurt. Kelly's relief didn't last long. With another loud bark, Boomer shot down the dark hallway. He vanished before Kelly could yell his name.

"Don't worry," Michael said. "He'll be fine."

"Yeah. He'll probably find his way out of here before we do."

"As long as we're in here," Michael suggested, "we should search every passage and check out every door. Then we can do something to block them so whoever is taking advantage of them won't be able to anymore. Stay behind me just in case we're not alone in here."

"I hope our mystery guest is long gone. Maybe he went straight for the exit after I spotted him. That would be the smart thing to do."

"No one said anything about this guy being smart. If he was, he would have left as soon as he realized I was on the job." Michael grinned at her as if trying to lighten the dark mood. "Look at the bright side—you have a lot more storage space than you originally thought."

"That's not funny."

"Now we know how the bad guy gets into your bedroom so easily."

"I can't believe I didn't figure it out a long time ago," she said. "And what about Wade? He's a genius when it comes to construction. He should have noticed."

"How do you know he didn't?"

Kelly didn't like what Michael was getting at. She glared at him through the darkness.

"Wade would have told me," she insisted. "I know him. You don't. Stop trying to make me doubt him. He's been a good friend."

"Fine." Michael sighed. "I just think it's a bit odd that such a 'genius' wouldn't notice the layout of the rooms didn't quite fit."

"I didn't notice it, either," Kelly said. "We broke through the side wall and put the new shower there, but we didn't push it far enough. If we'd just gone another inch or two, we would have found the passageway.''

"Hmm," was Michael's only comment.

Kelly decided to change the subject before they got into a major fight. Now was not the time for raised voices, not with the possibility of her attacker being nearby.

"I wonder how many separate passages there are in this place."

"I have no idea," Michael admitted. "I was in a hurry to find you, but I did glimpse a few side tunnels and intersections. I think these corridors were set up like a maze. Fortunately, I have a pretty good sense of direction."

Kelly placed her hands on Michael's back as they walked, afraid of being separated from him. The lighter barely lit a five-inch circle around his hand. She hung on to him, following him blindly, her trust in him intensifying with every passing second.

They found a few different doors on the second floor. Kelly was stunned each and every time. She was having trouble believing any of this was real; it just didn't seem possible. She had grown up in Moore House. She'd been a curious child. She should have stumbled across at least one of the doors while playing.

"Here," Michael said. "Hold this." He handed her the lighter.

She had no idea what he was planning to do, but she did as he asked, straining her eyes in the dark. There was a wide gap in the floor to one side of them. Michael latched on to a wooden beam nailed to the wall. Kelly realized there was a ladder leading down to the first floor. He descended slowly. Moments later she heard his feet hit the ground.

"Okay. Toss me the lighter."

When she allowed the flame to die, her surroundings went from dark to pitch-black, shocking her even though she had thought she was prepared for it. She couldn't see a blasted thing now.

"I don't know where to drop it," she complained.

"Throw it toward my voice."

She prayed she would drop it down the hole to him and not just lose it on the wood floor. It wasn't as if she could move around on hands and knees searching for the thing. The hole was big enough for her to fall through. Breaking her neck wasn't on the agenda.

"I got it," Michael said. "Now climb down the ladder. Take it easy, one step at a time. I'll be here to catch you if you fall."

It sounded like a promise to her.

Michael used the lighter to illuminate the hole so she could find it.

Kelly moved at a snail's pace, carefully placing one foot on the first rung, then gripping the edge of the floor as she lowered herself. The light died and her breath caught in her throat. Fearing something was wrong, she froze.

Had the bad guy found them?

Then Michael latched on to her waist, his fingers holding her with gentle pressure. Relief spread through her as her feet finally met solid ground. But Michael didn't let go.

Instead he pulled her closer. Their bodies touched, and Kelly instantly forgot about the madman lurking in the hidden passages. Desire blazed to life within her.

"Sweetheart," he said, "we need to have a long and serious talk."

"Now?" Was he out of his mind? "Here?"

"No. We'll take care of business first. But then I want to talk with you. Alone. As soon as it can be arranged."

"Sounds serious," she said.

"It is," Michael replied.

"You can't give me a little, tiny hint what you want to discuss?"

"Us. Our future plans. Yours and mine."

"Oh." She didn't get a chance to say more. Holding her hand Michael flicked the lighter back on and headed down the hallway, pulling her behind him.

"I don't believe it," Michael said. "There's a light here." He pulled on a dangling string and the lightbulb blazed to life. "I think there might be another exit here."

He dug at a deep grove in the wall. With an intruder in the house, she felt it was risky to stay in one place for too long. Since she didn't have eyes in the back of her head, she revolved slowly, scanning their surroundings. She tripped over something on the ground and fell right on top of a skeleton.

Kelly's face stopped a mere inch from empty eye sockets. Without flesh on bone, the skull seemed to be grinning at her. Or was it grimacing?

She bolted away from it, her mouth forming a scream, but Michael's hand covered her lips before the sound was even born.

"It's okay. I don't think it's anyone you know." He knelt beside the skeleton. "It could be that Barrington woman. Maybe she didn't escape after all." Rising, he took Kelly's hand and flicked the light off. "We'll tell the authorities about this later. Let's go."

They found a couple more secret doors. Eventually they exited the passageway through the opening in the study. They left the dark hallway as quietly as they had entered. Neither of them had seen a sign of another living soul.

Paddy was waiting for them in the study. He beamed at them, his gaze dropping to their interlocked hands. "I see you found her," he said.

Boomer raced out of the passageway behind them and straight across the room. Seconds later they heard his huge feet trotting up the staircase.

"There are doors everywhere," Michael announced. "I

want them all blocked. You and Kelly can take care of that while I search this entire house from top to bottom. There wasn't anyone in the passages. If someone is in this house, I'll find him.''

"You don't want me to go with you?" Kelly asked, trying to keep the hurt from her voice.

"I need you to go with Paddy, because I know the house and I don't need a guide. Paddy does. Simple as that.'' Michael lifted her chin with a strong finger, forcing her eyes to meet his. "We'll talk soon. I promise.''

She forced a smile. Waiting to speak to him was going to be like waiting for the dentist to begin a root canal. Especially since she didn't know what he wanted to say to her. It could be bad news or good news. Either he was going to declare his feelings for her or he was going to end their relationship and bring about some closure.

Relationship? He'd made love to her once. She would have to keep a careful rein on her tongue when they finally got a chance to talk. A word like *relationship* could scare a guy off faster than a double-barrel shotgun.

Kelly reluctantly led Paddy around the house to each of the rooms that boasted a secret door. She helped him block them one by one, using the closest piece of heavy furniture. Her thoughts were with Michael the entire time. He had taken on the most dangerous job himself. What if the killer was roaming around Moore House, waiting for an opportunity to kill again?

If she was going to lose Michael, she wanted to lose him to his job—not to a dangerous psychopath. Let him return home in one piece, wherever that turned out to be. She realized he hadn't even told her what state he resided in. Wherever it was, he could return there without a single protest from her. At least she would know he was alive and well. That way she could hold on to a glimmer of hope that someday he might seek her out. But even if he never did, she would be happy knowing he was out there somewhere.

Paddy's rough voice broke through her thoughts. "Hang in there, kid."

"What?" she said.

"With Michael," Paddy explained. "He's had a hard time of it. My wife Mary and I tried to love Michael as if he was one of ours, but he feels like he's somehow unworthy of love. I think you could change all of that."

Goose bumps broke out on her arms.

"I'm not sure what you mean," she said.

"Well, it's obvious to anyone with two eyes that that boy is crazy about you. I haven't seen him like this before. Give him time. Don't be afraid to open your heart to him. He'll come around."

"How did you first meet Michael?"

"I was working for the Chicago Police Department and Michael was assigned to be my partner. He was a rookie, and I was considering a change in career. He was a good cop with sharp instincts, but he was hard to get to know. He doesn't open up easily."

"I've noticed. Did he ever talk about his childhood? His father?"

"Yes, ma'am. He spoke to Mary more than to me. His father was a real piece of work, the bastard. I wasn't too broken up when I heard about his death."

"Did Michael's father ever hit him?"

Paddy seemed surprised. "Not that I know of. I think the jerk abused his sons verbally, mentally, but not physically. Why? Did Michael say something to the contrary?"

"No." Kelly glanced at the door, hoping Michael wouldn't overhear them. He wouldn't like it if he knew she was asking questions about his past. "But then he doesn't open up easily. You said so yourself."

"Mary has a way of getting people to talk to her. Michael

told her about his childhood. His mother was a mess. She was scared to death that her husband would track her down, so they moved around a lot. They were always looking over their shoulders.'' Paddy's lips tightened into a pained grimace. ''His mother eventually shacked up with another jerk. Michael's father probably didn't hit him often, but his stepfather did. Michael used to get between the creep and his mother, try to protect her.''

''Oh my God.'' Kelly covered her mouth with a trembling hand. ''No child should go through that.''

''Michael got bigger, stronger, and finally put the guy through a window. It was the last time the man ever laid a hand on either one of them.'' Paddy looked toward the ceiling, remembering. ''Michael has trouble trusting. He doesn't love easily, but when he does give you his love, it's yours for life. He looks at Mary like a second mother, and she spoils him with home-cooked dinners every time he's in town.''

''And I thought I'd had a rough life. At least my father loved me and took care of me. I didn't have to protect him.''

''Give Michael some time. Be patient with him. He watches you with a spark in his eye.''

''What about Michael's love life?'' she asked. ''Has he ever been married?''

''Michael? Married?'' Paddy laughed. ''Hardly. Oh, he's been with a bevy of beauties over the years, but none of them have been smart enough to snag him.''

''Snag him?'' Kelly snickered. ''You make it sound so romantic.''

''Don't let Michael's tough-guy attitude fool you. Deep down I think he is a romantic. He wants what we all want— true love. I overheard him telling my Mary how he envied me once. He told her he wanted a woman like her, someone smart and compassionate.'' Paddy smiled at Kelly. ''I think he found that in you.''

"He doesn't want me. He used me. He lied to me. Am I supposed to forget that? How can I trust him now?"

"He wanted to tell you everything from the beginning." Paddy chuckled. "I wish I had a dime for every time he spoke about telling you the truth. I warned him not to, of course. You were a wild card. We had no idea what you might do. You could have gotten us all killed."

"Thanks for the vote of confidence."

"I'm going to step into the hallway and call Michael on my cell phone, now, okay? Two more doors and we're done. I want to check how he's doing."

She nodded in agreement, but after Paddy left her side she was hit by a sudden wave of panic. She was alone in the study. They hadn't blocked the secret panel here. Except for the heavy desk there wasn't anything to block it with. She was going to suggest they nail the corner bookcase shut.

A loud grunt followed by a thud reached her ears.

"Paddy?"

There was no answering call. She headed for the foyer, the hairs on the back of her neck standing at attention. Something was horribly wrong. She shouldn't have let Paddy leave her side. They were supposed to stick together as per Michael's orders.

Paddy was on the floor, slumped against the wall, head hanging forward. He was unconscious. There was a telltale patch of blood on the back of his gray head.

She shouted Michael's name. There was no reply.

"I'm going to get Michael." She reassured Paddy. "He'll know what to do. I'll be right back…I promise."

She raced upstairs and called Michael's name again. He could be in any of the rooms. She checked them one at a time, peering inside as she came to them. They were all empty. There was a possibility he'd already made it to the third floor and was checking out the ballroom.

But he would need a key to get in there. She didn't use the ballroom. The huge room with its ten-foot dome ceiling, crystal chandeliers and smooth hardwood floor was probably still locked. She couldn't remember the last time she'd been there. Of course the key was just above the door on a small hook. He might have found it.

Fear chilled her to the bone. What if the killer had gotten to him before attacking Paddy? She couldn't stand the thought of something happening to Michael. In a short time he had become the most important person in her life. She couldn't lose him.

"Kelly?" The voice was weak and female, and sounded like Margo. "Kelly? Help me."

The words floated down to her from the attic. The door was open an inch or two. That was odd. Kelly was sure she'd locked it and put the key back in the library.

She took a reluctant step toward the stairs leading to the attic. The whispered voice pleaded with her for help. It seeped through the crack, beckoning to her. Like a moth to the flame, she followed. *It* sounded like Margo. Could she be alive, after all?

Kelly froze at the top of the stairs and glanced down them. She should run for help, get Michael. But what if Margo couldn't wait?

"Kelly, please. Help me."

Kelly moved closer to the opening. She had no idea what to do next. Someone had knocked Paddy out cold and could be somewhere behind her, following her, maybe in the hallway just beyond the stairs. Margo was inside the tiny attic, quite possibly injured. The woman might have escaped from her captor long enough to call for help. If that were the case, why didn't she come out into the light? Kelly was beginning to wonder if it was Margo's voice she'd heard.

She wrung her hands, undecided on her next course of action. She knew what Michael would tell her to do, but he wasn't anywhere in sight. If she ran to him, the bad guy could catch up with Margo and hurt her. Perhaps even kill her this time.

"Margo, I'm coming."

Kelly took a deep breath and plunged ahead, entering the dimly lit space.

MICHAEL FROZE in midstep, straining his ears. Had he imagined someone calling his name? He started back in the direction he'd come from, heading for the staircase. He'd been gone long enough. He needed to check on Paddy and Kelly.

Moore House was designed like a maze. He had stumbled across the back stairs leading to the third floor by accident. So far he'd counted three sets of stairs leading to the top level. Although Kelly had insisted the doors were locked, he pushed them open with no trouble. There was a grand ballroom with a broken chandelier and a scratched up, wood plank floor. He thanked God he wasn't allergic to dust. There must have been at least an inch of the stuff on everything he touched.

Michael neared the stairs.

A door opened as he passed by it, to a room he had checked earlier. He turned to greet the person, figuring it had to be Kelly. She was a stubborn woman. He had expected her to follow him, and he didn't mind one bit. It was time for him to tell her about his decision regarding the future.

Elvin Grant stood in the doorway holding a gun. It was aimed at Michael's chest.

"Don't try anything," Grant said. "My partner has your little girlfriend."

Michael's mouth went dry and his heartbeat tripled in tempo. He should have kept her close to him. Paddy was getting older. His reflexes weren't what they used to be. If anything happened to Kelly, Michael wouldn't be able to forgive himself.

Another awful thought occurred to him. Grant hadn't mentioned Paddy. His old friend could be seriously injured. Or worse.

"You have a partner?" Michael asked. "Your boss, you mean. Right?"

"Yeah. My boss." The man gestured with the gun, indicating that Michael should walk down the hallway. "Go on. We'll see your darling soon enough."

"If anything happens to her," Michael promised, "I'll kill you. And it won't be easy or quick for you."

"Oh, I'm so scared. I'm positively shaking in my boots." Grant hid behind false bravado, but Michael saw the fear and the uncertainty in his eyes. "On your way now."

Michael obeyed the orders. He moved down the hallway, but kept his eyes open and his mind alert. He would figure out the best course of action. Then, without hesitation, he would deploy his plan.

"Who is your partner?"

Grant laughed. "As if I would tell you. Keep moving. We're going to the master bedroom."

The master bedroom? What was the fascination with that room?

Upon entering, Michael saw two chairs with rope draped loosely around them. There were only two. Either Paddy was dead or the bad guys weren't planning on tying one of them up. Were they planning on taking a hostage? He would die before he allowed them to take Kelly away.

"Sit," Grant snapped like a vicious bulldog.

Michael headed for the chair. A way out formulated in his head. If he could catch Grant off guard, he could grab the gun and surprise the man's boss. The only problem was he didn't have a diversion. He wished Paddy was with them. His old friend could read a look better than anybody.

"I assume your boss wants the diamonds," Michael said.

"Yeah, that's right. We want the jewels. Where are they?"

"You mean you don't know?" Michael stalled for time.

"They were supposed to be in the bathroom, hidden behind the shower wall. At least that's what Fuller wrote in a letter to his daughter. But we already looked there." Grant shrugged. "Go ahead. Check it out. Somebody beat us to it."

Michael went to the master bathroom and his mouth dropped open. The fire must have been set to get them out of the house for a while, long enough for the perpetrators to bust through the shower wall. Dust and debris covered the floor near the tub. He drew closer. There was a gaping hole where the faucet and showerhead used to be.

"You didn't find them?"

"No, we didn't find them," Grant retorted mockingly. "If we'd found them, we wouldn't be here anymore, would we?" he motioned for Michael to return to the bedroom. "Go on. It won't be long now."

"Is your partner going to join us?"

Grant stared at Michael in silence, refusing to answer. He lifted the ropes and motioned impatiently once again for Michael to take a seat in one of the chairs. The two men stood facing each other.

Michael's fists were tight at his sides. He weighed his options. If he allowed Grant to tie him to a chair, he probably wouldn't get a chance to jump the man. It was now or never.

THE ATTIC'S OVERHEAD light flickered. The bulb was dying. It glowed brighter for a second before dimming once again. Kelly crossed the floor with cautious steps, not wanting to trip over a discarded box or miscellaneous junk. She made a mental note to clean the attic later, after life got back to normal.

A sudden tingling sensation at the nape of her neck sent a warning through her nervous system. She wasn't alone. There was somebody standing behind her. She prayed it was Michael.

Kelly turned slowly, trying to prepare herself for the worst.

Relief washed over her.

Margo had closed the door. Her neighbor stood in front of it, looking a bit worn around the edges. The woman was pale. Her clothes were dirty and torn. Other than that, she seemed fine. Physically at least.

"Margo, I'm so glad to see you."

"I'm glad to see you too, dear. You have no idea what I've been through."

"It's okay now," Kelly said. "Michael and I will help you."

"Yes. I know."

"We need to go find Michael," Kelly said, striding forward to hug Margo.

"I don't think so, dear."

Kelly stopped halfway across the floor. "What? Why not?"

Margo pulled a gun from behind her back and held it steady with both hands. She aimed it at Kelly with a maniacal laugh.

Chapter Fourteen

"What are you doing?" Kelly barely got the question past her numb lips. "If you're afraid that whoever kidnapped you is coming back, don't be. Michael and I will protect you. Michael's one of the good guys. He's an agent with the CIA. He can protect you from the bad guy."

"You silly girl." Margo laughed, but it sounded more like a witch's cackle. "You don't get it, do you? I am the bad guy."

"But the photograph? We thought you were dead."

"I faked it, you harebrained twit. I pretended to be dead so that you would stop looking for me. No one, not even a CIA agent, would suspect a corpse."

Time spent with Margo at her home, drinking her tea and eating her homemade cookies, scrolled through Kelly's mind. She remembered their heart-to-heart talks at the kitchen table. Margo had been so sweet, so concerned. Had it all been a lie? Was Margo just one more person who had lied to her?

"I can see the wheels turning in your pretty little head," Margo said. "You're trying to figure out my motive. Well, let me help you. You stole my home from me."

"No, I didn't. I sold you the guest house. It's yours. didn't threaten to take it back."

"Mine?" Margo yelled. "Screw the guest house! *This* house is mine. Moore House belongs to me."

Kelly had no idea what the woman was babbling about. Moore House had been in Kelly's family for three generations. No one could have stolen it from Margo, because she'd never owned it.

Kelly shook her head.

"It's true!" Margo shrieked. "This house was taken from my father by the stupid court system after his death. They took me away and gave me to strangers to raise. Mean strangers. But I've come back, and I want my house."

"You're Fuller's daughter?" Kelly remembered her mother talking about the jewel thief's offspring.

"That's right, dear." Margo's voice dropped. Her hands wavered a bit. Kelly could tell the gun was getting heavy. If she could keep Margo talking, the woman wouldn't have the strength to continue and Kelly could wrestle the gun from her. "We need to get going now."

"Going?" Kelly shook her head again, backing away from the other woman.

"We're going to meet up with your nosy cop friend in the master bedroom. We have some questions to ask you."

We? Kelly didn't understand what was happening. Every word that fell from Margo's lips sent her into a deeper state of confusion. The woman was insane. Kelly's faith in her own instincts withered. She had trusted Margo, had taken her neighbor into her confidence.

An epiphany hit Kelly like a brick to the head. Margo couldn't have done everything on her own. She had to have had help. A partner perhaps. Kelly's mind began formulating a long list of people who could be working with Margo. The last name she came up with was Michael.

Kelly didn't want to believe Michael was involved in trying to drive her crazy, but she had caught him in a lie already. He had gone to a lot of trouble to cover up his brother's murder. If that part of the story was true.

Did Jimmy even exist?

It was possible there was no Jimmy, and Michael had set the whole thing into motion. He could be after the mythical diamonds.

No, Michael was an honest man thrust into a position that left him with no choice but to lie. It wasn't his fault. Since she'd uncovered his true identity he hadn't lied to her. She was sure of it. The truth sparkled in his eyes whenever he spoke to her. His feelings for her were real. She would bet her life on it. She trusted Michael.

He was the only one who had lied to her in an effort to help her.

"What do you hope to gain by this, Margo? Do you want me to sign the house over to you?"

"Do you think I'm stupid or just crazy?" Margo chuckled. "I gave up on getting my house back. I just want the jewels now. They belonged to my father, and now they're mine."

"Take them," Kelly said in desperation. "I don't care. Take whatever you want. Just please leave me and Michael alone."

"Your darling Michael is waiting for us. We'd better hurry before my partner gets an itchy trigger finger."

Knowing Michael was in danger spurred Kelly to action. She hurried from the attic and down the hallway to the master bedroom. Margo was on her heels, keeping up a good pace for such an elderly woman. Kelly was still having trouble believing she was behind all the awful things that had transpired.

Angry curses filtered out of the bedroom's open door. There were grunts of pain and sharp bumps. Glass shattered. Margo grasped Kelly's hair and yanked her backward, holding her close. The muzzle of the gun pressed against Kelly's temple.

"Don't get any ideas," Margo warned. The woman took a deep breath and shouted, "Whatever you're doing in there, you'd better stop! I have the girl. I'll shoot her if you don't stop fighting the inevitable, Mr. Taggert."

The noises immediately ceased.

"Okay," a familiar male voice called. Kelly assumed it was the voice of Margo's partner, Elvin Grant. "It's safe to come in now."

Margo released her hold on Kelly's hair and pushed her inside. Michael was sitting in a chair near the closet. Elvin Grant was tying him up with a sturdy rope.

Kelly frowned. Her surprise was mirrored in Michael's eyes. They were both stunned by the turn of events. Neither of them had guessed the truth.

"You're Grant's boss." Kelly made it a statement. There was no need to sound as stupid as she felt. Obviously Margo was holding the thin man's leash.

"Yes, dear." Margo smiled widely as if she was giving Kelly an old family recipe. "Elvin was quite helpful. I tried to buy the house."

"You have enough money to buy Moore House?"

"If you were reasonable on the price, yes. The people who adopted me were well off. They died a few years ago. Terrible fire. I inherited." She pointed at the unoccupied chair with her gun. "Your turn. Elvin will tie you and then we'll get to the question and answer part."

"Question and answer?" Kelly tried to be brave, but she could hear the tremor in her own voice. On the outside she was calm, but inside she was nearly hysterical. "What are you talking about?"

Kelly put up a minimal amount of struggle when Elvin shoved her into the chair. He wrapped a rope around her waist and pulled her arms back to tie them securely. It hurt.

The rough rope bit into her tender flesh. She clenched her jaw, refusing to cry out and give the terrible partners in crime any sort of satisfaction.

"It's okay," Michael told her. "Trust me. Everything will be okay."

She nodded, tears in her eyes. Looking at his handsome face now, she realized she loved him. She truly loved him.

She didn't know exactly when it had happened. It was before they had made love but after he'd saved her life in the garage. Because of their extreme circumstances and her doubts about him, she had fought her feelings for him. Only now could she admit to herself that she loved him with all her heart. Too bad love wasn't enough.

Margo stopped her frantic movements. Her expression changed, became wary as she sniffed the air. "Do you smell something?" she asked.

"No," Elvin whined. "You know I can't smell anything with my allergies."

"Everything will be okay," Michael repeated.

"I wouldn't count on it," Margo said. "Let's begin. Which one of you has my diamonds?"

"Diamonds?" Michael said the word as if he hadn't heard of the gemstone before.

"Don't play games with me," Margo said. "I've been listening to conversations, following the two of you around with hidden cameras. You know all about the jewels, Taggert."

"First, why don't you clear up a few things for me?" he asked. "How did you trick Kelly in the garage? She claims she saw someone go inside, but no one was in there."

"Easy," Margo said. "The house isn't the only building with secret doors. There's one inside the garage, hidden behind the metal tool shelf. Next question."

"Who wrote on the mirror when I was in the shower?" Kelly asked. "That was a pretty good trick. I thought I was losing my mind for sure when I brought Michael in and there were two words instead of one."

"Also simple," Margo replied. "Elvin entered through the secret door. You didn't bother to shut the bathroom door. When you took off screaming, he went inside and added a word." Margo clenched her teeth. "Anything else?"

"I assume he sent me the threatening note when I was in town," Michael said.

Margo nodded.

"And the tiny pearls that were on my grandmother's wedding gown? What about them? Did you take them?"

"I took more than that from your bedroom," Elvin said. "Just a few trinkets here and there to make you think you were going crazy."

Michael frowned in puzzlement. "Wade found a pair of glasses in the study. Do they belong to either of you?"

"If they were found in the study, they belonged to my father," Kelly said. "Why didn't you ask me if you were worried about them?"

"Angel, I hit a new clue every time I turned a corner and I was trying to keep my head on straight when it came to you. I guess I forgot about them. I put them in a drawer in the nightstand next to my bed."

"What about my wedding gown, Michael? Was that you or them?"

"That was me." He smiled sheepishly at her. "Sorry. I put it in an empty closet in one of the spare bedrooms the night Jimmy died. Later, after you let me know inadvertently that Jimmy got it from the attic, I returned it."

"But the attic is always locked."

"It wasn't locked when I went up there," he replied.

"That's because I was using it and the ballroom to hide out in," Margo said. "This house is really much too big for you, child. You should think about moving."

"How many employees do you actually have?" Michael asked. "Grant here told us there would be others to take his place if I pulverized him."

"I was bluffing, you twit," the thin man said. He sighed in frustration, waving his gun around like a madman. "Can we get on with it? I want those damn jewels."

"Patience," Margo said. She turned to Michael, a wide smile stretching her lips. "Wait a second. I have an idea. If you tell me what I want to know, I'll tell you who killed your brother."

Kelly gasped.

Michael stiffened beside her, and a muscle twitched in his lower jaw. "You're bluffing." He forced a strained smile. "You don't know anything."

"But I do," Margo said. "I've been at Moore House off and on for weeks now. I got that particular night on videotape. I know who killed your brother."

"Prove it," Michael said.

"Fine." She drew closer to them and hovered over Michael. "Do you remember that night? You found your brother's body lying in front of the closet. Your friend left for a while, but you stayed. You knelt next to his body and cried. I heard what you vowed to your brother that night."

Michael remained silent, but his eyes blazed to life.

"I saw it." Margo added, "I can give you the tape. Evidence for the trial. If you ever catch up with the man, of course. But first, you give me what I want. Who has my diamonds?"

"I don't know," Michael said.

"Liar!" Margo lowered the gun to point it directly at his head.

"*No!*" Kelly screamed. "I'll tell you where they are."

The words were out before she could swallow them. She had no idea where the diamonds were, if they even existed.

But she had captured the woman's attention. Margo walked away from Michael, leaving him alive and well.

Kelly's mind whirled in a violent circle. Margo would kill them both if Kelly didn't think of something logical and believable to say.

"Tell me," the older woman demanded.

"Don't forget I get a cut," Grant said.

"Shh!" Margo waved the gun at him. "I don't have anything to give you a cut of yet." She stood over Kelly, her wild eyes staring holes into her. "Give me what I want. Where are my diamonds?"

"*Your* diamonds?" Michael snorted in disbelief.

Kelly prayed Michael wasn't going to push the woman too far. Margo was walking the thin line of insanity and Kelly feared she was about to tumble off. Then what? Would she shoot both of them? Would she leave them to die, another two tragic victims of Moore House?

"That's right!" Margo returned to lean over Michael. "You heard me. Those diamonds belong to me. My father was Walter Fuller. This house and those jewels are my inheritance. Your idiot brother found the letter from my father before I could. He was going to steal my diamonds." Margo pointed at Kelly. "She stole my home, but she won't get my diamonds. I want them now."

"You don't want to hurt Kelly," Michael said. "If you did, you would have killed her a long time ago. You tried to buy the house. When that didn't work, you tried to scare Kelly off. You aren't a cold-blooded killer."

"You're right," Margo admitted. "I didn't want to hurt anyone. But that was then." She pointed the gun at Kelly once again, returning to stand in front of her. "This is now. Now I'm angry. I'm tired of playing these games. You tell me where my diamonds are or I'm going to shoot one of you. Maybe both of you."

Michael leaned back in his chair, an easy smile on his

face. He winked at Kelly and said, "Go ahead, angel. Give the lady the information she wants."

Kelly stared at him blankly. What was he expecting her to say? Did he actually believe she knew where the diamonds were hidden? No, he was up to something. Kelly saw the gleam in his dark eyes.

Michael glanced at the bedroom door, so quickly Kelly almost thought she'd imagined it.

She turned her head and coughed into her shoulder. She looked in the direction of the door. She followed Michael's example, only sparing the door a quick glance. It took everything she had in her to school her expression. Excitement pulsed through every one of her nerves. She wanted to scream for joy, but she couldn't even smile. If she gave Paddy away, he would be killed. Paddy's injuries had obviously not been serious enough to prevent him from backing up Michael in their time of need.

"Okay," she said. "I'll tell you exactly where the diamonds are."

Margo's face lit up. She allowed the gun to drop back to her side, ready to hang on every word. Kelly licked her lips as if they were too dry to speak. She stalled until she knew Margo was about to crack.

"They were behind the shower wall," Michael prodded. "Isn't that right?"

"Yes, I found the diamonds when I tore the original shower down."

"What?" Margo laughed so hard tears came to her eyes. "Did you hear that, Elvin? We didn't find the diamonds because she remodeled the bathroom."

"I don't see the humor in it," Elvin said.

"Oh, Elvin, don't be such a stick-in-the-mud. It's funny. We tore the shower wall out looking for the diamonds, but they weren't there because she'd already found them. She found them before we started hiding in the house. We didn't need that sledgehammer, after all.'' Margo returned her attention to Kelly. "I'm surprised at you. I thought we were friends, but you didn't confide in me.''

"Sorry," Kelly mumbled. "I suppose I was a little paranoid. It's not every day that a girl finds a fortune in jewels hidden in her bathroom wall.'' She added, "I guess we know now why Boomer wasn't barking.''

"That's right. My dog wouldn't bark at me.''

"Where is Boomer, by the way? I haven't seen him in a while. He might be hurt.''

"He isn't," Margo said. "I took him back home. He's fine there.

Kelly silently prayed for Paddy to make his move. Whatever the man was going to do, he needed to do it fast. She couldn't hold Margo off for much longer.

KELLY WAS DOING a brilliant job keeping the crazy lady distracted, and she didn't even know it.

Michael almost winced in pain as the small, flickering flame burned his wrist.

He had managed to dig Grant's lighter out of his back pocket. The two perps were so busy counting their millions, they weren't paying enough attention to him. Michael lit the lighter and burned the rope around his hands one thick strand at a time. He was determined. If he was going to die today, it certainly wouldn't be while he was tied to a chair.

He was nearly done. Just a few more seconds and he would be free. Michael tried to rush the job but only burned himself more. He had to be careful. If his shirt caught on fire, Margo and Elvin might notice.

Keep talking, baby.

Kelly was doing a wonderful job stalling, but Margo seemed to be running out of patience. Michael didn't have much faith in the woman's self-control. She might freak out at any moment and shoot them both. At least Paddy was nearby. The old Irishman hovered near the bedroom door, hanging back enough so he wouldn't be spotted by Margo or Elvin.

"Your diamonds aren't in this room," Kelly said.

"Where are they?" Margo practically screamed the question in her face.

Michael burned through more of the rope. He pulled his hands apart, and the rope stretched. He felt several strands break, but there were a few stubborn ones that wouldn't give. He held his breath, hoping his hands were far enough apart to slip the rope off.

It worked.

His hands were free. He allowed the rope to quietly fall to the carpet. His eyes focused on the thin man. Margo was preoccupied with questioning Kelly, but her partner looked bored. Grant's gaze drifted to Michael every couple of minutes.

Michael gave a short nod to Paddy.

It was now or never.

Paddy rushed forward to grab Margo from behind. He lifted her arms into the air, the gun pointed at the ceiling. A shot rang out. Bits of plaster crumbled around them.

Michael jumped up from the chair. With fists together, he swung upward to strike Grant in the jaw.

The thin man flew backward and landed on the mattress. He tried to get off the bed before Michael could reach him, rolling to one side and hitting the floor with a dull thud. He struggled to stand, but Michael straddled his back and tied his hands behind him. There wasn't anything Grant could do. His movements were feeble and weak.

The old lady was fighting harder than her partner. Margo stomped on Paddy's foot and bit into his arm. He screamed in agony. His hold on the woman loosened enough for her to lower her gun and aim. She was going to shoot Paddy square in the chest, and Michael was too far away to stop her. He grabbed Grant's gun, praying he would have time to fire it.

Kelly's feet shot out, striking Margo in the back of the knees. The old woman crumpled with an angry cry.

Paddy snatched the gun from her grasp.

"No!" Margo cried. "It isn't fair! Those diamonds belong to me."

Michael untied Kelly's hands. He couldn't wait to hold her in his arms. For a few tense minutes he'd thought that wouldn't be a possibility again. Now, as she stood, he wrapped his arms around her tightly. The embrace was warm and sweet, fraught with emotion. He didn't want to let her go.

Paddy seemed to realize that. He called the police and the agency from his cell phone after tying Margo up so she wouldn't cause them any more trouble. He dragged the two bandits out of the room and closed the door with a wink in Michael's direction.

"Wow," Michael joked. "I thought they'd never leave."

Kelly trembled with laughter as she ran her hands over his back. He loved the feel of them, of her. Nothing else in this world could feel so good.

"I was scared out of my mind," she said. "Are we going to have that talk now?"

"Soon," he promised. "Right now I need to give Paddy a hand."

Michael slowly, reluctantly, released her and took a step backward with a sigh. He headed for the door.

"I can't be with you," Kelly blurted out.

Michael froze with the doorknob in his hand. All of his fears resurfaced with a vengeance. He wanted to turn around and pledge his love to Kelly Hall for an eternity, but the words wouldn't come. She had already made her choice. She didn't want him.

This wasn't how he had pictured their ending. It was supposed to be a happy one. He had thought there would be an exchange of kisses, promises, and maybe he would even get the nerve up to tell her he loved her.

"We shouldn't talk about this right now," he cautioned. "You just stared death in the face. You're upset. You can't make life decisions in this state of mind."

"I didn't," Kelly said. She sank down on the mattress and took a deep breath. "I knew all along that we couldn't be together."

He could see the tears beginning to form. She didn't want to turn him away. She was scared. He didn't want to upset her further. A few hours or days to mull things over and she would see how right they were for each other.

She looked so beautiful perched on the edge of the bed with her golden hair flowing over one shoulder. He wanted to wrap the strands around his hands and kiss some sense into her. She had to know she was killing him.

"I need to help Paddy with the prisoners," Michael said. He went to the window and glanced out. "I hope the police can get through. The snow is really starting to come down."

"Please, don't change the subject. I'm trying to be honest with you here. I don't want to hurt you."

"Then don't do this to me!" He turned on her. He hated emotional scenes, but one was brewing here like a violent storm. The backs of his own eyes were beginning to sting. The emotion in his heart boiled to the brink of spilling over, and there wasn't anything he could do to stop it. He lowered his voice. "Don't do this to us."

"I'm sorry." She sniffed. "I can't be with you."

"Is it because of the scars?" He went to her, kneeling beside her near the bed. His hands rested on her legs. His fingers burned and began to stroke their way up her thighs, a reflex action. The scent of her filled his nostrils. It took every bit of strength he had not to lay her down and make love to her. "I don't care about them. They're not as bad as you seem to think they are. You are the most beautiful—''

"Stop," she begged, trying to cut off his words.

"—incredible, wonderful woman I've ever met. You are the only one I've ever loved."

She cried out in pain and leaped to her feet. Tears cascaded down her face as if there was no end in sight. She put distance between them, both physically and mentally.

Michael could feel himself losing her, but there wasn't anything he could do about it beyond appealing to her heart.

"I know you love me," he said from his vantage point on the floor. He felt as if he wouldn't ever stand upright again; how could he when he'd been cut off at the knees? "I see it in your eyes every time you look at me. We belong together."

"We would never be happy." She spoke softly, condemning their future with her prediction. "How could we be? I can't leave Moore House, and you can't live here with me."

"This *is* about your scars. Dammit to hell! I thought you were getting over that."

"I'm not going to get over it." She turned her blue eyes on him. "But it isn't about the scars. It's about trust. I couldn't trust you."

"Angel." He stood on legs he could barely feel and crossed the room to stand beside her. She turned her back on him, but it didn't stop him from touching her. He stroked her upper arms and wondered if she felt the tingles in her blood, too. "I know I hurt you, and I know I don't deserve you. But if you're worried you can't trust me, that's ridiculous. I swear I won't lie to you again. Not ever. Not if we both live to be a hundred. You have my word."

Her shoulders shook, her entire body racked by violent sobs. "It isn't you," she cried. "It's me. I don't have it in me to trust anyone again, not after what happened here.

Look. Everyone I believed in has lied to me, fooled me, used me. I married your brother. Then he stood over me in this very room, after drugging my champagne, and laughed at me. He called me names, belittled me.''

Michael muttered an emphatic curse. ''I'm not Jimmy.''

''I know you aren't. I'm not confusing the two of you anymore.'' She paused for a second before continuing. ''I'm sorry. I want to be able to love you like you should be loved. I would give anything to be a normal person again, to be able to trust you and not wonder if you were lying to me or using me.''

''What do I have to do to convince you my love for you is real?'' Michael asked urgently. ''I would do anything.''

''There isn't anything you can do, because the problem is inside of me.''

''But you trust Wade. He hasn't lied to you. If you can believe in him, maybe someday you can believe in me, too. We can have a future. It doesn't have to be now. I can wait until you're ready.''

''I don't want you to do that.'' Kelly shook her head vehemently. ''Don't wait for me. I want you to be happy, have a good life.''

''How the hell am I supposed to do that without you in it?'' He raked a hand through his hair in frustration. He could feel her slipping away a little more with each passing second, and he was helpless to stop it.

Desperate, Michael grabbed Kelly by the shoulders and forced her eyes to meet his. Sensual awareness burned a pathway to his heart. He had to have her. In such a short time she had come to mean everything to him. He stared into those incredible blue orbs and repeated the words he hoped would make the difference.

''I love you.''

''I'm sorry.'' She shook her head, sending her hair flying. ''I can't love you.''

Michael didn't know what to do. He wanted to shake her until her teeth rattled. But the ugly facts weren't going to vanish just because he wanted them to. She was right. She was light and he was darkness. They couldn't possibly make a marriage work. What had he been thinking? He'd allowed himself to believe in the impossible.

"I'm sorry, too," he said as he released her and turned toward the door. "The police will want to talk to you. I'll make sure they don't harass you too much. You'll be fine here on your own."

"Goodbye, Michael." Her lower lip quivered, and she hugged herself. "Thank you for everything. You'll never know what a difference you've made in my life."

He wished that were true. If he had made a difference, she would be in his arms right now instead of on the other side of the room.

Michael took a last look at his angel. She wasn't wearing the white gown now, but she exuded that ethereal beauty all the same. Her eyes shone with tears, looking like bright sapphires in the darkness. Her petite frame trembled beneath his gaze. The picture seared deep into his brain. This was how he would remember her.

He shut the door softly, knowing she would be safe now. They'd caught the bad guys. Kelly would hide in her little world, safe from feeling too much, safe from pain. He was going to keep his mouth shut and let her live her life the way she wanted to. After all, he wasn't the foremost authority on living a happy life. She needed to follow her own path.

Maybe she knew what she was doing.

She wanted honesty and trust, and his world was built around lies.

KELLY WALKED THROUGH the next couple of days like a zombie. She hadn't seen Michael or Paddy. They were busy with paperwork and debriefing. Her life was getting back to normal, but it felt wrong. In her entire life she couldn't remember being truly lonely, until now. Every time she glanced at the door, she expected Michael to stroll in. Each time she heard a noise, she expected to see him.

She and Wade were hard at work restoring the kitchen to its original beauty, so she was keeping busy. But her thoughts returned to Michael over and over again. There wasn't anything she could do about it. She couldn't shut her mind off. Everything reminded her of him, from the snow covering the ground outside to the pitcher of iced tea in the refrigerator.

The doorbell rang one lazy Saturday afternoon as Kelly finished paying her bills. She wasn't expecting Wade, and he was the only one who visited now that Margo was gone. Kelly raced to the front door, her heart in her throat. The feeling that she would find Michael standing there sent her running at breakneck speed.

She opened the door. Boomer bolted, knocking into Michael's legs. Michael lost his balance and almost fell on the front porch. The dog happily romped in the snow.

Michael smiled and nodded at her. "Can I come in for a second?"

"Of course," she said. Her heart soared at the sight of him, then plummeted when she remembered they weren't together anymore. They wouldn't be together again, thanks to her. She had no idea what to say to him.

He looked better than any man had a right to. His dark hair spilled over his forehead, partially shading his dark, sultry eyes. The lines around his mouth seemed deeper now, as if the strain of everything that had happened had sliced into him, bleeding him dry.

She felt the urge to brush her hand against his face, wiping the weariness from his eyes and giving him a moment of comfort and peace, but she didn't do it. She wasn't sure if he would accept even the smallest gesture from her. She watched for a signal—something, anything that would tell her he wanted her to.

Kelly stared at his body in wonder. One word from him and she would bolt into his arms, holding him close. She wanted to meld her thin form against his tall, muscular frame. His broad shoulders strained against the black T-shirt. She'd been a fool to walk away from him.

She prayed he would reach out to her.

"I wanted to fill you in before I leave town," Michael said. "Since you were the intended victim, I thought you should know. Margo was not Fuller's daughter, after all. Margo roomed with your mother at the hospital for seven years, and your mother talked about the history of Moore House nonstop." He shrugged. "Margo was in and out of hospitals her whole life. She's even suspected of killing her adoptive parents by setting fire to their home."

Kelly gasped. She had been living next to a lunatic, having lunch with her, and she hadn't suspected a thing.

"Did Margo set fire to Moore House?" she asked.

"She actually had Grant do it. He's also the one who screamed 'Fire!' at the top of his lungs. She didn't want to kill anyone, just scare us off."

"Did Margo have a tape of Jimmy being killed?"

"If she did, I haven't seen it. The woman is babbling in a padded cell right now. She isn't making sense to anyone."

"I feel like such a fool," Kelly admitted. "I told her about my fear of getting sick like my mother, and she used it against me. What is it about me? Why do I attract the nuts and the con artists?"

"It's not you, honey. It's the house. Both Margo and Jimmy wanted the diamonds."

"Yeah," Kelly said with a fluttery laugh. "The invisible diamonds."

"That was a real good story you used to stall Margo.

Hearing that you found the diamonds already kept her distracted, but how did you come up with it?"

"It was true in part. Wade and I did tear out the old shower, but we didn't find anything. If there were diamonds hidden there, you can believe we would have found them."

"Yeah," Michael chuckled. "Wade is good at finding things."

They both stopped breathing for a shared moment and their eyes connected. Kelly knew he was thinking the same thing she was.

"What do diamonds look like when they're uncut?" She asked even though she knew what the answer would be.

Michael sighed. "They look like rocks."

Wade had a box full of rocks in his lost-and-found.

"I've told him several times not to take things from my home without asking," she said. "Oh, well. He can have them. I don't really care about the diamonds."

"But other people do," Michael reminded her. "If we could figure it out, so could somebody else. Wade could be in danger. Besides that, people won't stop treasure hunting in your house until everybody knows the diamonds have been found."

Kelly nodded. Michael was right. Wade had no idea what he was sitting on.

"We need to go to Wade's and get those diamonds right now," Kelly said. "Then we can take them to the proper officials."

"Do you have any idea how deep the snow is out there? If I hadn't rented a jeep, I wouldn't have made it here. Call Wade. I doubt he's in any danger. If we can't get to him, neither can anyone else."

She nodded in agreement, then offered, "Would you like some coffee?"

"No, thanks." Michael turned to the door. "If I'm going to get out of here, I need to go now. The snow has started

to fall again. They think we'll have several inches by night-
fall. Will you be okay here on your own?''

"Of course." She watched him head for the door, and
every fiber of her being told her to call him back. She could
make him stay with three little words. If she admitted she
loved him, told him she couldn't live without him, he would
stay. There wasn't a doubt in her mind.

But it wouldn't be fair to him. Try as she might, she
wouldn't be able to completely trust him without reserva-
tion. She was a horrible judge of character, as naive as they
came. How could she love and trust him? Or anyone else
for that matter?

Michael stopped at the door. He turned to face her and
their eyes locked for one long, painful moment. He hesitated
as if he was hoping she had changed her mind about them
being together. They stood for several silent seconds.

He mumbled goodbye and left.

Kelly stretched out her hand, wanting to reach for him.
Call him back, her mind shouted at her. *It isn't too late.* She
ran to the door and yanked it open, but Michael was gone.
The Jeep was heading out the wrought-iron gates, taking her
only chance at happiness with it.

She softly closed the door.

It was over. She had lost Michael, and it was her own
damn fault. Blinking back the tears, she remembered Wade.
She needed to call him, warn him.

"Kell?"

She jumped and spun around to find Wade standing in
the library doorway. He looked more frightened than she
felt.

"Wade, what are you doing here?"

A stranger with a dark complexion and horribly cold eyes
emerged from behind Wade. He held the biggest gun she'd
seen in her life, and it was pointed straight at her. Instinc-

tively she knew who the man was without him introducing himself.

Zu Landis had returned to finish the job.

"Michael is gone," she declared. "You can't hurt him. He'll be with his friends, his fellow agents, before you can do anything to stop him."

"Wrong," Landis said with a heavy accent she couldn't label. "I have taken care of Taggert. I removed the gasoline from his vehicle. He will return to us shortly." The man smiled. "And then you will all die."

Chapter Fifteen

Kelly stared at the barrel of the gun in disbelief. Any second a bullet would emerge from the chamber, and she would be dead. She marveled at the truth about death. Your life really did pass before your eyes, and her life was sadly lacking. Michael was right. While hiding from the evil in the world, she had hidden from the good things as well.

Her one true regret was letting Michael go without telling him she loved him.

"He's a bad man, Kell."

"I know, Wade. It's okay. You did the right thing. I wouldn't want you to get hurt because of me."

"How touching," Landis said with a sneer.

"He tricked me," Wade whined. "He said he wanted to help you. He was at my house. He wouldn't let me tell you. He said you'd die if I told anyone."

"It's all right, Wade. I understand."

"I'm sorry," Wade cried. "I was bad. I lied. Friends don't do that."

"Sometimes they do," she admitted, to herself as well as to him. She could see Michael's side for the first time. "Sometimes friends have to lie or keep secrets in order to protect you. I understand that now."

Wade shook his head repeatedly.

"Get over there," Landis ordered as he shoved Wade

forward. "Stand by the girl. Either of you does anything dumb and you both die."

Kelly slid a comforting arm around Wade, her mind whirling. She had to think of a way out for all of them before Michael returned to the house. If need be, she would give her life to save his. But she hoped it wouldn't come to that.

Landis was an assassin. He was here to do a job, nothing personal. The man worshipped money. If she offered him enough, perhaps he would go.

"Do you like diamonds, Mr. Landis?"

His dark eyes snapped to attention. "Pardon me?"

"Diamonds? I know where you can get your hands on ten million dollars worth of diamonds, and no one is looking for them. They were stolen in my grandfather's day. They've been forgotten, turned into legend. If you were to take them and leave the country, no one would be the wiser."

"I was paid to do a job. I was hired by a rival government to kill certain CIA operatives. I haven't finished it."

"You killed Jimmy. Didn't you?"

"Yes. Although at the time I was under the impression he was Michael Taggert."

"You did your job. It's not your fault the government faction who hired you didn't do their homework. They should have known Michael had a twin. They should have warned you. You could leave here ten million dollars richer, and there would be no risk involved."

"Keep talking."

"Taggert isn't a stupid man. He's trained by a top government agency. He could kill you."

"Not likely," Landis said.

"But it's possible. Why take the chance? Grab the diamonds and go."

"What about my reputation? I didn't assassinate my target."

"You did what you were paid to do. Killing two men wasn't part of the deal. You would be killing Michael for free. Do you do charity work, Mr. Landis?"

"No." His eyes hardened. "I do not." He lowered the gun a fraction and stepped closer. "Where are these diamonds?"

Should she tell him? Kelly didn't trust the man. He might kill them faster if he knew there were diamonds at Wade's house. She wouldn't give him the actual jewels. She would lie, throw him off track long enough for her and Wade to escape.

"They're in the study."

"If this is true," Landis said, "and you have diamonds, then why does the dummy look so baffled? Didn't you tell him?"

"No."

"Why not?" Landis glanced from one to the other. "Ah. I see. You were afraid the dummy could not keep a secret. You are a greedy bitch, aren't you?"

"Do you want the jewels or not?"

"If you have diamonds, I want them, of course." Landis raised his gun, aiming it at her heart. "Lead me to this study."

Kelly led the way, with Wade directly behind her and Landis following closely, his gun ready to fire. Kelly wanted to tell Wade the truth. She was sure the killer's words had cut her friend to the quick, but she couldn't say anything. Landis would overhear. She prayed Wade would be able to understand.

They entered the study as a group, but Kelly pulled Wade to the side. They stood in front of the bookcase where the secret door was located.

"The diamonds are behind a book." Kelly pointed to the

bookcase on the opposite wall. "One of those encyclopedias on the third shelf."

"Do you think I am an idiot?" Landis's face turned a bright red. "You want me to fish for jewels that are not there so you and the freak can make a run for it. I was not born yesterday, as you Americans are fond of saying."

"It isn't a trick," Kelly insisted. "The diamonds are there. Wade and I will stand right here. You can lock the door if you want. You have a gun. Surely you aren't afraid of us."

"Afraid? Zu Landis afraid?" His voice rose in anger. "I am not afraid of anyone. Fine, I will lock the door. If either of you moves, I will kill you both. There is nowhere you can hide from me."

Landis locked the door before examining the bookshelf closely. He pulled out one large book after another and dropped them to the floor below with no regard for their brittle pages or leather covers.

Kelly gestured for Wade to lift her.

Frowning in confusion, he obeyed. His huge hands circled her waist and he lifted her high into the air. She pulled the metal spring, opening the secret door. The two of them entered the dark passageway without a light. Kelly prayed she could remember her way to the master bedroom. It had the only other secret door that wasn't barricaded, as far as she knew.

"Hey!" Landis's furious scream followed them into the darkness. "What is this? A trick? You cannot run from me. I will find you."

Kelly had to practically drag Wade behind her; he was too frightened to move. If it wasn't for her frantic hands tugging at him she was sure he would return to Landis with an apology on his lips.

Somewhere along the line, Kelly made a wrong turn. She didn't find the ladder leading to the second floor. Instead she found a ladder going down. Wade used the ladder first. Kelly followed him, holding tight to the rungs. They both made it safely to an underground tunnel. Kelly was stunned, amazed the place existed.

At the end of the tunnel they found another secret door. She wouldn't have seen it except for a crack of light along one edge.

"Help me, Wade! We have to find a way to open this."

In desperation they felt along the splintered wood for a way out. They bumped into each other a few times. Kelly was about to give up hope and pull Wade in another direction when he yelped. "I hurt my hand. I'm bleeding!"

"I'm sorry, Wade, but we can't worry about that right now. We need to get out of here. He could be right behind us."

"Stand back," Wade said.

Kelly took a step backward, feeling the seconds of her life tick away. Landis would figure out where they were eventually. They had to get out.

Wade took three steps away from the door. Then he raced forward, throwing his weight against the wood. It splintered, flying open. They were free.

Kelly moved through the doorway and found herself in the garage. So this was how Margo or Elvin had managed to vanish after entering the decrepit building. She turned to Wade, giving him a quick hug.

"Wade, you need to go find help. Head for home. Call the police or go to a neighbor's house." A dreadful thought occurred to her. "You do have your keys, don't you?"

"Yes. I don't lose things. I find them. I take care of my things like my mama always told me to."

"I know you do. Hurry, okay?"

"Come with me." Fear entered his voice. "I'm scared. That bad man might find me."

"You'll be okay, Wade." She held his arms in a tight

grip, hoping some of her strength would flow into him.
"The bad man won't find you if you hurry. I need to hunt
for Michael. His car must have run out of gas by now. He'll
be heading back to Moore House."

"The bad man will shoot him."

"Not if I can help it, Wade. Now go. Hurry, please."

Wade nodded. He stuck his head out, looking both ways
before he darted outside. Kelly watched with dread as he
left. She was alone now, with only herself to depend on.
She had to locate Michael before Landis stumbled upon
him. Michael didn't even know he was in danger.

She ducked back inside the tunnel and raced down it.
When the light from the opening faded into darkness, she
felt her way along the wall. Splintered wood jabbed at her
delicate fingertips.

In the distance she heard Landis growling like a wounded
bear. As long as he kept making noise, she would be able
to avoid him. Moore House was big enough for the two of
them to run in circles and not bump into each other. She
had to find Michael. If he hadn't entered through the front
door yet, he soon would.

Kelly found the ladder again. Hesitating long enough to
catch her breath, she placed a foot on a knotted rung. Using
her hands along with her feet, she quickly inched her way
up the ladder to the second floor.

She found a door and pushed against it. It wouldn't
budge.

Of course it wouldn't open. In her haste to escape she
had forgotten about blocking the secret doors earlier. Now
she was trapped. She had two choices. She could return to
the study and hope Landis was searching for her somewhere
else in the house. Or she could return to the garage.

Decision made, Kelly found the opening in the study
without too much difficulty. The room was empty. She
strained her ears and was rewarded with the frustrated grunts

of a man on the edge of losing his temper. Landis was nearby. She would have to be careful. If he caught her, Michael was as good as dead.

Kelly slipped from the study, walking in the opposite direction from the annoyed mumbling. She heard Landis curse as he knocked something over. It broke. Glass shattered.

Kelly hurried to the foyer. The front door lay just ahead, unobstructed. She ran across the marble floor, desperate to escape. Nothing could stop her now. She would race down the driveway to the place where Michael's car had stalled. He had his gun. They would be safe if they were together.

INSTINCT TOLD MICHAEL something was wrong when the dial on his fuel gauge registered empty. He had filled the car not too long ago. It couldn't possibly have run out of gas yet.

A boulder settled in his stomach as he gazed up at the dormer windows at the front of Moore House, watching him like black eyes void of emotion. Kelly was somewhere deep inside the bowels of the Victorian monster. He had to find her before something unthinkable happened to her.

Michael entered the foyer with his gun drawn. His feet tapped against the marble, echoing loudly.

Just then Kelly stepped in front of the library doors, and a huge smile lit her face. The relief that flooded through his tightly coiled muscles reflected in her eyes.

He held his arms wide.

She rushed toward him.

Arms snaked out of the library doors and caught her, wrapping around her waist like steel manacles. A dark shadow moved into the light, an evil demon taking shape before Michael's startled eyes. *Landis!*

A glint of silver appeared over her shoulder, catching Michael's attention. The muzzle of a gun pressed into the soft flesh of her temple.

She gasped. Her startled eyes begged Michael not to do anything stupid.

"Let her go," Michael demanded, lifting his gun. He aimed carefully, but he could barely see the top of Landis's head. If he pulled the trigger, there was a distinct possibility he could hit Kelly. "She has nothing to do with this."

"She's in the way," Landis said. "Like you. You were warned not to play games with me, but you didn't listen. You thought you were going to set a trap for me, but the trap is for you."

"You killed some important people, top agents with the CIA. Did you actually believe we wouldn't come after you?"

"No matter. Once you were the hunter. Now you are the prey."

Michael asked, "How long have you been here?"

"Here?" Landis raised his eyebrow as if he didn't understand. "In town? In this house?" He laughed softly. "Actually, not long, but I was here before. I came here to do a job and someone got in the way. I thought I was shooting my target, fulfilling my contract. I was mistaken. Now I'm back."

"You killed Jimmy." Michael hissed between clenched teeth and aimed his weapon again. "That was a bad move on your part."

"Yes, I killed him," Landis admitted with pride. "He was living here under your name. I listened and I watched. He was the stupid one. He made the bad move, not me."

"I'm only going to say this one more time. Face me like a man. Let Kelly go. Are you going to hide behind a woman's skirt? Coward!"

Landis clicked his tongue. "Sticks and stones, as they say." He lifted Kelly off her feet and moved sideways, carrying her with him. He circled around Michael. He was almost to the front door.

Michael moved, too, keeping his gun steady. He would probably get only one shot. He couldn't risk hitting Kelly, but he couldn't allow Landis to leave with her, either.

"Where do you think you're going?" Michael asked. "You wanted to kill me. Here I am."

"No," Kelly cried. "Michael, stop. I don't want you dead."

"Shut up," Landis shouted. "Let him talk. He's going to die, anyway. Like his brother. Like a dog."

"You aren't leaving this house with her," Michael said.

Landis dragged her past the tall arched window.

Kelly suddenly twisted in the killer's arms.

Landis was obviously unprepared for the attack. Surprise registered on his face. He tried to regain control—too late.

She kicked out with her foot and sent Landis's gun flying. Then her body went down. She hit the ground with a grunt and rolled to the side before Landis could grab her again.

Michael pointed the gun at the place where the killer's heart would be—if the man had a heart. Michael's finger tightened on the trigger. Landis was the bastard who had killed his brother. Michael desperately wanted to kill him, but first he wanted answers.

"How did you kill Jimmy?" he demanded.

"I bashed his head in with a hammer." Landis shrugged. "I know it isn't my usual way. I was going to shoot him, but I did not realize the woman was drugged. I didn't want to wake her. There was a hammer nearby. I used it." Landis laughed, taunting Michael. "He begged for his life. It was pathetic. He cried like a woman. You should thank me for killing him. He was nothing but a bug under my foot."

"You knew he wasn't me." The gun in Michael's hand started shaking. "I wouldn't have begged for my life. You knew he wasn't me before you killed him, and you still did it."

"Yes." Landis smiled, his black eyes dancing with madness. "That's right. I killed him for the pure pleasure of it."

With a shout of fury, Michael dropped his gun and launched himself at Landis. He hit the other man square in the gut. They flew through the window behind Landis, landing hard in the snow. The soft powder exploded around them.

Michael struggled for the advantage. He tumbled Landis onto his back, but then Landis flipped him over. They rolled across the snow-covered flagstones, battling for the upper position. The position of power.

Kelly's terrified scream barely registered.

Michael used the strength of his legs to shove the man away from him, sending Landis flying backward, sailing through the air. He landed on the ground with a loud grunt of pain.

Michael struggled to his feet and charged like a bull.

Landis threw a handful of snow into his face.

Michael staggered. Painful grit made his eyes water and burn, obscuring his vision. He quickly swiped at his eyes with the backs of his hands, trying to get a visual on his enemy.

Landis swung a heavy fist.

It connected with Michael's jaw. His head snapped backward. Blood rolled down his chin.

Michael hit Landis in the face and in the stomach, then jumped into the air, executing a perfect karate kick that Landis blocked like an expert.

From the corner of his eye, Michael saw Kelly run out of the house with a gun in her hand. He couldn't tear his eyes away from Landis long enough to see if she had his gun or the enemy's. He wanted to yell at her to get her butt back inside just in case he lost and Landis decided to make good on his threats against her.

In that split second, Michael was distracted.

Kelly screamed a warning, but it was too late.

Michael took a hard fist to his cheekbone. He stumbled, almost losing his balance completely. Landis took advantage, swinging his legs out and knocking Michael off his feet.

The two men struggled, trading blows.

"Move away from him!" Kelly yelled.

THE MEN ROLLED ACROSS the snowy flagstones, tumbling so fast that Kelly couldn't aim the gun. They shuffled positions again and again, one man on top, then the other. Kelly grew dizzy watching them. She didn't want to accidentally shoot Michael. She would rather die herself than hurt him.

She held the gun tightly in both hands. Her finger trembled on the trigger. "Move away from him," she repeated.

Landis heard her, too. He made certain he didn't stay in one position for more than a split second.

Kelly lowered the gun. She desperately tried to think of a way she could help Michael without putting him into more danger.

Turning the gun around, she launched herself at Landis. She straddled him from behind and hit him repeatedly with the butt of the weapon.

He swatted at her, knocking her off.

Kelly landed on the ground and struck her head. Pain lanced through her skull and her vision blurred for a second.

Michael stood, gripping the other man's shirt in his hands. Spinning around, he tossed Landis against the side of the house headfirst. The other man slammed against Moore House and fell like a stone.

Kelly held her hand out to Michael. He grasped it and pulled her to her feet. Her legs wobbled beneath her, but she smiled. "Are you okay?"

"I should be asking you that. Are you crazy? What pos-

sessed you to run out here and physically attack a man twice
your size? You could have been killed!''

''We both could have been killed. I think that's the
point.'' She nodded at Landis's seemingly lifeless body.
''What are we going to do about him?''

''I'm going to tie him up,'' Michael said. ''You are going
to go inside and give Paddy a call. Tell him to send a squad
car.''

She squeezed his hand before releasing it. They had won.
Finally, the dark cloud that had hung over their lives was
gone. There was just one thing that worried her. Would
Michael walk out of her life forever?

Maybe if she told him she loved him he would stay. They
came from different worlds, but if there was a chance they
could work it out, didn't they owe it to themselves, to each
other, to try?

Kelly turned slowly, a smile firmly in place.

Michael was looking at her with a questioning gaze.

Behind him, Landis shot to his feet, the gun magically
materialized in his hand. As he raised it, time seemed to
switch into slow motion, but still moved too fast for Kelly
to scream a warning.

She didn't have to. Michael's brows drew together in a
frown as he read her expression. He turned around.

A loud explosion ripped through the air.

Michael jerked as he was hit in the chest. His hands went
to the wound, catching the blood. He turned slightly on one
foot, disbelief on his handsome face.

''Run!'' he ordered.

The word was barely audible over the crashing sound of
the blood in Kelly's ears.

She raced forward, catching Michael in her arms as he
fell. They both tumbled to the ground. High-pitched screams
filled the air; Kelly didn't realize they were coming from
her. Her soul had detached from the rest of her body, aban-

doning her. She watched the scene play out from somewhere just beyond reality.

Landis smiled and winked at her, then aimed the gun. She braced herself for the impact of the bullet, sure she wouldn't be able to feel it. If Michael died, so would she. It was as simple as that.

Landis did a strange dance. He collapsed, a look of surprise in his black eyes. The gun fell beside him. He landed facefirst in the snow.

Kelly tugged at Michael as someone tried to take him away from her. She yelled at the angel of death, refusing to release Michael into its greedy arms.

"Let me see him!" Paddy shoved her out of the way. He laid Michael on his back and ripped his shirt open, exposing the bullet hole.

Blood flowed from the wound.

Paddy removed his own shirt and wadded it up. He put a mound of snow on Michael's chest, then put the shirt over it. He grabbed Kelly's hands, placing them over the bloody mess.

"We've got to stop the bleeding. The ice might freeze the blood. It'll give us time to get him to the hospital," Paddy shouted. "Push down! He's going to die if we don't stop the bleeding. Snap out of it, dammit!"

Kelly steeled herself against the sight of Michael lying helpless at her knees. She did as Paddy ordered, pushing as hard as she could. She lifted her face and shut her eyes. Snowflakes fell on her cheeks.

Paddy grabbed his cell phone and called for an ambulance.

Kelly couldn't do anything but pray as she watched Michael's lips turn blue.

She was losing him.

"DON'T YOU LET HIM DIE!"

Was that Kelly shouting at the top of her lungs?

Who was she yelling at? It didn't make sense. His angel didn't scream. She was sweet and patient, loving and kind. He wanted to hold her hand, but couldn't find it in the darkness. He wanted to ask her to please stop shouting. Her voice, although lovely, was plunging into his sweet dreams, pulling him back into a painful world.

His chest was on fire.

Michael forced his eyes open.

Lights rushed by his face, one melding into the next. He saw shadows hovering nearby. Kelly was among them. He was sure of it, but he couldn't reach her. She floated over him, around him. Her voice found him even though her hand didn't.

He wanted to ask the people who were dragging him down the never-ending corridor to stop, but he couldn't speak. They were taking him away from Kelly.

"Michael, you're going to be okay," she said. "I promise. Just hold on. Don't leave me."

Where did she think he was going? He wasn't planning on leaving her. Why would he? She was his world. But he heard the insecurity in her voice. If he could, he would tell her how important she'd become to him. In their short time together, she had gotten under his skin and into his blood. He could no more leave her than he could stop breathing.

He smiled, allowing the darkness to suck him under again.

KELLY HAD DRIVEN like a maniac all the way to the hospital, praying she would get him there in time. She almost got the truck stuck twice. Luckily, Wade owned a monster, with the biggest wheels she'd ever seen. Once they made it to the hospital, she pleaded with the doctor to save the only man she'd ever love. Losing Michael would rip a hole through her life, dead center. She needed him.

At first she had resented the feelings Michael stirred within her. She didn't want to rely on anyone, especially not someone she'd known for only a week. Was it possible to fall in love in such a short time?

Yes, absolutely. She silently answered her own question.

Michael was the most wonderful man. If she had been handed a catalog of male parts and told to assemble the perfect man, he would have been Michael Taggert, without a doubt. He was not only an incredible male specimen physically; he was just as good on the inside.

Paddy approached with two coffees. He handed her one before sitting beside her. His warm eyes settled on her face, and he smiled at her. His hand covered her own, and he patted it.

"Honey," he said, "relax. Michael will be fine. He's young and strong."

"I know. I keep telling myself that."

"You love him."

It was a statement, not a question, and Kelly wondered if it was written on her face. Paddy was the second person to tell her she was in love with Michael. Did everyone know? Was she that obvious?

Paddy asked, "Have you told him? Does he know how you feel?"

"He knows." Her voice came out quiet, barely audible to her own ears. "I'm sure he knows."

"He loves you, too."

Her eyes misted over. Yes, he loved her. He had told her he loved her. She could still hear the quiet desperation in his voice. She had hurt him.

She swallowed the lump in her throat and tried not to cry. Somehow she was going to make it all up to him. As soon as he was on his feet again she would tell him she loved him, and beg him to forgive her. She would be a good wife to him, if he would have her.

"It was my fault," she said. "I was the one who carried the gun outside."

"You didn't shoot him. Landis did."

"You saved my life." Kelly placed a hand on Paddy's weathered one and asked, "How did you know to show up when you did?"

"It was your friend Wade. We ran into each other, almost literally. I was on my way to your house, anyway. I wanted to have a talk with you and Tag."

"What about?"

"I wanted you two kids to wise up and admit you have feelings for each other. Life is too short." He nodded to the doors that led to the operating room. "As you can see. When you have a chance at happiness, you take it."

. "Things are complicated," she said.

"How so?"

"I have scars." She blurted the words out before she could restrain her tongue.

Paddy appeared taken aback by the news. He shifted uncomfortably in his seat, and she realized he hadn't known. Michael hadn't told him.

"Well," he said, "we all do. We all have scars of some sort. Don't we?"

"Mine are on my arms. It's a long story. The short version is I was burned by scalding water when I was twelve. I hate it when people stare at me and feel sorry for me or make fun of me, so I hid out at Moore House. For years... How could Michael live a life with me?" she asked. "I'm afraid to go out in public."

"You're in public now."

"Yes, but my arms are covered."

"You stood up to those nurses and that snooty doctor. I saw and heard the whole thing. That was something to watch. I think you're a lot stronger than you give yourself credit for."

"I don't know about that," she said.

"I do. That wasn't a shrinking violet I saw dealing with the medical staff."

"Those were extraordinary circumstances. I was worried about Michael."

"Answer me this. When was the last time you walked around in public with your burns showing?" Paddy asked. "How old were you the last time someone made you feel bad because of your scars?"

"I don't know." She closed her eyes and tried to think back. "I guess I was a teenager in high school. My father made me wear short sleeves. He wanted me to confront my fears."

"And?"

"It was horrible. I cried almost every night."

"What about after that?" Paddy asked, "What changed?"

"I became an adult. My father couldn't make me dress a certain way anymore, so I wore long sleeves. I didn't go out much. After he died, I moved back into Moore House."

"Don't you think things might have changed since then? You're an adult now. You don't seem like the type of gal who would shy away from a confrontation."

Kelly digested the information slowly. Could he be right? It had been a long time since anyone had stared at her scars. Was she hiding for no reason at all?

She glanced at her watch for what must have been the tenth time in as many minutes. She wished somebody would report to them on Michael's condition. He had been in surgery for over two hours.

"It always takes this long. Don't worry," Paddy said. "I've had to sit vigil more times than I can count on fellow officers who were shot in the line of duty. The longer the surgery, the better the guy's chances. That's what I think." He smiled at her. "Now, back to you. Where do you see yourself in five years? Do you honestly want your life to stay as it is?''

"You're saying I should take a chance, face the world?'' A tremor sizzled through her body, but the idea of giving up her peaceful way of life didn't chill her as it used to. "I don't know if I can."

"You can do anything you want," Paddy said. "You survived a professional killer. What could be worse?''

"You're right about that." A smile curved her mouth. "Maybe it's time for me to take control of my life. Michael suggested I get a job. I think I can do it.'' She nodded forcefully. "I'm going to do it.''

"Good for you, honey. You've just taken the first step to a new life."

She leaped to her feet, looking down the long white corridor. "I can't sit around like this. I'm going to go to the chapel to say a prayer for Michael.'' Her chin lifted with the newfound strength coursing through her veins. "Then I'm going to visit some people, maybe the children's ward, see if I can do something to make them feel better. It'll keep my mind off my own worries."

"Michael was right. You are a marvel.''

She smiled dimly. She was going to be the woman that Michael deserved, but she wasn't doing it just for him. Her scars weren't important. More than anything, she realized, her scars had been emotional ones connected to her mother. Once she had let go of her resentment and fear of her mother, she was able to see herself in a different light, as well.

THE NEXT TIME Michael opened his eyes, the world wasn't so comforting. Pain, nearly unbearable pain, screamed from each nerve ending, setting it ablaze. His entire chest felt as if it was going to literally explode if he took too deep a breath. He drew short, shallow breaths instead.

His eyes were heavy, but he forced them to open.

Kelly stepped into view. She was beautiful with the light shining in her golden hair like a halo. For one drug-induced moment he thought he was dreaming. His hand stretched out and she took it. Her flesh was warm, comforting.

"Don't speak," she said. "You're going to be okay. Landis shot you. But Paddy got there in the nick of time and shot him. Landis wasn't as fortunate as you are. He died."

It was a relief. Landis hadn't managed to hurt Kelly. She was okay. In fact, she was stunning, staring down at him with those incredibly blue eyes. Michael could drown in those eyes. And her smile. It lit up his heart.

He opened his mouth to confess his love for her and ask for her forgiveness. He had put her through the proverbial wringer. He'd been a fool to keep her at bay for so long. Life was too short to waste, too short to live without love. He opened his mouth to tell her how he really felt about her.

"Tag!" Paddy appeared on the other side of Michael's bed. "You had us worried."

"Now that you're here and he's awake," Kelly said, "I'm going to step out. I need to get some air, maybe some coffee."

"Go right ahead, hon," Paddy said. "We'll be fine here, just the two of us."

Michael wanted to call out to her, stop her from leaving, but he didn't have the strength. So he tried to relax. She would be back. He smiled up at Paddy, giving the man his undivided attention.

"We found the hammer that killed Jimmy. That nut Wade Carpenter had it. Landis killed Jimmy, no doubt about it. He couldn't have known about the hammer otherwise. Forensics tested it. Jimmy's blood is on it." Paddy's gaze drifted to the door for a second. "You know, that little gal didn't leave your side the entire time. It's nearly been a week. You've been out of it, although you opened your eyes a few times. She's unbelievable. She had those doctors and nurses hopping.''

Kelly? His little angel had stood up to the medical staff for him?

"The nurses were impressed with her. They offered her a volunteer position here at the hospital, working with sick kids."

Michael smiled. He had known Kelly had it in her to do something great, given the right opportunity. She was smart and compassionate. The lucky kids were going to adore her.

Paddy went on. "I haven't seen a woman so dedicated to a man since I met my own dear, sweet Mary." He paused for a moment. His eyes were moist. "That girl loves you. I hope you know that."

Finding his voice at last, Michael whispered. "I love her, too."

"Good. I hope you aren't going to let her get away."

"Not as long as I can draw a breath."

They talked for a few more minutes before the nurse interrupted them, anxious that her patient get some rest. Michael made Paddy promise to give Kelly a message for him. He wanted her to be there when he woke up. He had something important to talk to her about.

Michael drifted off to sleep rehearsing what he was going to say to Kelly the next time he saw her.

KELLY FLOATED INTO Michael's hospital room wearing a pair of tight jeans and a pretty top that would have given a healthy man heart failure. Her blond hair fell in gentle waves over her shoulders, ending at the soft contours of her breasts. She wore a touch of cosmetics—an innocent pink shade of lipstick and a smudge of silver near her eyes— even though her face didn't need any enhancements.

Michael beamed in delight at her. She was his angel. He

couldn't wait to get out of the damn hospital bed and take her into his arms again.

She set a bouquet of flowers on the table near his bed.

Michael opened his mouth to tell her how glad he was to see her, but she held a hand up, instantly capturing his attention.

"Please, let me say what I came here to say." She spoke quickly, as though she was reciting a long scene from a play she couldn't wait to be done with. "This isn't easy for me. I hope you don't think it is. I was up all night thinking about it. There's nothing else we can do."

"What are you talking about?" Michael struggled to sit up in bed. He had the awful feeling he was about to be dumped. "Just say it."

"We haven't known each other for very long. Have we?"

"No. I suppose not."

"We met during extreme circumstances. We had to rely on each other to stay alive."

"I know all of this, Kelly. What did you really come here to say?"

"We need six months apart." She blurted out the words and then stopped pacing. She waited at the end of his bed for his reaction.

"Six months? Why?"

"There are a number of reasons." She started counting on her fingers. "One, I need to get my life in order. I've made such a mess of it. You deserve better than that. I want you to have a woman who is complete and happy and ready for anything."

"I don't want you to change because of me." He sat up straighter. Pain tore at his chest. "Did I ever ask you to change for me?"

"No. Of course not." She was at his side in an instant. "What do you think you're doing? You need to rest. You're going to hurt yourself."

"If I'm going to fight for my life, I prefer to do it on my feet."

"Your life?"

He cupped her face between his hands and stared deep into her lovely blue eyes. "You are my life. Don't you know that?"

"You don't have to fight for me, Michael. You already have me."

"Then what's all this talk about six months?"

"I need the time for me. Okay? I need to see what I can do on my own, without you there to catch me if I fall. Six months isn't a lifetime."

"It'll seem like it," he mumbled.

Michael lay back down, a wave of dizziness leaving him weak. He didn't want to be vulnerable, not in front of Kelly. He wanted to be strong for her, her knight in shining armor.

"Number two." She bent back another of her fingers, continuing the count. "If we're going to be together, you have things to work out. You'll have to figure out what you're going to do about your home, friends, job. I want you to be sure you want to be with me. Because it'll be for keeps. For always."

"I wouldn't have it any other way."

"Number three," she said. "Maybe we don't belong together. It might be true love. But what if it isn't? I think we need the six months apart to regain our composure and common sense. Love makes people blind, deaf and dumb."

He was afraid to ask, but... "What happens in six months?"

"You come to Moore House for dinner. We'll talk. We'll compare notes. If our love is real, it'll still be real in six months."

"I'm not going to be able to talk you out of this, am I?"

She shook her head slowly yet deliberately. "Not a chance."

"What if one of us has a change of heart?"

"Better to know before we make a commitment. Don't you think?"

He kissed her fingers, each in turn. His lips lingered on the digits. He sucked one fingertip lightly into his mouth.

Michael had the horrible, sinking feeling he was losing her. But what could he do? She'd made up her mind. The backs of his eyes stung. He blamed it on the drugs in his system.

"Promise me something," he said.

"What?"

"Promise me you won't change too much."

She smiled and leaned in for a bittersweet kiss.

Chapter Sixteen

Six months later

Chimes rang throughout Moore House, filling the air with whimsical notes. Candlelight and glowing flames in the parlor's hearth gave off a golden hue. The smell of cinnamon and fresh baked ham floated from room to room.

Butterflies danced in Kelly's stomach. She wanted to run to the door, but she forced herself to walk instead. Her day of reckoning had finally arrived. It was evening and Michael had come for dinner as promised. As agreed, neither of them had contacted each other during the past months. There had been no letters, no phone calls.

Kelly pulled the door open wide, a cheerful smile in place.

Michael grabbed her, lifting her off the ground, and swirled her around on the marble steps.

"Michael!"

"I've missed you!" He set her down, but seemed reluctant to let her go. His hands remained on her waist. "If you ever suggest we spend time apart again, I'll throttle you. It was pure torture."

"For me, too."

"I want to look at you," he insisted.

Michael pushed her away. His eyes traveled the length of

her body and then repeated the journey as if he couldn't believe what he saw.

She was glad to note her trip to the beauty salon in town hadn't been in vain. Kelly rotated in a slow circle for him. Her new tea-length black dress hugged her petite figure. The thin spaghetti straps bared her arms for the world to see.

Her blond hair was swept up in a flattering style and secured with decorative pins. She wore a little more makeup than usual—in pink tones, because the saleslady had told her it suited her complexion better than the darker colors.

"Well? What do you think?"

"You are stunning."

"Now it's my turn."

Kelly's eyes devoured the sight of him. He was even more handsome than she'd remembered. His dark hair had obviously been cut recently. It was a lot shorter than it had been before, but it suited him. His dark eyes crinkled at the sides as they swept over her yet again.

He removed his long black coat and casually dropped it to the floor.

Her eyes widened. He was wearing a suit—a gray suit with a crisp white shirt and a dark tie. He looked incredible in it. The suit must have been tailored just for him. It outlined his broad shoulders and muscular body perfectly, causing her mouth to go dry.

Michael's hand swept one of the spaghetti straps off her shoulder. He kissed the skin there and she shivered. His warm mouth burned the area and then his tongue soothed it.

"Shouldn't we talk?" she asked.

"I'm not stopping you." His hands slid up the sides of her silky black dress until they rested beneath her vulnerable breasts. "Go ahead. I'm listening."

"I'm a nurse now."

"That's great, angel. I knew you could do it."

His mouth found the delicate shell of her ear. He sucked the earlobe into his mouth, causing her to squirm. It tickled, but she didn't feel like laughing. She was on fire, burning with the desire denied her for six months.

He moved on to her throat, as if insatiable.

"Well, I'm not actually a nurse yet. I'm in school for it." He swung her around to face him. "I volunteer at the hospital twice a week."

Michael's mouth explored her neck from a different angle now.

"What have you been doing?" she asked in a breathy voice that couldn't possibly belong to her.

"I quit my job." He sucked on the tender flesh above her carotid artery. "I gave up my apartment." His hands slid around her waist and dipped down to caress her bottom. "I packed my bags, and here I am."

"The skeleton in the passageway belonged to none other than Elizabeth Barrington. Another mystery solved." She kissed his throat in turn and smiled against his flesh. "You know, you may look like Jimmy and sound exactly like him, but your heart is undeniably unique. You actually fell in love with me. I still can't believe it."

"Why wouldn't I? You have no idea how incredible you are."

"Tell me," she whispered, leaning into him.

"I'd rather show you."

He lifted her, pulling her tight against the evidence of his arousal.

She sighed. "I made dinner."

"You want to eat now?" His hips rocked against her in a sensual rhythm. "I'll stop if you want to eat."

"I'm not really hungry. Unless you are."

"This is what I'm craving."

He slid down her body, kissing her exposed skin until he reached the material of her dress.

Kelly had had enough teasing. She wanted him more than she'd wanted anything or anyone in her entire life. She tugged him up until he stood over her again.

She kissed him full on the mouth, thrusting her tongue between his parted lips. She wanted him just as badly as he wanted her. Food could wait. She couldn't.

Kelly stepped out of her high heels and kicked them to the side. Her trembling fingers ripped at his shirt until she had mastered the buttons, sliding them through the tiny holes and freeing his solid chest. He was every bit as beautiful as she'd remembered.

"Before I forget, Mary and Paddy send their love," Michael said. "They bought the cabin in Montana. They want us to visit in the spring."

Kelly's mouth went to work on his chest. She teased him with her tongue, lapping at his nipples.

He groaned and added, "That was a generous gift you gave them. Five million in diamonds is a lot to give up."

"Wade has the other half," she said. "He found them. He deserved something."

"You're a crazy lady. I'm in love with a nut."

She smiled at the gentle teasing, freed at last from the bonds of her mother's insanity. She didn't worry about losing her mind anymore.

"I have money. I don't need more."

He tilted her head back and kissed her hard on the mouth. At the same time, his hands were pulling at the fabric of her dress. He lifted the hem until her thighs were exposed to the cool air.

He released her mouth, his breathing harsh.

"The sheriff in Tinkerton is retiring," Michael said. "How would you feel about marrying a local lawman?"

Kelly froze. Had she heard him right?

"You want to marry me?"

"What did you think I was here for? Your cooking? Of

course I want to marry you." He pushed her toward th
parlor door. "Come in here with me."

Michael froze in the doorway. His eyes scanned the room
and Kelly glowed with pride. She'd made changes while h
was away. Changes to herself and changes to the house.

The sheets were gone, exposing the beautiful wood fur
niture to the light of day for the first time in years. Every
thing was polished. She had purchased a leather sofa for th
room and a matching chair. There were filmy white curtain
in place of the heavy drapes. Now sunlight spilled into th
room during the day, giving it life and color.

Michael turned to her slowly. "Did you do this your
self?"

She nodded.

"It's amazing." Michael took her hand and pulled he
forward. "You are amazing."

He pushed her down on the sofa and knelt beside he
Reaching into his pocket, he produced a black velvet bo:
Opening it, he showed her the most magnificent ring she'
ever seen. It was gold with sparkling diamonds in a simpl
breathtaking setting. "Kelly Hall, will you marry me?"

"Yes. Yes. Yes." Tears of joy flooded her eyes and sh
wrapped her arms around his neck, nearly strangling him.

Michael stood, lifting her with him.

She clung to him, silently vowing to never let him g
again.

"Will you live in Moore House with me, Michael?
know it's got a bad history, but I think we could be happ
here."

"I wouldn't have it any other way."

"Are you sure? Not one couple ever found happines
here."

"We will. We're going to fill this house with love an
laughing children and sweet memories." He took anothe
look around the room. "I think the house wants us here."

She beamed. "So do I."

"Are all the rooms different now?" Michael asked.

"Are you interested in one specifically?"

"I think I'd like to see the master bedroom. What changes have you made there?"

She swallowed, feeling giddy. "I bought a new bed. A bigger one."

"Really?" Michael shrugged off his shirt. "Maybe we should try it out. Make sure it's sturdy. I wouldn't want you to get ripped off."

"You're always thinking of me," she teased.

"Always." He answered sincerely. "You have no idea how often I thought about you while I was away. I couldn't sleep without dreaming about you being in my arms again."

"It was the same for me," she said. Her hands went to his belt, fumbling with the clasp. "I regretted sending you away. I was afraid I'd made a huge mistake."

He lifted the dress over her head as she pulled his belt free and went to work on the button that held his trousers in place. His hands smoothed over her bare flesh. Two wisps of lacy material covered her in strategic places.

"You could have called," Michael said. "I would have returned in a flash."

"After making such a big deal about being apart, I didn't feel like I could call. Besides, my reasons were valid. We needed the time to straighten out our lives."

"Now we can be together."

His hands covered her breasts, molding them with growing urgency.

"Yes," she gasped. "Now we can be together."

His pants fell to the floor, and he stepped out of them. He wore striped boxers. Other than that, only his socks remained.

Kelly couldn't wait anymore. If she didn't have him now, she was afraid she would burst into flames.

"Forget the bed," she breathed. "Take me here."

"In the parlor?"

"Yes. I want you to make love to me in the parlor and in the foyer and in the library. Everywhere. I don't want a room left untouched by our love."

Michael laughed. "We'd better get busy then. With over forty rooms, we have a lot of work ahead of us."

He grasped the top of her bra and tugged it down, exposing her creamy flesh to his heated gaze. He leaned forward, taking one of her breasts into his mouth and then the other. Back and forth he went, lavishing them with searing kisses.

Kelly threw back her head, crying out for release. She sank down on the sofa, pulling him with her until they were lying side by side. His mouth continued its exquisite torture. He didn't seem in any hurry to complete the journey.

A thought occurred to her. "You haven't said the words yet. At least not today."

"What?"

"That you love me."

"Neither have you," he reminded her. "You know I do."

"Say it." Her eyes focused on the ceiling above. Her hands delved into his hair. "Tell me."

He pushed himself up on his elbows and hovered over her. "I love you with everything that's in me. I loved you yesterday. I love you today. I'll most certainly love you tomorrow."

"I love you, Michael."

"I know." He grinned and returned to his wicked administrations. His tongue lapped at her nipples, making her want to scream in frustration. Her hips bucked beneath him, silently begging for more.

"When do you want to get married?" he asked.

"I don't know." Her forehead wrinkled. "There's a lot of planning to a wedding."

"I want to take it slow. I want to woo you. I'm going to seduce you on a daily basis, shower you with gifts and make certain you know you're loved. You'll never have to question that again."

"Sounds wonderful."

"Now," Michael said, "shut up and make love with me."

With a happy grin she kissed him full on the lips and pulled him back down to her quaking body. Her hands roamed every inch of him. She memorized everything about him. He belonged to her now. No one, nothing, would ever threaten their happiness again.

Michael took his angel to heaven.

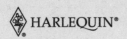

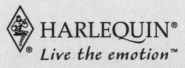

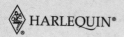

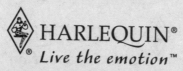

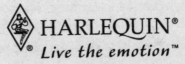

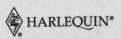

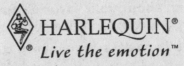